OF MICE AND MURDER

NEVERMORE BOOKSHOP MYSTERIES, BOOK 2

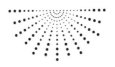

STEFFANIE HOLMES

BACCHANALIA HOUSE

To all the book boyfriends
who keep me up at night.

"There are always plenty of not quite certifiable lunatics walking the streets, and they tend to gravitate towards bookshops."

– George Orwell, *Bookshop Memories*, 1936.

CHAPTER ONE

"*How* does it look?" Morrie yelled from his precarious position atop the wooden ladder as he held the painting of a rampaging Godzilla cat terrorizing a town filled with fleeing mice against the dark paneled wall above the staircase.

"Like the entrails of one of Grimalkin's eviscerated mice," Heathcliff growled.

"Meow," Grimalkin echoed from her perch on Heathcliff's shoulder.

"Hey," Quoth pouted. He sat on the bottom step, his black hair hanging over his face, draping him in shadows. "I worked hard on that painting."

"Ignore Heathcliff, he's no bloody help." Morrie steadied himself against the wall as the ladder wobbled. "Mina, your thoughts?"

"I think that ladder doesn't look structurally sound."

Morrie gritted his teeth as his arm muscles strained from holding out the canvas. "I'd like to remind you that I'm risking my beautiful neck up here for *your* genius plan. We don't *have* to hang Quoth's paintings all over the shop—"

"Fine. Move it over two inches so it's centered on the panel."

Morrie leaned out, his arms stretching the last inch. I nodded and he reached for his hammer and—

Something warm streaked across my boots. A tiny white shape darted up the staircase and along the frame of the ladder. A twitching nose sniffed the air as the mouse surveyed its next move.

"Yeooow!" Heathcliff moaned as Grimalkin's claws dug into his shoulder. She launched herself across the room, flying up the staircase and landing on the bottom rung of the ladder just as the mouse darted up Morrie's trouser leg.

"Help, it's in my trousers!" Morrie lurched forward, hopping from foot to foot as he swung the painting at his leg. The ladder wobbled across the step and lurched toward the edge of the staircase.

"Morrie, watch out!" I yelled. Morrie leapt off the top of the ladder just as the leg went over the edge of the step and the whole thing crashed down the stairs. The painting flew from his hand and sailed through the air.

Feathers flew in all directions as Quoth transformed into his raven. He darted out of the way just as the ladder slid over the bottom step. I sucked in my breath.

Quoth soared overhead and captured the frame between his talons just before it hit the ground. He flapped his wings and set it down against the wall.

The mouse streaked past him. Grimalkin bounced back down the stairs and bounded after it. Quoth stuck out a talon to capture the critter, but the mouse slipped through his grip and disappeared under a shelf.

Grimalkin's front paws slid on the floorboards. She howled as she skidded into Quoth, sending the pair of them tumbling across the room in a furious ball of fur and feathers.

I raced up the staircase, my heart pounding as I wrapped my

arms around Morrie, who was still frantically beating at his trouser leg.

"Get it out, get it out, get it out!" he howled.

"It's gone." I grabbed him under the arms and hauled him to his feet, surprised to feel wet patches under his arms. *Is James Moriarty, criminal mastermind and eminent mathematics professor, afraid of a tiny mouse?*

It appeared so. Morrie buried his face in my neck. "It had little scratchy legs," he whispered into my hair.

"Don't be so dramatic. Where'd it go?" Heathcliff wrenched Grimalkin and Quoth apart.

"Into the stacks. I'm sure it's nothing to worry about. It's just a wee mouse." I wiped a strand of hair out of Morrie's face. His lower lip quivered, and it was totally adorable. "Judging by the row of tiny trophies along the perch over the door, Quoth and Grimalkin will make short work of it sooner or later."

"That was no mere mouse," Heathcliff growled. "He is the White Fury, the Mouse of the Baskervilles, the Demon Mouse of Butcher Street."

"Now who's being dramatic?"

"Didn't you read the paper?" Morrie slumped onto the front step, folding his hands over his long legs. "This little fellow has been doing the rounds of all the shops in town, chewing his way through power cords and ductwork, terrifying customers, creating health code violations. It looks like the blighter has decided to take up residence in our shop. I don't like this. I don't deal well with *vermin*."

"A *mouse* made headlines in the Argleton *Gazette*?" Four years in New York City had made me forget the insanity that was village life.

"Not just the headlines. Front page." Morrie winced as he pulled himself to his feet and dusted off his trousers. "These trousers are contaminated now. I'll have to throw them away, and they cost four hundred pounds."

"You have four hundred pounds to spend on trousers?" I don't think I'd ever had four hundred pounds in my life.

"Forget his bloody trousers. Look what you've done to my shop!" Heathcliff folded his arms and glared at the ladder, which had smashed a wooden panel and left a long scratch along the balustrade.

"It wasn't me," Morrie protested. "It was the mouse!"

"Meeeooooow!" howled Grimalkin.

My temples throbbed. *Just another day in Nevermore Bookshop.*

The shop bell tinkled. Heathcliff frowned as the sound of clomping orthopedic shoes signaled the arrival of an elderly customer. These were his least favorite types of customers, after children and Millennials and everyone else.

Heathcliff was the only shop owner I knew who wished customers would just leave him alone. We'd been getting a steady stream through the doors ever since I started working at Nevermore Bookshop, but I blame that on the recent murder in the Sociology section. Even though the police solved that crime over a month ago (with a little help from Heathcliff, Morrie, Quoth, and myself), the villagers still made a beeline for the upstairs room where it had taken place.

Believe it or not, a murder during my first week on the job had so far been the *least* of my problems. It turns out the murder victim was my ex-best friend, Ashley, and since I'd been one of the people to find the body, the police were convinced I'd done it. Luckily we'd managed to clear my name and got a dangerous killer locked behind bars.

It *also* turns out that my new boss and his two flatmates are actually the fictional characters Heathcliff, James Moriarty, and Poe's raven, Quoth. And the bookshop I'd loved since I was a kid was no ordinary bookshop – it was plagued by some kind of curse, had a hidden occult book collection, and a room that moved forward and backward in time.

4

And *then*, because my life wasn't already crazy enough, I sort of… *slept* with Morrie. Well, there wasn't much sleeping happening. He'd taken me hard against one of the hallway bookshelves. My cheeks reddened just thinking about it. Ever since then we'd been doing it everywhere we could – in the storage room, on his perfectly-made bed, on Heathcliff's chair in the living room. My body tingled just thinking about Morrie's hands sliding over my skin. My life may be insane, but it had never been more perfect… *except* for the tiny, unresolved issue of me not wanting to be with a master criminal, and of Heathcliff kissing me, and Quoth declaring he had feelings for me, and me not knowing which of them to choose…

Oh yeah, and I was going blind. That was also a thing.

Quoth fluttered away to greet our customer while Morrie scrambled to right the ladder. Heathcliff slouched back to his desk and slid his muscled frame into his chair, flipping open a book in front of him with a heavy thud.

I guess I'll help the customer, then. I turned to see who'd come through the door.

"Oh, hi, Mrs. Ellis!" Mrs. Ellis was the hilariously horny old biddy who used to be my school teacher. She'd encouraged my love of reading, always giving me books far above my level, usually featuring muscled men and swooning women on the covers in various states of undress. She'd retired years ago and now lived in a small flat above the chippy across the road, which suited her perfectly as it gave her the ideal vantage point to eavesdrop on conversations in the street and gather all the village gossip.

"Hello, Mina, dear." Mrs. Ellis wrapped her arms around me in a motherly hug. I sucked in a mouthful of hyacinth perfume and tried not to gag. As I pulled away, a pair of beady grey eyes met mine from over Mrs. Ellis' shoulder.

The eyes belonged to a sour-looking woman in a fuchsia-pink suit, complete with matching handbag and hat. She leaned against a crutch and peered down at me through a pair of horn-rimmed glasses.

"That's a provocative outfit for working a retail job," she frowned, sweeping her judgmental gaze over my body.

I smoothed down the front of the t-shirt I'd screen printed the night before. It read, 'I like big books and I cannot lie,' with the OO's in the word BOOKS strategically angled across my chest. Morrie and Quoth thought it was hilarious. Heathcliff didn't seem to have noticed it yet. "What do you mean, ma'am?" I asked, all sunshine and innocence. "I'm declaring my love of the written word."

"It implies you're sexually excited by books, like some kind of perverted *lesbian,*" she sniffed.

"Oh no," Morrie called from the top of the stairs. "I can assure you, she's a big fan of the cock."

Mrs. Ellis snickered. She squeezed my hand. "I *knew* you'd land one of those handsome beaus, dearie. Tell me, is he long and lean in all the right places?"

My face flared with heat. *Could the floor just swallow me now?*

The woman's face turned beet red. She called up the staircase. "Young man, that is inappropriate language in front of your elders, and you—"

Sensing a lecture coming on and Heathcliff's anger sizzling in the background, I jumped in. "Ma'am, I'm sorry about my friend, and my t-shirt. I'm happy to help two such lovely young ladies with their book-buying needs."

Mrs. Ellis tittered. Her companion didn't look nearly so amused, although she did brush an invisible speck of lint from her shoulder.

"Oh, dear me, where are my manners. Mina, this is my dear friend, Gladys Scarlett. We're on the Argleton Community Fundraising Committee together." Mrs. Ellis beamed, clutching Gladys' hand. "Don't mind her. She approves of provocative outfits and beautiful bookish men, don't you, Gladys? She's just a bit under-the-weather today."

"I *chair* the committee, thank you very much," Gladys Scarlett corrected her.

"Yes, of course. Gladys is very involved in the community. She's on all sorts of committees; I forget which ones are which."

"It's nice to meet you, Gladys," I held out my hand and the old woman shook. She had a firm grip. "I'm Wilhelmina Wilde. I used to be one of Mrs. Ellis' students—"

"Wilde?" Mrs. Scarlett's eyes lit up. "Are you any relation to our Oscar?"

"Um, I don't think so." My heart skipped a beat. My mum ran away from home when she was sixteen to be with my dad, who abandoned her shortly thereafter while she was pregnant with me. She still didn't talk to anyone in her family, and I'd never met any relatives. "I don't know anyone by that name—"

"No, no, no, *Oscar Wilde*, the great Victorian writer and provocateur. We studied *The Picture of Dorian Gray* in the book club last month, didn't we, Linda?"

"We certainly did. Although I must admit, it wasn't as vulgar as I expected."

"This month's choice should be more to your taste," Mrs. Scarlett declared. "It's one of the most banned books in America since its release in 1962 because of its vulgarity and language. That's what makes it so *invigorating.*"

"You're both in a book club?" I asked, interested.

"But of course! I'm surprised Heathcliff hasn't told you about it," Mrs. Ellis was busy scanning the books on the fiction shelves, probably looking for more of her favorite bodice-rippers. "Gladys here has been running the Argleton Banned Book Club for the last year."

"Banned Book Club? So you read only banned books?" The idea intrigued me. Heathcliff stomped on my foot in an attempt to get me to hurry the conversation along, but I ignored him.

"Yes. It was all my idea. We feel it's important to ensure that censorship continues to be challenged," said Mrs. Scarlett. "Each month, we choose a different book that has been banned in some way, and we read and discuss its merits and characters over high tea."

"We come in every month to collect the books for our members," Mrs. Ellis waved at Heathcliff. "Mr. Heathcliff is so good to put our requests aside for us. That's why we're here, for our six copies of *Of Mice and Men*."

"Don't talk about mice!" Morrie yelled from upstairs.

"He's a bit sensitive at the moment," I stage-whispered, loud enough for Morrie to hear. "A tiny mouse ran up his trousers, and he hasn't been the same since."

"It wasn't a tiny mouse. It was enormous, like all things in my trousers!"

"I can see why you feel at home in this shop, Mabel," Mrs. Scarlett huffed, tapping her crutch against the floor. "Young lady, please tell me you've got all six copies. I can't stand for something else to go wrong."

Heathcliff dumped a stack of books on the desk. "There. Six copies in near perfect condition. If you find any mouse droppings, you can have the books half-off. Now, can we move this along? This is a bookshop, not a bloody social club—"

"What else has gone wrong?" I asked as I elbowed Heathcliff out of the way to ring up the books.

"We used to meet in the village hall, but some workmen on the King's Copse development lost control of their earthmoving machine and drove it straight through the wall." Mrs. Ellis' face lit up with delight. "So of course the place is in a right state, and Health and Safety won't allow us to meet there until it's fixed."

"We asked about using the youth group room, but some members of the church committee objected," Mrs. Scarlett declared. "Apparently, our book club has a corrupting influence on the community. Personally, I think it's an attempt to oust me from my seat and replace me with that rotten Dorothy Ingram."

"Well, we *are* reading books the church considers objectionable," Mrs. Ellis clucked. "Although how anyone can object to Harry Potter is beyond me. Young Harry never gets his end away—"

"Yes, and how they can object to fine literature and yet support that hideous development is beyond me!"

"Development?" I asked. I'd been out of the loop of Argleton news in New York City. I didn't know anything about a development.

"Grey Lachlan, a big city developer, purchased the old King's Copse wood. They're building a huge housing development behind Argleton." Mrs. Ellis made a face. "Several houses are already going in on the clear strip between the wood and the village. That's how the village hall got knocked through."

"I bet they did it on purpose. It's a dreadful business, that development. They want to expand right through the old wood!" Mrs. Scarlett tsked. She leaned closer and whispered conspiratorially. I caught the faintest whiff of garlic on her breath. "But we'll soon be putting a stop to it."

"How?" I tried to picture Mrs. Scarlett and a horde of formidable old biddies chaining themselves to trees.

"Grey Lachlan may own the land, but if they want to put anything on it, they'll have to go through the planning process just like everyone else," Mrs. Scarlett declared, puffing out her chest. "As the head of the planning committee, I don't intend to allow their modern monstrosities to sully our quaint local vernacular. Argleton is a popular destination for tourists and locals because of its old world charm, and this development threatens that. I'm surprised you're not more concerned about it." She glared at Heathcliff. "They'll drive away your customers!"

"Good," Heathcliff muttered. "I hope they start building tomorrow."

"Gladys has collected a petition of supporters from the local community to block the plans until a design is submitted that's more in keeping with our heritage. She's really very clever," Mrs. Ellis put in. "I'm looking forward to the meeting next week where she will present it. Grey Lachlan will be there. He's rather handsome."

"He's a *scoundrel*," Mrs. Scarlett hissed. "If his wife wasn't in our book club, I'd see him driven out of this village. But that doesn't solve the issue of a meeting place for our book club. Do either of you happen to know of any spaces to rent in the village? If we don't find anything, we shall have to meet at the Lachlan house, and I won't be having with that."

"Why don't you meet here?" I asked.

Heathcliff's boot slammed down on my foot. I masked the pain with a sweet smile.

"Oh, that would be wonderful!" Mrs. Ellis clapped her hands together. "How appropriate to have our book club in an actual bookshop!"

Mrs. Scarlett sniffed as she surveyed the rows of shelves stuffed with books, the torn leather armchair beside the window, and the stuffed armadillo in the center of the display table. "It's rather dark in here. One needs to be able to read *Of Mice And Men* in order to discuss it."

I agreed. I'd been slowly adding lamps to the upstairs rooms to brighten the place up so I could actually see, but I hadn't told Heathcliff that yet.

Instead, I said, "How many are in your book club? You could all fit into the World History room." Nevermore Bookshop was divided into several tiny rooms and pokey corridors. The World History room was the largest space on the ground floor, dominated by the bay window that formed part of a pentagonal turret on the western corner of the building. Floor-to-ceiling windows and pastel yellow wallpaper gave the room a cheery quality. "It's lovely and light in there."

"Let's see," Mrs. Scarlett ticked off her fingers, "there's the two of us, and Sylvia Blume – she's the local medium, bit of a daft lady, but she brings the most delicious homemade tea selection. Mrs. Lachlan, of course, wife to the hated developer. They live in the big house on the hill, pretending they're old money when really they're just scrubbers from the East End. Then there's young Ginny Button and my dear friend Brenda Winstone. She's Mabel's cousin, isn't she?"

"She is. A lovely lady, although she married a lug of a man – the famous historian, Harold Winstone. No doubt you'll hear all about him. Poor Brenda is so smitten with Harold, but he's an utter womanizer and a terrible writer to boot. I'm glad *he's* not in our club." Mrs. Ellis wrinkled her brow. "We'd love to host the Banned Book Club in the shop, and I hope you and the hand-some Mr. Heathcliff will join us."

"Not happening," Heathcliff growled, thumping a dusty stack of books on the counter.

"I'd love to," I beamed.

"Oh, how wonderful." Mrs. Ellis clapped her hands together. "We always get Greta at the bakery to cater our meetings. She makes the most amazing cream doughnuts. Gladys and I have one every morning after our walk, don't we? We're popping over after we've paid for our books and we'll make sure she includes enough for everyone."

"You'll need to read the book by Wednesday—eeeee!" Mrs. Scarlett clutched her chest. Her face puffed up, her already red cheeks darkening. "A mouse!"

I whirled around just in time to see a white streak fly across the floor and disappear behind Heathcliff's desk. He leapt to his feet, cursing. Quoth swooped down from the chandelier and dived after the rodent. The mouse disappeared into the stacks of books, but Quoth wasn't small enough to fit into the gap and he couldn't stop in time. He smashed into the shelf and tumbled across the floor in a flurry of feathers.

"Quoth!" I picked him up and cradled him in my arms, feeling his body for broken bones.

He blinked his eyes at me, preening as I stroked the top of his head.

I meant to do that, his voice landed inside my skull. I was still getting used to Quoth's occasional telepathic interjections when he was in his raven form.

I smiled. "Well, you're just fine."

"Help! Gladys!" Mrs. Ellis cried.

I whirled around. Mrs. Scarlett had dropped her crutch and sunk to her knees, one hand gripping the edge of Heathcliff's desk, the other clutching her stomach. She leaned her head against her shoulder and sucked in deep, garlicky breaths.

"I'm fine," she wheezed. "Give me a moment."

"Gladys isn't well," Mrs. Ellis cooed, rubbing her friend's shoulder. "The doctors think it's her heart. She gets these dizzy spells, and—"

"Make way, doctor coming through." Morrie clattered down the stairs. He dropped to his knees beside the old lady and peered into her eyes, sniffed her garlic breath, pinched her earlobes, and slapped her cheeks.

"I'm fine, don't fuss." Mrs. Scarlett gripped Morrie's shoulder and hauled herself to her feet. "I just had a fright."

"The bloody mouse," Morrie swore. "You saw it, didn't you? It wasn't a mouse so much as a vicious *dog*—"

"Yes, well." Mrs. Scarlett leaned against her crutch and dabbed at her cheeks with her handkerchief. "I think we'll be going now. Just be good and make sure that mouse is taken care of before our meeting."

"Did you hear that?" Heathcliff growled at Quoth, who'd perched on the top of the register.

"Croak!"

CHAPTER TWO

"*Y*ou're late home again tonight," Mum complained as I walked through the door and dumped my bag on the sofa.

"Sorry. Mr. Dennison's widow brought in a huge box of railway books, and Heathcliff wanted them shelved as soon as possible." We'd also drunk a bottle of wine and Morrie and I had a pretty heated make-out session, but I decided not to mention that. "Did you know that railway books basically pay for second-hand bookshops to remain open? Ishtar bless those anoraks—"

"I don't like you walking through the neighborhood at night." Mum still lived in the same council flat I grew up in, on the far edge of the estate. Our next door neighbors were gang members, and a house down the road exploded last year when a meth-cooking operation went wrong. It was that kind of neighbor-hood. But since our car only worked on alternative Tuesdays, I'd been walking about at all hours for as long as I could remember and she never commented on it before.

"I wasn't alone." I headed to the fridge and pulled out a block of cheese. "Quoth walked me home."

"One of your new friends?" Mum raced to the door and

peered out into the darkness. "I can't see him. Did he leave without coming in again?"

He flew away. "Yeah, sorry, Mum. He's really shy. You want a cheese toastie?"

She followed me into the kitchen. "I don't like this, Mina. You're spending every spare moment with these men, and I've never met them."

"You know Heathcliff Earnshaw."

"Yes, and that worries me. He's a gypsy. You know what they're like."

"Mum, that's racist, and I'm not talking about this now—" My knife hovered over the cheese as I spied a suspicious-looking set of boxes shoved up against the telly. "What are those boxes?"

"Oh!" Mum bounded over and lifted the flaps, holding up a tiny book. "I've been waiting to tell you. They're my new business."

"What happened to the wobblelators?" My mum was convinced that she was meant to be a millionaire, and that the way to make her dream a reality was to sell useless crap to unsuspecting people. Over the years she'd tried every get-rich-quick scheme out there, and her latest attempt was wobbling exercise power-plate machines.

"They were just so *heavy*. And I couldn't compete against the young, fit salespeople. But with these, I think I've finally found my calling. Even you have to admit that this time I'm onto something special."

She tossed a tiny book onto the table. I picked it up and gaped at the title.

Cat Language – a Cat-to-Human Dictionary.

I flipped the book open. It was a dictionary, all right. Only it translated the language of cats into English. Apparently, 'mew-mew' meant 'I am hungry' and 'meeeeorrrrw,' was 'feed me now, or I'll claw your face off.'

I stifled a laugh. "Mum, these are... um..."

"I know, they're genius! Everyone has a pet they want to understand. And all those cat videos on the internet mean I can try some *search engine marketing.* Plus, the animal behavioral doctor who put these together has no idea how to run a successful business, so it's an absolute steal. I'm not locked into purchasing a certain amount of books. I lease the rights to the dictionary file, have the local printer make up the copies, and then I get to keep *all* the profit." She dumped a box on the table. I winced as hundreds of books spilled out – not just cat dictionaries, but dogs and hamsters and mice and goldfish. *Goldfish? What noises do goldfish even make?* "I thought you could set up a display on the counter at Nevermore Bookshop, maybe push them to anyone who buys pet books."

"Mum, *no.*"

"But you work at a bookshop. Mina, it's perfect."

"I'm not taking these to Heathcliff. No one will buy these."

"I've got ones for dogs and gerbils and mice, too—"

"I said *no.* Can we drop this?" I slid two pieces of bread into the oven and turned on the grill. "I've got a lot of reading to do tonight. I'm hosting a book club meeting at the shop and I need to finish the book they're studying. If you need me, I'll be in my room."

Mum frowned, flicking through the cat dictionary. I knew I hadn't heard the last about it.

～

I managed to shower and crawl into bed without getting into it with Mum again. Our flat was technically only a one bedroom, but we'd blocked out the windows in the tiny conservatory off the living room and added a cheap standing wardrobe Mum found on the side of the road. The room was barely big enough for my bed and clothes, but I'd managed to cover every spare surface in band posters and ticket stubs and Polaroid pictures of Ashley and me as rebellious teens pouting and making rude hand gestures at the camera. Mum hadn't changed a thing since I left for New York City. Looking at the walls now gave me a weird feeling in my gut. I felt like I hardly knew the person staring back at me. She was another Mina, from another world.

I jammed my headphones in my ears, cranked up a playlist of Nick Cave and The Sisters of Mercy, and opened *Of Mice and Men*. Bugs slammed into the windows outside, attracted to the too-bright bulb hanging over the bed.

Halfway into the first chapter, I lost touch with the outside world. The words and the music carried me away, and I forgot that I was Mina Wilde, failed fashion designer and soon-to-be blind bookstore assistant sleeping in her old childhood bedroom in the dingy flat she swore she'd never return to. Instead, I was on the cotton fields of southern America with migrant workers George and Lennie as they toiled and dreamed of a future where they owned their own plot of land. A dream so remote and impossible it clung to them like a shroud.

I knew what that was like.

One thing that jumped out at me in the book was how loneliness shaped many of the interactions between characters. George and Lennie's friendship came about because of loneliness. Candy lost his dog. Everyone had aspirations that drove them from true human connection. Even the nearby town in the story was called Soledad, which a quick Google search revealed means 'solitude' in Spanish.

All that loneliness reminded me of myself and the guys. I'd carried loneliness with me my entire life. I thought I'd found a real friend in Ashley, but New York City and her own greed and a knife in the heart had put paid to that. Like me, Heathcliff, Morrie, and Quoth each bore their own loneliness. Heathcliff wore his like a badge of honor, Morrie buried his deep and covered it with cocky jokes and power games, and Quoth... Quoth used his as a shroud.

Loneliness... and powerlessness. Every character in *Of Mice and Men* suffered from some lack of power, and each had a scheme by which they could attain more power and status. By the end of the book, every one of those schemes had been torn down and dashed to pieces. Even Lennie, the strongest physical character in the book, had his inherent power stripped away by his intellectual disability. There was no way to halt to march or time or the inevitability of the natural order.

I finished *Of Mice and Men* around midnight, tears streaming down my cheeks as (spoiler alert) George gives into the futility of his powerlessness and kills Lennie. The TV still blared in the living room. I desperately wanted to pee, but I didn't want another confrontation, so I turned the light off, lay down on the pillow, and stared at the ceiling.

I must've fallen asleep, because the next thing I knew, grey light streamed through the gaps in my moldy curtains. Rain pattered against the glass, and a cold chill nipped my bare skin. I crawled out of bed, tiptoed to the bathroom to relieve my now bursting bladder, pulled on some clothes, and snuck out of the house before Mum could bug me about cat-language dictionaries again. I opened my bag to throw in my phone and found she'd stuffed three inside. I tossed them on the sofa where she was sure to see them, and left.

I hurried through the empty streets. The early hours of the morning were some of the most pleasant on the estate. If I squinted hard enough, I could pretend I didn't see the hollowed-out cars on the neighbor's lawn or the windows covered with sheets at the dealer's house, and that I really lived in a picturesque American candy box suburb.

Not that I'd have to squint much longer.

And just like that, the grief and panic hit me, rolling through my body like a wave. How much longer would I be able to see the world?

How many more days would I be able to put together a killer outfit like the cuffed red tartan pants, white sleeveless shirt, and leather suspenders I now wore? How many nights would I be able to stay up late reading in bed? How many more times would I be able to stare into the icy depths of Morrie's eyes, and see him staring back?

I opened my eyes as wide as I could, and took in every detail of the passing flats. Would I miss their drab, peeling paint and the rows of overflowing bins lining the footpath? I didn't want to find out.

But sooner or later it would happen, and I... I wasn't ready. I felt like I'd created a little world for myself inside the bookshop – the kind of family I'd never had when it was just my mum and me, the friends I'd been so desperate to have back in secondary school. But then I remembered why I was back in Argleton in the first place, and the dread settled on me and took away all the happiness I'd managed to claw back.

And when you added in all the messed-up feelings I had for the guys... For Morrie, whose touch made my body sing but whose criminal escapades terrified me. For Heathcliff, whose dark heart begged me to save him but whose story I knew contained another that he would always love. For Quoth, whose kind heart melted mine but who would never be able to lead a normal life.

All perfect guys, and any relationship I had with them was doomed to fail. The inevitability of that failure hung in the air between us, unspoken, like the characters in *Of Mice and Men*. It left us with what Morrie and I had – fuck buddies, friends-with-benefits. It was fun... the most fun I'd ever had in my *life*. But how long was that going to last before it destroyed all our friendships?

What the hell am I doing?

You could just not sleep with any of them, a voice inside my head reminded me.

I almost laughed. Yeah, because that was an option. Clearly, my conscience had its eyes closed whenever I entered the shop because hot damn, I wouldn't be saying no to any of them.

You could be with all of them, the voice offered. *Quoth said—*

Also not an option. That just would never work.

Wouldn't it? Why not?

I reached the village and crossed the green toward the shops. Quoth's words from a month ago reverberated around in my head. It was after he saw Morrie and me together, and he'd followed me and told me how they all wanted me to be happy and safe, about how none of them wanted to compete for me. As if they'd discussed it, as if they were okay with it.

Obviously, Quoth knew about Morrie and me, and I had to assume Heathcliff did, too. We hadn't exactly been quiet this last month. But neither of them had said anything about it. In fact, Quoth flirted with me the other day. Heathcliff was a big grump, but that was no different from usual. In fact, he'd even gone out – of his own volition – and brought back lunch for me last week. So maybe they really did want to share me. Maybe it really *could* work.

This is insane. I've got to stop thinking about this as if it's an actual option.

The bakery across the road from the shop wasn't open yet. I could see Greta – the German girl who owned the bakery – through the window, sliding trays of pies into the ovens and dusting her cream doughnuts with powdered sugar. I waved at her and she waved back. I couldn't help but grin. Back in New York City, you'd never wave to shopkeepers or bakers, because everyone was a stranger.

I slid my key into the front door and pushed it open. The floorboards creaked under my feet as I entered the darkened shop. I fumbled along the shelf and flicked on the small lamp I'd installed by the front door the other day. It was shaped like an old, bent pipe, with a funky Edison bulb to illuminate a small circle around my feet. Heathcliff hadn't noticed it.

"Meow?"

"Hey, Grimalkin." I bent down and brushed my hand over her soft fur. She leapt into my arms, butting her head against my chin.

"Fine," I laughed, stroking her under the chin until her body vibrated with purrs. "I can see no one else is up yet. I'll get you something to eat."

I walked into the main room, flicking on the lights as I went. Behind Heathcliff's desk was a bowl for Grimalkin and one for Quoth, who liked to snack on berries during the day while he was in his raven form. I filled Grimalkin's bowl with a packet of wet food, and she chowed down hungrily.

"Did you catch that mouse yet, girl?" I asked her as I stacked the papers on Heathcliff's desk and made a new line in the ledger for the day's sales.

Grimalkin looked up from her bowl and gave me a pained look. *Don't ask me about that bloody mouse,* she seemed to be saying.

"Oh well. I couldn't catch it, either. Better luck next time." I rubbed her head. She purred against my hand. "See? I don't need a cat dictionary. We understand each other perfectly."

The World History room was behind the main room. It had probably been the ballroom during the Victorian period of the house, judging by the expensive flocked wallpaper, baby piano piled with books beside the imposing fireplace, twin chandeliers hanging from the high ceiling, narrow doorway leading off to what had once been the kitchen, and the original chaise lounge and Chinese tea table in the pentagonal alcove. Two rows of shelves along the center of the room held volumes on archaeology, military history, and British/Scottish/Welsh history. A small display in the corner held popular conspiracy theory books –

Heathcliff's idea of a joke. Random chairs and haphazard stacks of books lined the walls.

If we rearrange the shelves so they run the opposite way, we'll have more room in the pentagon for some extra chairs and a table for the Banned Book Club. My mind whirred at the possibilities. In fact, the dimensions of the room were much more generous than I remembered. *If we pushed the shelves right back against the walls, we could hold other events in here... book readings, exhibitions, even a gallery opening for Quoth—*

"You know, for sleeping with the world's foremost criminal mind, you need to work on your breaking and entering skills."

I whirled around. Quoth perched on the edge of the chaise lounge, hugging his feet to his chest. A couple of black feathers stuck to his hair, which caught the light streaming in through the windows, shooting jets of color through the obsidian strands.

"Technically, I'm just *entering,*" I held up my key. "I didn't even hear you come downstairs."

"You must have been lost in thought, because I've been tapping on the chamber door for a while now." He rapped his knuckles against the doorframe.

"You're so funny. Hey, do you have to poop on yourself for quoting that poem?"

"Nope." Quoth stepped into the room and came up beside me. Today he wore a black singlet speckled with paint, and a pair of black cargo pants, also paint splattered. On any other guy that would've looked scruffy, but Quoth made it appear dark and mysterious. "So what are you doing?"

"I wanted to get the room ready for the Banned Book Club tomorrow. I know Heathcliff doesn't want it to succeed, but I think we should give it a shot. This bookshop could be a really amazing community space. It's already brighter with your artwork on the walls. Imagine if we had book clubs and author readings and art shows as well?"

Quoth gave me a sad smile that broke my heart. "I'm sure Heathcliff would just love all that."

"I'm hoping to convince him." I grabbed the end of one of the bookshelves. "The first step is to make this book club go off without a hitch. Can you get the other side of this?"

"Only if you tell me why you're *really* here."

"I told you. I want the meeting to—"

"*Mina.*"

I groaned. "Fine. I wanted to escape my mum."

Quoth tilted his head to the side. He didn't ask me to elaborate, but something about the way his silence filled the space between us made me desperate to fill it.

"My mum is…" I tried to think of the words. "You'd have to meet her to understand."

"I'd like that."

I shook my head. "*Not* happening. I need my home life and my bookshop life to remain separate. Mum is… she's amazing and so selfless. She did everything for me so I'd have a better life and opportunities she never had. But I think deep down she believes she failed. I think she feels responsible for my eyesight. It's hard because I want to make her feel better, since it's not her fault, but also… sometimes it feels like everything is about her. I can't be upset about it around her because it makes her feel bad, and right now I'm so upset I want to scream all the time."

Quoth didn't say anything. We shoved the bookshelf against the wall and started on the other. The silence welled up between us, and more words tumbled out of me before I could stop them. "Mum grew up in Liverpool, in the worst house in the poorest neighborhood. Her father was in and out of jail for aggravated assault and drug dealing. Her mum was a junkie. She stopped going to school at fifteen and got pregnant a year later. Mum decided she didn't want her parents' life for us so she ran away, followed my dad to Argleton, and cut her parents off completely. My Dad abandoned her shortly after, but she never went back to them. She said my grandmother came to look for us once, but she told her to piss off."

"I'm sorry," Quoth said.

"Don't be. At least I had a family. I had Mum, and she's always been there for me and she's always done the best for me, but… she hasn't been able to throw off her past. She's uneducated. She can't hold down a real job – instead, she reads tarot cards for the rich ladies on the hill, the ones with more money than sense. She's obsessed with the idea of being wealthy, but she thinks she's entitled to the perks of being a CEO without the work. She encouraged me to go to fashion school because she believes I'll make us millionaires, which is the complete opposite of what most parents would've done, especially since I also had scholarship offers from Oxford and Cambridge for English."

"Your mum sounds fascinating," Quoth laughed.

"She's got a new get-rich-quick-scheme – selling dictionaries of cat and dog language, can you believe it? They're completely ridiculous. The dumb thing is, I think she's chosen it because I work in the bookshop. Like, she thinks these stupid books she gets made at the local printers are the same thing as this." I held up *Of Mice and Men*.

Quoth said nothing.

"It's probably that I'm too old to be living at home, but she's been winding me up lately. She's got a bee in her bonnet about my job and you guys. She keeps trying to see you when you drop me off, and asking me hundreds of questions. I bet she'll start dropping by the shop just because she's 'in the neighborhood'." I used air quotes. "Why can't she just leave me alone?"

"Do you want me to come inside and meet her?"

"No." The word came out harsher than I intended. I imagined my three intelligent guys meeting my ditzy, riches-obsessed mother, and an old, deep shame flared on my cheeks. "I mean, thank you for the offer, but there's no point."

"We *could* meet her, you know. If it would help."

I snorted. "Yeah right. 'Hey, Mum, here are my friends, the grumpy antihero, the supervillain, and the bird.'"

Quoth looked away. Regret swelled in my chest.

"Quoth, I'm sorry. I didn't mean that."

"Yeah, you did." His voice was small.

I sighed. "Look, it's not that—"

"Let's just get this room cleaned up." Quoth avoided my eyes as he reached for the shelves. As he placed his hand on the top, a white streak darted down his arm, launched itself into midair, performed a perfect series of somersaults before landing on all fours, and disappeared into the stacks.

"Bloody hell." Quoth leapt back, feathers exploding from his cheeks.

"You haven't taken care of that mouse yet!" I wailed.

"Morrie put down some traps," he mumbled, trying to rein back his forming beak. "But apparently our mouse friend doesn't have the palette to appreciate a fine French *Bleu d'Auvergne*."

I groaned. Of course, Morrie would choose some expensive cheese for a bloody mousetrap. I'm surprised he hadn't set down tiny glasses of wine and crackers for the mouse.

"Relax," Quoth wrangled his jaw back into place. He grinned at me, but the smile didn't reach his eyes. "Grimalkin and I will see to it that it doesn't go anywhere near this room. Now, how about giving me a hand with this bookcase?"

CHAPTER THREE

"Good morning, sleepy." I slid onto Morrie's bed and placed a steaming cup of coffee on his bed stand.

A pillow crease ran along Morrie's cheekbone, accentuating his aquiline features. He opened one eye, and an ice-blue orb swiveled toward me with a hunger that had nothing to do with the anticipation of caffeine. "Mmmm, it is now."

Morrie wrapped his arm around me and pulled me against him, throwing the duvet over us and enveloping me in his warmth. His naked chest fitted around me, and his hardness pressed against my thigh.

"I have to be at work in fifteen minutes," I warned him, sinking into his body.

"I know the boss," Morrie murmured, kissing a trail of fire down my neck. "I bet he'll understand."

"I know the boss too, and I bet you he won't."

"Then we'd better be quick." Morrie rolled me underneath him, grabbing a condom from off his nightstand. His other hand cupped my cheek, tracing the line of my jaw as his lips devoured mine.

Morrie's kisses swept me away – any thoughts or worries or

fears I had disappeared the moment his full lips met mine. That was why I hadn't managed to ask him about his criminal dealings to assuage my moral misgivings.

And it wasn't going to happen this morning, either. Not with his fingers dancing over my stomach, reaching down, *down...* I let my legs fall open, and Morrie rolled the condom on and slid inside me.

I gasped as he filled me, every inch of him touching long-sleeping parts of me, awakening my whole body and bringing me to life. I clung to his sinewy frame, moving with him, settling into his rhythm, trying not to race ahead, to show him how much I wanted him to lose control, because that made him tighten up and grasp his control even tighter.

Even though we were on the clock, Morrie kept up his languid, steady pace. Everything about him was a battle between his two natures – the cool, calculating mathematician who desired total control, and the criminal who embraced chaos at every turn.

My body betrayed me, writhing beneath him, pressing back against him, begging him to go faster, harder. Morrie kept his relaxed pace, as if he were in no hurry at all, as if he were exactly where he wanted to be. I ground my hips against him, driving him deeper.

"Now, now, gorgeous, there's no fire."

There was a fire – in my veins, in my heart, in all the hidden parts of me he'd stoked to life.

Morrie knitted his fingers in mine, pressing my hand into the pillow above my head. The gesture was both intimate and controlling. My eyes flicked to the hook on Morrie's ceiling, and I imagined his cheeky smirk as he locked me into it, and what he might do to me if I dared relinquish all my control...

An orgasm hit me, shocking in its suddenness. I leaned into the pillows as I clenched around Morrie, allowing the waves of pleasure to roll over me. His own body stiffened, and with a final shudder, he came as well, tightening around me, his jaw clenching and twisting.

I loved that twist in his jaw – the slightest imperfection hinting at a loss of control, only for a fraction of a second. Then my Morrie was back, grinning wickedly at me like the cat that got the cream.

Morrie rolled off me, his fingers trailing over my skin. He reached across me and turned his phone screen toward him. "Look at the time, you still have three minutes."

"There's a hook on your ceiling," I murmured.

"I don't know what that doctor of yours is on about – your eyes work perfectly fine."

"*Why* do you have a hook on your ceiling?"

Morrie's eyes bore into mine, the corner of his mouth flicking up into that infuriating smirk of his. "Do you want to find out?"

My stomach plunged to my knees. My eyes trailed to the leather and steel apparatuses hanging beside his bed. I didn't live under a rock. Ashley and I had giggled our way through the *50 Shades of Grey* movie. I knew Morrie was pansexual and had some kinky proclivities. Did I want to be part of that? Was I that kind of girl? Most importantly, did I trust *James Moriarty* to truss me up on his ceiling?

His fingers brushed over my clit and my body answered for me. *Yes, yes, yes.*

"Yes," I whispered.

"Couldn't quite hear you, love." Morrie dragged his teeth across my earlobe.

Fuck, I have to... There was something that had to happen first. I needed control of my body back. My brain had some questions that needed answering first.

I forced myself to shuffle away from Morrie's touch, rolling over to face him. "What are we?"

"*Homo sapiens,*" he replied without missing a beat, his hands roaming down my shirt. *By Astarte. Be strong, Mina.*

27

"No," I slapped his hand away. "I mean, you and me... what is this thing we're doing?"

"Right now I'm trying to make you come with one-and-a-half minutes on the clock." Morrie's hand burrowed between my legs again.

"Morrie," I warned.

He didn't stop stroking me. "Mina, I'm not going to be your boyfriend."

"Oh." Disappointment surged through me. *Why not? Why don't you want me? I thought we had something more than sex going on here, but maybe I read it wrong? By Aphrodite, I'm hopeless.*

Morrie laughed. "If you could see your face, you look like I just told you the Sex Pistols broke up."

"They *did* break up." I slapped his hand away again, but he was relentless, and his finger... *oh, oh...*

"I mean to say, I'm not going to be your boyfriend because that's not what you want."

"You don't know what I want."

"I know that you flirt with Quoth. I know that you make those big doe eyes at Heathcliff whenever his back is turned. I can read you like a book." Morrie kissed a trail along my neck. "A good book, with lots of naughty parts."

"I'm not sleeping with either of them."

"Why not?"

He plunged a finger inside me. I moaned, gritting my teeth. *Focus.* "Because I'm not a slut."

"Slut is such a loaded word, Mina. Aren't all those punk rock songs you love about sex and rebellion?"

"Yeah, but..." Morrie's finger drummed against my clit. My body exploded with a second orgasm. I arched my back against the pillow, letting the pleasure wash over me. Morrie withdrew his hand and cupped my cheek, his icy gaze arresting me.

"Exactly." Morrie's wicked smile lit up his entire face. "You don't have to compromise by choosing one of us. I never did.

Honestly, Quoth could do with having a woman to share his deep and meaningful feelings with, because neither Heathcliff nor I care. And maybe you could fuck some happiness into surly McGrumpyface."

"I don't…"

"Sorry love, I've decided these are my terms," Morrie grinned. "I'm not going to commit until you at least know what you're missing. Sample the wares. Be like the customers who read all the juicy bits before they decide which book to buy."

"I don't understand. You want me to…"

"I want you to fuck Heathcliff and Quoth. In fact, I insist upon it. Now…" he thrust his hand back under the sheets. "I've only got thirty-five seconds left, but I think I can work a miracle."

"That's fine." I slid out of bed, diving for my clothes. My cheeks burned. I dressed facing the wall, unable to look Morrie in the eye. He chuckled behind me, and the back of my neck flared with heat.

I can't believe him. Who asks the girl they're sleeping with to shag their two best friends?

James Moriarty, apparently.

And who am I that I'm even still here? Why do I want to do it so bad?

Great. Just great. I'd tried to get some clarity, and now I was more confused than ever.

CHAPTER FOUR

"*Y*ou reprehensible cur! You mewling quim! I'll smash you open like a rotten hazelnut."

I raced downstairs in time to see Heathcliff yank the monitor off his desk and hoist it over his shoulder, as though he intended to dash its brains out on the ground. "No!" I leapt across the room and flung myself in front of him, catching the corner of the monitor. Heathcliff stumbled back in surprise. I grabbed the monitor from his hands before he could protest and set it back on the desk.

"What did you do now?" I plugged the screen back in and rescued the computer mouse from under the armadillo's tail.

"I did nothing!"

"Then why were you about to smash the computer on the floor?"

"The-Store-That-Shall-Not-Be-Named informed me that our customer rating has been downgraded from good to poor," Heathcliff yelled. "All because some roving cumberworld complained that the six-hundred-year-old bible he purchased was *written in bloody Latin*. In addition to being nice to customers,

I've now got to hold their hands and wipe their snotty noses and burp them, too?"

"Yes, yes, The-Store-That-Shall-Not-Be-Named is evil, and customers are dumb. I get it. Can't you wait for me before you throw expensive equipment across the room?"

"I hate computers! The world was better when we didn't have computers and *apps*." Heathcliff said that last part like it was a curse word.

"No, it wasn't. The world sucked back then, too – it just sucked without Uber Eats." I switched the monitor back on. Our online book catalog flashed in front of the screen, and the message from The-Store-That-Shall-Not-Be-Named flickered across the top. Scanning the text, I found that all we needed to do to get the rating back up was obtain two more positive reviews, which would happen naturally as we sent out our next batch of online orders. Heathcliff always saw the negative side. "Besides, if we didn't have apps, I might never have seen your job ad. Think of how dull your life would be without me."

"Your shirt is on inside out," he muttered without looking up from his book.

"Shite!" I darted into the World History room, tore off my shirt, and put it back on the right way around. Heathcliff glanced up when I walked back in. His eyes met mine and my breath hitched. I remembered the fierce kiss we shared the day he found me inside the occult room, the way he'd grabbed me as though he couldn't control himself. The way he devoured me with all the fierce passion that had fueled the torrid romance of *Wuthering Heights* and made him such a beloved antihero.

My heart pattered faster. Morrie's insane challenge played over in my mind. One way or the other, I had to get this Heathcliff thing out of my system. *I need to find out if what I'm feeling is for this Heathcliff, here and now, or if I'm lusting after the character I fell in love with as a teenager.*

I squared my shoulders and sucked in a breath. *Here goes nothing.*

"Heathcliff, um…"

"What?" His head snapped up again, his black eyes staring straight into my soul.

"Can we… can I… take you out for dinner on Friday night?"

"Why?"

Why? What kind of answer is why? "Because… you never leave the shop. I'm worried you don't have enough fun. Or enough nutrients."

"I have fun." Heathcliff thumped the stack of books on his desk. "I'm pricing stock, aren't I?"

"That's not exactly what I had in mind. I was thinking more the kind of fun where you hang out with a person you like and get to know them a bit better. It wouldn't even have to be crazy. I'm not talking about going skydiving or getting matching tattoos. Just dinner. Maybe a drink. Do you want to go or not?"

Heathcliff's black eyes studied me. After a long time, he said. "As long as I don't have to wear anything fancy."

I glanced down at his wrinkled white shirt, waistcoat, and old-fashioned trousers. With his heavy boots and long, messy hair, he already looked like he was the lead singer of the world's hottest rock band. "I think you're good."

I was just about to say something else, but the bell tinkled. I poked my head into the hall. "Welcome to Nevermore Books—"

My words were lost in screams of delight. The front door banged open and a deluge of screaming, laughing, childish voices poured into the shop. I glanced up just in time to see a wave of young faces run in all directions and disappear into the shelves. Their delighted squeals bounced off the high ceilings and echoed around the darkened corners.

"What the fuck?" Heathcliff growled. "It's like the Mongols are invading."

"Careful, children, behave yourselves," a matronly voice called after them. Being children, they completely ignored it.

I whipped my head back just as two boys crashed past me, arms swinging as they kicked a soccer ball between them. Heathcliff stood up, scooping books into his arms. "You deal with this mess. I'm going upstairs to get some peace."

"But—"

"The whole reason I hired an assistant was so I don't have to deal with customers. *Especially* not the ones with snotty noses and jammy hands." Heathcliff picked up his book and ducked into the storeroom behind the desk. "Have fun."

"Wait—"

He slammed the door behind him. I heard a bolt slide into the lock.

"You bastard," I hissed at the door, then turned around just in time to see a young girl scrambling onto the table to grab the stuffed armadillo.

"Don't climb on that!" I yelled, rushing over and scooping the child off the table before she fell and cracked her head open.

"But I wanna!"

"Come on, Trudy," An older girl, about fourteen, rushed in and grabbed the child's hand. "Let's look in the children's section. I bet we'll be able to find some lovely illustrated biblical stories for you."

They raced off, brushing past a round woman who stood in the doorway. She ducked as a paper plane flew over her head. Her face crumpled apologetically and her rosy cheeks reddened as she held out her hand to me. "Hello, my dear. I'm so sorry for all the noise. The children are very excited to visit a bookshop. Many of them don't have books in their homes, you know. I believe reading is just so important, so I thought I'd bring them over."

"It's fine," I said, straightening the armadillo and taking her hand. "If you could just remind them it's a bookshop and not a jungle gym, everything will be fine."

"I'll do my best, although I'm afraid sometimes they get the better of me." She patted her thigh. "These old bones aren't as fast as they used to be. They're a rambunctious bunch, but they're good souls. It's nice to see them learning and experiencing something new. If I can turn just one of them into a reader, well, I'll have made a difference."

"I was a reader growing up," I smiled at her. "I've never forgotten the feeling of diving into a book and escaping to another world. Is this a school group?" The kids were a range of different ages, and there were far too many to be her children.

"Oh, heavens no. These are my youth group. I'm Brenda Winstone, and I run the youth group activities at the Argleton Presbyterian Church," the woman frowned. Her rosy face instantly aged, and a look of sadness came over her kind green eyes. "I haven't any children of my own, you see. My husband is Harold Winstone – you might know him, he's a very famous historian. He travels all over the world writing books about interesting buildings and their history. Right now, he's writing a history of the old Argleton hospital, the one they're tearing down? A lovely man is my Harold, but he dedicated his life to his research and didn't want children distracting him. So I donate my time to young ones in need."

"It's lovely to meet you, Brenda. Mrs. Scarlett mentioned you the other day. You're in the Banned Book Club."

Mrs. Winstone's eyes bugged out. "Please, don't say that so loud."

"Oh, I'm sorry. I didn't realize it was a secret."

Mrs. Winstone opened her mouth to say more, but the older girl poked her head in the room and said that a boy named Thomas had thrown up on a George Eliot. Mrs. Winstone dashed off to deal with that particular disaster while I rescued a terrified

Grimalkin from where the boys had her cornered on top of a bookshelf.

As Grimalkin's claws dug into my shoulder, I watched Mrs. Winstone scurry around after the children, who ran circles around her. *What an odd woman.*

Half an hour, a broken chair, one slammed door, and three squashed fingers later, Brenda Winstone paid for a huge stack of children's books and bustled the youth group next door to terrorize Greta at the bakery. I went across the hall to straighten the Fiction room and discovered the teenagers had moved every one of our copies of Darwin's *On The Origin of Species* into the General Fiction section.

Who says religious people don't have a sense of humor?

I'd nearly finished re-ordering the books when Heathcliff emerged from hiding. "So what did they break?"

"Nothing."

"And?"

"There *may* be a tiny scratch on a chair in the Children's room."

"*And?*"

I sighed. "The chair's broken. One boy slammed his friend's fingers in the door, but I think they're just bruised."

"Just you wait, I'll have an HSE officer and the parents' lawyer in here by the end of the day." Heathcliff noticed the stack of Darwin books by my feet. "Church group, were they? Stick all the Darwin in the fiction shelves, did they? If any one of the little bastards sat in my chair, I'll be breaking fingers for real."

I threw a Darwin book at him. He ducked and slipped away, humming under his breath.

He's in a remarkably good mood, considering a horde of marauding children just destroyed his shop and we're hosting a book club tomorrow. It's not... it's not the prospect of our date that's making him almost cheery, is it?

No.

It can't be.

But maybe...

A broad smile crossed my face. After a shaky start back in Argleton, things really were looking up. I had a date with Heathcliff, Morrie was making me feel all kinds of good, no one had been murdered in the shop in over a month, and we were about to host the first of what I hoped would be many events.

I thought back to all the gossip about the King's Copse development, and Mrs. Winstone's reluctance to talk about the book club. Mrs. Scarlett seemed like a harmless old woman, but the more I heard about her and her book club, the more I wondered if I might be running with the badass old biddies of Argleton. *It's just a group of women chatting about books over high tea... it isn't as if the Banned Book Club is dangerous, is it?*

CHAPTER FIVE

"*O*h, this is a lovely room," Mrs. Ellis clapped her hands with glee. "You've done a wonderful job, Mina."

I had to agree. Yesterday, after he sheepishly came out of hiding and forgave me, Quoth and I finished flipping the bookshelves around to create more space and arranged the most comfortable chairs in a semicircle in the bay window. A table with ornate legs held a tray and kettle. I'd managed to locate enough un-chipped teacups and saucers in the guys' flat. I even created a banned books display featuring some other censored titles we have in stock – *The Picture of Dorian Gray, To Kill a Mockingbird, The Handmaid's Tale, Harry Potter.* Alongside it, I added two of Quoth's smaller paintings and a selection of my book art – origami shapes and hollowed books I'd made from discarded stock that Heathcliff had reluctantly allowed me to sell in the shop.

Mrs. Ellis admired one of my hollowed books, trying to see if her hip flask would fit inside the velvet-lined compartment, when Greta bustled in carrying platters of sandwiches and pastries. She arranged them on the table, placing a single plate in front of the wingback chair.

"Mrs. Scarlett has specific dietary requirements," Greta explained when I asked about the plate. "She's been very sick lately with an upset stomach, so she's on a detox diet. Gluten free, egg free, dairy free. I've made special versions of all the treats here for her."

"Thank you so much, Greta. You're a genius. Hey," I had an idea. "Are you sure you don't want to stay for the book club?"

Greta shook her head. "No, no, I've got so much work to do at the bakery. And my English is not good enough to read the books so fast. But thank you, perhaps another time."

She hurried off. I watched her go, feeling like I should go after her and say something else. She was around my age, and like all Germans I knew, her English was flawless, even better than mine. Working all day and night in that bakery... I never saw Greta with an assistant. She must be lonely, especially since people in the village could be unfriendly to outsiders.

Footsteps creaked over the floorboards and Brenda Winstone entered, wearing a long floral cardigan over a pair of tan trousers. "Is this the place? Oh, look at those lovely sandwiches!"

Mrs. Ellis bustled over to introduce us. "Mina, this is my cousin, Mrs. Brenda Winstone."

"We met yesterday," I smiled. "Hello again. How are your charges liking their books?"

Mrs. Winstone's kind face fell. "I'm afraid I won't have a chance to ask them. I've—I've been replaced as youth group leader."

Mrs. Ellis stared in shock. "But why? You're the best thing to ever happen to those children."

Mrs. Winstone sniffed. "One of the dears told that nasty Dorothy Ingram I was in the banned book club and took the youth group to this shop, and that little Billy Bartlett had his fingers smashed and the parents were making trouble. Dorothy got the church committee behind her, and they forced me to resign as the youth group coordinator."

"I'm so sorry!" I cried, thinking it must've been one of the kids overhearing my words. "I didn't mean to get you fired!"

"Heavens no, Wilhelmina, dear. It's not your fault." Mrs. Winstone picked up a sandwich and took a huge bite. "Dorothy's wanted me out for years – she finally had the perfect excuse. I'm trying not to let it bother me, but I'm sure we don't want to bring down the meeting with my sad news. Thank you so much for the use of your shop. The room is absolutely beautiful."

"It's Mina, actually," I smiled. "And I don't own the shop. I just work here. I loved the idea of a Banned Book Club, so I convinced my boss to let us host the event. You can use this room as often as you like."

"Well, it's marvelous. Simply a magical place. Say, do you have a children's story time?" Mrs. Winstone beamed, her rosy cheeks glowing an even deeper red. "I love helping children to read, and I'm certain I could find a lovely tale that would satisfy the parents, too—"

"After your neglect nearly cost poor Billy his fingers, there's not a parent in this village who'll trust their children with you," a cold voice from behind her said.

I glanced up at the elegant young woman who'd just entered the room, her blonde hair perfectly in place and a mink stole hanging around her narrow shoulders, just low enough to reveal an impressive necklace of clustered diamonds and rubies around her neck. She swept past us in a cloud of cloying perfume and settled herself on the end of the chaise lounge, placing both hands on her rounded stomach and peering up at Mrs. Winstone with a smug expression.

"Hello, Brenda, Mabel," she purred.

"Ginny," Mrs. Winstone said, her voice clipped.

"Hello, dear. How is the baby?" Mrs. Ellis sat down beside this newcomer, Ginny, and touched her stomach.

"He's perfect. We've just had our latest scan and the doctor says he'll be strong and healthy, just like his father." Ginny picked up one of the teacups and held it up to the light, frowning at the pattern.

"These aren't Royal Doulton," she pursed her lips.

"Nope," I said, already disliking this posh bitch. I picked up a cupcake and took a big, messy bite. "But they hold liquid, which is the important thing, wouldn't you agree?"

"I… I think I'll go find myself a seat," Mrs. Winstone whispered. She hurried off to take a place on one of the armchairs, as far from Ginny as it was possible to be while still remaining in the circle, and piled sandwiches and cakes onto her plate.

"What's up with those two?" I whispered to Mrs. Ellis as Ginny and Mrs. Winstone glared at each other across the cake stand.

"That's Ginny Button," Mrs. Ellis whispered. "She's unmarried, with a long string of lovers. She loves rubbing Brenda's nose in the fact that she's pregnant."

"Oh, no."

Mrs. Ellis nodded, her face lighting up at the chance to impart some fine gossip. "Ginny's a rotten piece of work, saying what she said. Poor Brenda lives for those children. She desperately wants one of her own, you know, but her husband Harold has given his final word on the matter. Ginny, of course, lets Brenda know every meeting how much of a mouse she is. Ah, I think I smell Sylvia now."

I sniffed as a haze of musky perfume wafted into the room, followed shortly after by a middle-aged woman with a jangle of jewelry and flouncy black peasant skirts. An enormous tie-dyed tote bag slapped against her side. "Am I late?" she wheezed, tucking a strand of frizzy hair behind her ear. The gesture was of little use since the rest of her hair stuck out at all angles, as if she'd just inserted her finger into an electrical socket. Something about her wild eyes and the millions of beaded bracelets stacked up her arms seemed familiar to me, but I couldn't place her.

"Calm down, Sylvia. You're on time. Gladys isn't even here yet." Mrs. Ellis patted her arm. "Dear Sylvia is always running late."

"I'm never running late!" the woman protested. "Modern society places too much importance in the arbitrary passing of time. Why, if we were to follow the rhythms and cycles of nature, then—"

"You'd think with your powers of divination, you'd be able to predict when you needed to leave your stinking little cottage," Ginny simpered from the sofa.

The woman's face reddened, but she didn't say anything. Neither, I noticed, did any of the other ladies. *Ginny Button must have a lot of power in the village.*

"Mina, this is Sylvia Blume. Sylvia, this is Mina Wilde—"

"You're Helen's daughter," Sylvia Blume beamed, throwing her arms around me like we were old friends. "I remember you when you were just a wee girl, reading books in the corner of my shop. Look at you now, all grown up!"

Now I remembered where I'd seen Sylvia before. She owned the shop where Mum did her tarot readings for suckers who liked being parted with their money. I used to spend time there after school before I discovered Nevermore Bookshop. I vaguely remembered the cloying smell of incense clinging to everything and a frizzy-haired woman who used to pinch my cheeks and feed me candies from under her fortune-telling table.

"Yes, er, hello again."

"It's a real shame about your eyesight. Helen told me all about you having to give up your fashion job."

My cheeks flushed. "It's not like that."

Only it was. That was exactly what had happened. I mean, yes, I'd intended to just muddle through as well as I could until my eyesight got worse – which could've taken years or even decades – but Ashley went and blabbed it all over the fashion world. But when Sylvia Blume spoke of it, I felt embarrassed, and I didn't like that.

"I know. I can do an aura healing for you!" Sylvia grabbed my shoulders, snapping my neck forward. "I'm an accomplished healer. I can perform a cleanse that will banish the evil energies that are at war within your body and restore your sight!"

No way. "I think if modern medicine can't do anything for me, then you're probably not going to have much luck."

"Nonsense." Sylvia dropped her tote bag on the floor with a bang, grabbed my wrists, and yanked them above my head. Her earrings clattered together as she shook her head from side-to-side and started to chant.

Quoth, if you can hear me, get me out of this.

I glanced around the room in a panic. Another woman walked in and bent her head to speak to Mrs. Winstone – I guessed it was Cynthia Lachlan, the wife of the developer, judging by her expensive clothes and affected posh accent. I jumped when I noticed Quoth was still hanging around in his human form. He'd been holed up in the corner by Mrs. Ellis, who was busy braiding his hair.

"Ooooooooohm," Sylvia moaned, swinging my arms around. "Spirits, unleash the demons inside this girl…"

Outside the window, I spied a figure limping down Butcher Street. "Oh, here's Gladys." I managed to wrench my wrists from Sylvia's grasp. "I'd better go see if she needs any help."

I'd never been so grateful to see an old lady in my life. I bolted toward Mrs. Scarlett as she bustled into the room. She looked even worse than the other day, her cheeks flushed, her eyes unfocused, her hair hanging lank against her forehead. She gripped the edge of the doorframe and swung her crutch in front of her.

Mrs. Ellis rushed over. "Gladys, dear, you look poorly. Are you sure you're up to the meeting?"

"I'll be fine, Mabel. It's just my stomach upsets as usual. Do stop fussing." Mrs. Scarlett leaned over her crutch and heaved herself into the room. Mrs. Ellis bustled around to her other side and after a few faltering steps, Mrs. Scarlett took her arm. Quoth rushed over and guided her other arm. Finally, she sank into the wingback chair, leaned her walking stick up against the wall, and surveyed the room with pursed lips. She picked up a sandwich from her plate of special food and sniffed it suspiciously before taking a dainty nibble from the corner. "Why hasn't the tea been poured yet?"

"Oh, I've brought some of my herbal blends." Sylvia dug around in her bag and handed me two jars of dried tea.

"Coming right up." I steeped the tea and arranged the cups and saucers. The ladies shuffled in their purses, pulling out their copies of the book. Mrs. Scarlett unfolded a pair of glasses from a leopard-print case. While I poured the tea, Quoth leaned against the chair arm to look over my shoulder. His arm brushed mine and his rich scent – of earth and chocolate and fresh-cut grass – invaded my nostrils, and my stomach did that flip-flop thing.

I'd set my date with Heathcliff, but I hadn't yet figured out how to approach Quoth. I knew I had to pick my moment just right, or he'd spook. I glanced up at him, catching his kind brown eyes as they swooped over my body. Beneath him, my skin sizzled. Under his avian gaze, I was naked and exposed, even in the midst of the book club.

I dared a smile for him, my heart pounding. Quoth smiled back, and the corners of his eyes flared with fire. The fact that he'd stayed for the meeting, risking the chance that he'd shift, filled me with gratitude and hope... and desire.

Mrs. Scarlett's sharp voice jolted me back to reality.

"Welcome, ladies, to the December meeting of the Argleton Banned Books Club. The good Lord has seen fit to provide us with a new venue. Although it may be a bit dusty..." she sniffed disapprovingly at the shelves Quoth and I had painstakingly cleaned. I shifted uncomfortably in my seat. "It has a certain charm. I'm hopeful it could continue to accommodate the book club while repairs are made to our beloved hall."

"Are you sure this place is up to code, Gladys?" Mrs. Lachlan said, frowning at a crack above the window. Beside me, Mrs. Ellis tensed.

But Gladys Scarlett didn't seem to have noticed the question. She set down her teacup and rubbed her fingers against the palm of her hand.

"You okay, Gladys?"

"Of course. I've just got pins and needles in my hand. I'll be fine in a moment." Mrs. Scarlett ate a sandwich and a cream doughnut from her plate, then fumbled for her teacup, closing her eyes as she sipped the hot liquid. "Enough about me, let us get on with our business. *Of Mice and Men* explores the intimate journey of two men who cling to each other in loneliness and isolation. The title, of course, is taken from the Robert Burn's poem, 'To a Mouse,' which translates to 'The best-laid schemes of mice and men / Often go awry.' It refers to the ambitions of the main characters in the book that are thwarted by their own *m-m-mouse!*"

"Exactly, Gladys," exclaimed Sylvia Blume. "The symbolism of the mouse was very interesting because—"

"No, a *mouse!*" Mrs. Scarlett thrust out a wavering finger across the room.

As I stared in horror, a tiny white blob with a brown patch rocketed up the corner of the bookshelf and darted along the tops of the books. It raised a pink nose, sniffed the air, then disappeared behind the shelf with a flick of its tail.

Mrs. Scarlett's face crumpled. She clutched her stomach. A strangled sob escaped her throat.

"Eeeee!" Mrs. Lachlan yelled, leaping from her own chair and dropping a red velvet cupcake on the floor. "Someone get that filthy rodent before it contaminates the food!"

I gripped Quoth's thigh, watching his face contort as his predator instincts took over. Feathers shot through his skin. Luckily, the other ladies were too distracted to notice. He dropped his cup – smashing the china and splashing hot tea across the rug – and dived behind the shelves.

"Ow, you burned me!" Ginny snapped, rubbing her leg.

CRASH! BANG!

Books toppled to the floor. The mouse darted out from behind the shelves and streaked across the floor, disappearing into the sofa and clambering up the curtain above Mrs. Scarlett's head. Her face froze in reddened horror, and her whole body heaved as though she struggled for breath.

"Croak!" Quoth flew out from behind the shelves and dived at the window. Tea cakes and old ladies scattered in all directions. Quoth's talons scratched the glass as he snapped at the curtains. The mouse poked its head out from the opposite end of the curtain rail, twitched its nose, and disappeared down the other curtain and into the stacks again.

I leapt to my feet and waved at the bird. "He's over there! Try to chase him into the corner. I'll get the broom and—"

"G-g-g-geeeeee…"

I whirled around. All thoughts of the mouse flew from my mind as I regarded Mrs. Scarlett's face. Something was seriously wrong.

Her eyes bugged out like a frog. One side of her face twitched uncontrollably, while the other stuck fast in an expression of abject terror. Her skin glowed red. Bile and spittle dribbled from her mouth. She clutched her stomach and doubled over, banging the table with her knee as she collapsed.

"Gladys, what's wrong?" Mrs. Ellis bent over her friend.

"I'm calling 999," Mrs. Winstone whipped out her phone.

With a final wheezing cry, Mrs. Scarlett collapsed forward, face-planting into the Victoria sponge cake. Ginny screamed as cream splattered across her silk blouse.

"Mrs. Scarlett? Gladys?" My heart pounded. I shook her shoulder, but she didn't move or react.

No, no, no, no. This can't be happening. I lifted her wrist and felt for a pulse. There was none.

She's dead.

CHAPTER SIX

"Just when I thought I'd seen the last of this bookshop, you're stacking up the dead bodies like unread Dan Brown books," Jo joked as she clattered down the hall, pulling on her rubber gloves. Her medical kit slapped against her thigh.

I managed a weak smile for my new friend. As the local forensic pathologist, Jo had a real gallows humor about dead bodies and grisly murders. I wasn't nearly so desensitized. Up until a month ago when my ex-best friend was found murdered in the shop, I'd never seen a dead body. I still pictured Ashley's prone form with the knife sticking out of her back in my nightmares.

"At least it's not murder this time. In here?" Jo pointed to the entrance to the World History room, where the EMTs were waiting with the stretcher to take the body away after she'd pronounced the death and examined the scene.

I nodded. Jo disappeared inside. I leaned against a bookshelf, trying to keep my wobbling legs upright. Another dead body in Nevermore Bookshop. How was this even possible?

Jo's right. This is completely different from before. It's not a murder.

This is just a horrible accident. It's what happens when you host book club meetings for octogenarians.

But no matter what I told myself, my legs kept shaking and my heart pattered against my chest. I knew something wasn't right here.

Of course not. Something isn't right with Nevermore Bookshop. It brings fictional characters to life. I've been so distracted by Ashley's murder and Morrie's cock that I haven't been focused on the biggest mystery of all. And now the shop has claimed another victim. Maybe it's too dangerous to be open to the public. Maybe its magic is out of control. Maybe—

A thick hand clamped down on my shoulder. "Mina," Heathcliff's voice boomed in my ear.

"I'm fine," I whispered. "It was just a shock."

"You're a shite liar. Quoth's bringing down some tea." Heathcliff swung around in front of me, his dark eyes boring into mine. For a moment, his expression distracted me from my thoughts. Heathcliff only had two emotional states – grumpy and grumpier. Right now, he wore neither. The edges of his hard mouth wavered, his eyes widened, his swarthy skin hung pale and limp. I studied his stricken features, trying to discern what had caused this shift. He almost looked… concerned. I knew it couldn't be for Mrs. Scarlett – was it for me?

The thought that I might be the object of Heathcliff's empathy, that I'd brought forward some deep-rooted, long-buried tender emotion, made my heart beat faster. My gaze flew to his lips – the lips that had one month ago met mine in a fierce kiss and had barely spoken to me since. A shiver ran through my body that had nothing to do with the chill in the shop.

"You are okay," he murmured, his rough fingers stroking my cheek. "You are not in danger."

I shook my head, unable to speak, unable to say to him that right now I was in danger of losing myself to him.

"Mina."

I jumped. My heart leapt into my throat. My eyes flicked to the place where the voice had come from. It took a moment in the darkness to resolve the shape of Quoth, returned to his human form, standing in the doorway with a tea tray in his hands.

The spell broke. Heathcliff's face boiled over into his usual scowl. Quoth stared at the floor. "I brought tea," he mumbled.

"Excellent!" declared Mrs. Ellis from her spot under the window. "We could all use a nice cuppa. Be a good lad and serve us old ladies. Isn't his hair beautiful, Sylvia?"

Quoth handed me a cup. His hand shook as I took it from his fingers. "I'm sorry," he whispered.

"You have nothing to be sorry about," I whispered back. Heathcliff grunted, slipping off into the shadows.

Quoth's eyes followed his friend's back, a million unsaid emotions passing across his face. He swiveled away. This time, his eyes darted toward the opposite corner, where the members of the Banned Book Club clung to each other, weeping and whispering. "If I hadn't shifted, perhaps the mouse would've—"

"It's not your fault. She was an old woman with a bad heart. I don't blame you." I sipped the tea, noticing my own hand trembled a little. "I just wish I could stop feeling like this was a sign, that bad things are destined to happen to me, or around me."

"Nothing is bad when you're around," Quoth whispered, backing away. "And you never have to be afraid. I'm always watching out for you."

Quoth scurried over to serve tea to the old biddies. As I sipped my drink, the EMTs removed the body in a white bag. Jo followed, peeling off her gloves and slumping down in the leather chair on the other side of the desk. I cast a look over my shoulder. Heathcliff was nowhere to be seen. I slid into his chair, grateful for the way his peat-and-cigarette scent rose from the worn leather. It steadied me.

"I was right. It looks like natural causes." Jo accepted a cup from Quoth's tray, folding her long fingers around the mug. "Probably a heart attack, but I'll know more after the autopsy. Did anything shock her before she died?"

"She saw a mouse," I shuddered at the memory. "She shrieked, then she started choking, and her face went all red and she fell over."

"That might do it." Jo picked up my copy of *Of Mice and Men* and flicked through it. "Say, this isn't the famous mouse, was it?"

"Famous mouse?"

"Don't you read the paper?" Jo set down the book and her bag and pulled out a copy of the morning's paper. Splashed across the page was the headline, £250 REWARD FOR THE HEAD OF THE TERROR OF ARGLETON, with an artist's rendering of a tiny white mouse with a brown patch.

"Apparently, the little bugger's been popping up in all the shops along the high street and Butcher Street. Greta from the bakery said it chewed through a bag of flour. Charles over at the newsstand said it nibbled the corners off a box of postcards. It even popped up beneath a chafing dish at the Indian buffet."

I squinted at the picture – it was an artist's reconstruction of a tiny white mouse with a pink nose and brown patch on its hind leg. "Yup. That's our little friend."

"Apparently, Mrs. Scarlett is only the latest in a long list of his victims," Jo grinned. "You've got a bird and a cat in here – you should have no trouble claiming that reward."

"I'll put it on a tab at the pub."

"Sounds like a plan. Hey, you want to grab a drink tonight?"

"Hell yes." If I couldn't get my fear under control, I was going to need it. Besides, maybe if I had a few drinks, I'd be brave enough to ask Jo what I should do about Morrie's challenge and my date with Heathcliff.

"Excellent. Meet you at the pub for happy hour." Jo drained her tea and left for the mortuary. The other ladies in the book club hovered, looking pale and lost. Quoth refilled cups of tea, his eyes focused intently on the teapot as though it would grant him the answers to the universe. I admired how hard he was trying to come downstairs and act like a normal human. I just hoped it wouldn't bite him on the arse.

"I just can't believe it," Mrs. Winstone sobbed. "One minute we were discussing our book, and the next minute, she's dead."

"Good riddance, I say," Mrs. Lachlan piped up. My ears perked up.

"Cynthia, how could you say that?" Mrs. Ellis admonished. "Gladys was our dear friend."

"She was a spiteful old hag who had to have her way with *everything*," Mrs. Lachlan spat. "Look at the farce she's made of the planning committee. Nature silenced her wicked tongue before someone thought to take matters into their own hands."

I shuddered at Mrs. Lachlan's cruel words. Mrs. Ellis stiffened. "Well, I shan't expect you to assist with the funeral preparations."

"Likely not," Mrs. Lachlan set down her teacup and stood up. "I think I'm quite finished here. Ladies, if you'll excuse me, my husband will need me."

"He'll need you to plan the celebratory party," Mrs. Ellis muttered as Mrs. Lachlan hurried off.

The other ladies finished their tea and headed off. Mrs. Ellis was the last to leave. She leaned over the desk and clasped my hands in hers. "I'm terribly sorry you had to see that today, Mina. It's the price you pay for making friends with old biddies like Gladys and myself. I want you to know that you had nothing to do with her death – it was just a horrible accident. Just yesterday Gladys told me how much she enjoyed meeting you and how she was looking forward to having young blood in the book club."

"Mrs. Lachlan sure seems to hate her."

"Oh, yes," Mrs. Ellis tsked. "It's such a shame. They used to be very good friends before that business with the King's Copse development."

"What was it that Mrs. Scarlett opposed, exactly?" King's Copse was part of the ancient wood just outside Argleton. Much of the original wood was cleared for forestry thirty years ago. Only a few acres of the original wood remained. It was a popular place for Argleton's youth to congregate to smoke weed and get up to shenanigans. If I didn't feel like reading or Mr. Simson closed the shop early, I often used to go to the wood and sit by the stream.

"A few years back, Cynthia's husband Grey purchased King's Copse with the idea of turning the cleared areas into a housing development. Well, as you know, Gladys heads up the town planning committee. She's an amazing civil servant. She sits on the hall repair fundraising committee, the town beautification league, the garden society, and our very own book club. She makes it her business to know everything about everyone in the village. Anyway, Grey applied for planning consent to build four hundred houses on the site. All modern homes, not at all in the traditional vernacular of the village. The committee isn't happy, of course. They've made so many complaints about the design. Grey had to redesign the site three times, but he won't let go of his ugly modern design," she wrinkled her nose. "Mrs. Lachlan isn't pleased the application keeps being kicked back, but it's not Gladys' fault. Gladys felt it was her duty to inform the committee about Grey's outstanding debts from a failed project in London. Now the committee wants to deny him outright. Of course, Cynthia told us about the debts in confidence at a book club meeting. There might have been some Champagne involved." Mrs. Ellis smiled sweetly. "She was ever so upset when she discovered Gladys told the committee. There's been a terrible tension between them ever since."

"Oh, that's a shame." In my head, I wondered if perhaps this planning committee was the reason Argleton seemed so frozen in time. The village, with its wattle-and-daub cottages and Tudor pub, was gorgeous, but that didn't mean modern design couldn't also look nice or be nice to live in. You couldn't spend your entire life looking backward at the past.

You're one to talk, I reminded myself, thinking about how much I still wished I could go back to the past, to before my diagnosis, when I was going to be a New York fashion designer.

"Don't take what Cynthia says to heart. I'm sure she's just in shock, like the rest of us. She'll come around. After all, the Lachlans live in a gorgeous Georgian manor on the top of the hill. They can't say they don't love traditional design." Mrs. Ellis winked at me as she looped her carpet bag over her shoulder. "I hope you'll continue to be part of our book club, Mina. Perhaps you can help us choose more *racy* reading material. Honestly, I don't know why anyone bothers banning half these books!"

Mrs. Ellis winked at me again as she left. As soon as the door swung shut, Quoth popped his head up from behind the desk. He must've just transformed from his raven form, because he was naked. My cheeks flared with heat as I tried not to look.

"So that's your old schoolteacher?" His eyes widened.

"She's something else. Apparently, she still volunteered to teach sex education classes right up until her retirement." I slid open Heathcliff's snack drawer and rummaged around, withdrawing a Wagon Wheel that was only slightly smushed. I unwrapped the chocolate and offered half to Quoth. He shook his head. "Not fruity enough for you?"

"I don't want to spoil my dinner. Morrie's cooking tonight."

"He can cook in that bomb site you call a kitchen?"

Morrie leaned his head around the door. "I heard my name."

"Hey!" I rushed over and embraced him, his steadiness drawing the last of the fear and anxiety from my body. "What did you get up to today?"

"A little consulting work for a private client." Morrie slid his tailored jacket off his shoulders, revealing a crisp white shirt that accentuated his height and slim muscles. With his pretty-boy good looks and love of fine fashion, Morrie would be right at home on a Paris runway.

"Counterfeiter or money-launderer?"

Morrie raised an eyebrow. "Do you really want to know?"

"Nope."

"Then don't ask. How was the book club?"

Quoth winced, but with Morrie's arm sliding around my waist, I managed to get the words out. "It started off well enough, but then the Terror of Argleton showed up and scared everyone, which gave Mrs. Scarlett a heart attack and she died."

Morrie shuddered. "That mouse was back? We need to call an exterminator. Or the SAS. This is not acceptable."

"Didn't you hear what I said? Mrs. Scarlett *died* with her face in a Victoria sponge cake. It was horrible."

"That *is* horrible." Morrie kissed my forehead. "I was looking forward to a slice of that."

I punched his arm. "Get upstairs and start dinner. What are you cooking, anyway?"

"It's something French and delicious. Do you want to stay? We could open a bottle of wine, and I can lick your whole body while you tell me grisly stories about old biddies keeling over into cakes."

"Not tonight. I'm going for a drink with Jo."

"Too bad." Morrie led me by the hand through the corridor behind the main room, into the Children's room, where he wrapped his body against mine and met my lips in a furious kiss.

"We can't do this in the Children's room," I panted, breathless, trying to shove him away. "We'll corrupt the books."

"Good." Morrie pressed his lips to mine, and I gave up fighting. James Moriarty was relentless when he wanted something, and right now, he wanted me. His hard cock pressed against my thigh, and my fingers itched to touch it, stroke it, and make him lose control again.

But there was something I had to do first. I whispered. "I'm going on a date with Heathcliff on Friday night."

"You work fast. Does Heathcliff know it's a date?"

"Unsure."

"Then wear that sexy jersey dress of yours. That way he won't be left with any doubt."

"Are you sure this is a good idea? You're not weirded out by me going on a date with Heathcliff?"

"I'd be more weirded out if you *didn't* want to date him." Morrie's hand drifted under my blouse, rolling my nipple between his fingers as I gasped. "I've read enough online fanfiction to know that he's the original brooding bad boy. I keep telling him he needs a motorcycle."

"Don't do that. If he has a motorcycle, he'll be impossible to resist."

"Are you sure you don't want to stay?" Morrie growled, a wildness in his eyes I'd never seen before – the beast within threatening to take over.

"Tempting." My body shivered as his teeth scraped along my collarbone. "But I want to hear about Mrs. Scarlett's autopsy."

"You're choosing riveting conversation about a dead old biddy's liver over a home-cooked meal and a night of unbridled passion with yours truly?" Morrie kissed my cheek and stepped back, though he looked as though it took all his self-control. "Well played, gorgeous. You really are my girl."

"Maybe not after Friday, if Heathcliff sweeps me off my feet."

"I'm not worried." Morrie darted from the room, taking the stairs two at a time. I wondered if he'd done it on purpose, just to leave me breathless and needy in his wake. I sucked in a breath and straightened my skirt, trying to get my heart rate under control.

"Mina."

I whirled around. Quoth stood under the arch that led into the main room. He was still completely naked. I opened my mouth to tell him to put on some clothes, that a customer could come through the door at any moment, but his beauty closed my throat. His pale skin contrasted against the gloom of the bookshop, making him appear to glow with a faint aura. Black hair hung in silken strands over his chest, reaching down to touch the edge of his pelvis and *oh...*

He was half hard. *For me.* Brown eyes ringed with fire regarded me with predator-like intensity. I gulped.

"Mina, you should stay for dinner," he whispered, his velvet voice caressing my skin.

I opened my mouth, closed it, and opened it again, trying to find the words to say what I felt, what wicked thoughts went through my head as my eyes trailed over his perfect body. But all that came out was a strangled cry.

Quoth unnerved me, not because I was afraid of him, but because my own pain reflected back at me in his eyes. I had to be careful around him, so careful, because I could fall completely for him – my sweet, broken boy – and I could break him, and he could break me.

So instead I stepped back and said the only thing I could think to say that would push him away. "I wanted you to hear this from me. I'm going on a date with Heathcliff on Friday night."

"Oh." His features didn't move. His half-hard cock bobbed between us. My fingers itched to touch it, to feel that perfect body against mine.

"Quoth, I want you to know that I'm not choosing—"

He shook his head. "I understand, Mina. I accept it. Heathcliff and Morrie can take you on dates. I cannot."

"That's not what I meant. I—"

Quoth's body exploded in feathers. His lips puckered out, forming a hard, curved beak. The last thing I saw was his face contorting in pain as his limbs snapped into place. My chest clenched. Was that pain caused by his shift, or by me? I didn't want to cause him pain.

He unfurled his wings and soared over my head and up the stairs, disappearing into the shadows.

"Croak," he called down, his voice tinged with sadness.

"That wasn't what I meant." Tears pricked my eyes. I turned away and gathered my things, my heart racing. As I flipped the OPEN sign to CLOSED and shut the bookshop door behind me, my stomach squirmed. Morrie's challenge might entertain him; it might be exactly what the guys wanted, but I wasn't sure I had the emotional fortitude to deal with all three of them and their issues.

CHAPTER SEVEN

"I'm surprised you've even out with me now that Morrie's at the flat all the time," Jo mused.

I sipped my drink. A week ago, I'd broken down and told Jo about Morrie and I sleeping together. I had no choice – Morrie and Jo were friends and he'd already spilled the beans, so she'd been making low-level suggestive comments about it for weeks.

When I told her, Jo squealed and bought me another G&T and made me tell her all the gory details. My heart soared because my only girlfriend in the world had been brutally murdered after we had a falling out, and now I had another who seemed to get exactly what I needed.

Ever since Jo knew about Morrie, a weight had lifted from my shoulders. Only a small weight, because I'd barely scratched the surface of the secrets I was keeping. I hadn't told Jo about the boys being fictional characters come to life, about the room in the shop that jumped through time, or about the various characters they'd help set up in stable jobs all over the world. I hadn't told her about my eyesight, but I guessed she knew from the way she'd steered us toward the table under the brightest light and started reading items on the menu out loud. And I definitely neglected to mention the kiss I'd shared with Heathcliff a few weeks back, the way Quoth had said some weird things, about how they all liked me, or how they all would happily... *share me*.

I mean, that's crazy, right? Who even does that?

Lots of people aren't in monogamous relationships, that niggling punk rock voice in my head taunted me. I knew. I Googled it. It was called polyamory or polyandry, and there were whole communities of people who believed that you could have more than one partner and it worked.

But was I one of them?

Punk rock Mina screamed that I should stop being a pussy and have them all. Book nerd Mina wanted to be cautious, because three times the cock meant three times the heartache, especially when your boyfriends were fictional characters with troubled backstories of their own.

I toyed with my napkin, but the urge to talk overpowered me. "Has Morrie ever said anything to you about polyamory?"

Jo leaned forward, sensing the whiff of good gossip. "Not really. He's made a few comments about being grateful to be free of repressive Victorian puritanical constraints. Why, are he and you..."

"I've got a date with Heathcliff on Friday night," I said.

Jo's eyebrow went up. "Morrie okay with that?"

"It was his idea."

"Ah. Intrigue." Jo leaned forward, her eyes glinting. "Morrie wants you to date his closest friend?"

"You don't seem surprised."

"I know. Weird, right?" Jo sipped her wine. "I've known Morrie for long enough to realize he's kinky as fuck. He goes down to London for sex parties at an exclusive club. He keeps inviting me with him, but honestly, naked men are kind of gross to me now."

After I'd spilled my secret about Morrie last week, Jo revealed a secret of her own – she preferred to date women. Now that I knew her better, this wasn't a shock at all, and I promised to keep an eye out for any hot and slightly morbid females who came into the shop.

"Sex parties?" I gulped.

Jo grinned, toying with her straw. "Has he used any of his bondage gear on you yet?"

My cheeks flushed. "No."

"But you want him to?"

"…maybe?"

We laughed. My whole face flared with heat. I tipped my head back and downed my drink in one gulp. Gin was the only sane way to deal with a conversation like this.

Jo agreed as she slung back her own drink. "Do you want my advice?"

"Yes, please."

"I say go for it. Sure, close off your heart a little bit if you need to protect yourself, but don't look two gift horses in the mouth. You only live once. Most of us dream of having two hot and interesting people meeting our every whim."

"Three."

"Three what?"

"Three hot, interesting people," I mumbled.

"That weird guy who was handing out tea? Okay, *definitely* go for it. He is fucking gorgeous, and I don't even like dudes. Who is he, anyway? I haven't seen him before, and I'd remember a face like that. He's a thing of beauty. What kind of a name is Quoth?"

"He said his parents were seventies goths," I went with the cover story I invented for Quoth. Jo snorted. "I know, right? He's a friend of Morrie's. He's staying at the flat for a while. He's an artist – really good one, too."

"He did those paintings hanging around the shop?"

I nodded.

"Okay, you *have* to date him. Artists are always good with their hands."

The heat crept down my neck. "This is insane."

"Not at all. Once you're sleeping with him, can you get me a discount? I've got my eye on that painting above Heathcliff's desk."

"I can probably get you a discount."

"And I want all the gory details. I've only ever had one three-some. It was with my last girlfriend, Dr. Adele Martinez, and her young technician, Michael Rousseau, at the annual digital pathology symposium. After one too many G&Ts at the confer-ence dinner, we decided to sneak into the mortuary for our dalliance. Rousseau got so freaked out when we told him to lie on the autopsy table that he ran away and myself and Adele continued on our own. So I guess it wasn't really a threesome at all. I want to know what it's like with all those dicks flying around—"

"Can we talk about something other than my sex life or three-somes or flying dicks? You did Gladys Scarlett's autopsy today. Was it a heart attack?"

"Nope." Jo tapped her nails against the stem of her glass. "It turns out your local busybody Mrs. Scarlett didn't die from natural causes."

"No?" My chest tightened.

"I found high levels of arsenic in her blood. She's been poisoned."

CHAPTER EIGHT

"*P*oisoned? But... how?"

"I'll know more once I get the toxicology results back from the lab, but a lethal dose of arsenic is usually administered in food or drink, because it dissolves easily in liquid and it doesn't have much of a taste."

My heart thudded. "But we all ate food at the meeting. Could we all be—"

Jo held my hand. "Relax, Mina. I'd have notified you immediately if that was the case. If you'd ingested any arsenic, you would have felt symptoms by now. The body tries to expel the poison by vomiting and diarrhea. Also, didn't Gladys only eat very specific food because of her intolerances?"

"Yes, that's right. We all drank from the same teapot, but she had her own plate of sandwiches and treats. But that means..."

After the food was delivered, only myself, Quoth, and the ladies went anywhere near it. Someone in the Banned Book Club must have administered the poison.

Jo nodded. "I can tell by your face exactly what you're thinking, and you're right. It means one of those kind old biddies is a cold-blooded murderer. Can I get you another drink?"

I pushed my empty glass away. "I'm not thirsty anymore."

"Really? I'm parched. Murder cases are thirsty work." Jo waved at the landlord, who ambled over with two more glasses for our tab. "This case is fascinating. Arsenic was actually one of the most common types of poison to be used throughout history. Murderers love it because it has no obvious taste, and the symptoms can appear similar to dysentery or cholera, which were pretty common."

"So it's not difficult to make?"

"Oh no. It's a simple chemical process that's been known to poisoners since Ancient Egypt, and it was a particular favorite murder method of the Borgia family. Apparently, they'd spread it on the entrails of a pig, leave them to rot, then dry what remained and grind it into a powder called *la cantarella*, which they added to the food or drink of their enemies."

"You sure know a lot about killing people," I mused.

"Hello, I'm a forensic pathologist," Jo grinned, pointing to her chest. "I've got loads more stories if you want to hear them, but you might have trouble holding down your dinner. This is actually my first arsenic poisoning. You don't see it used much anymore. During the Industrial Revolution, arsenic was as common as mud because of the huge demand of iron and lead – the extracted ore contained arsenic, and during smelting, the arsenic would condense in the chimneys as a white solid that could be scraped off and sold. Every household had arsenic for killing rats and mice and other vermin. Now, of course, you'd need a special license to purchase it, or access to an industrial plant where it's stored. It's not a very common poison anymore, which means it should be easy to figure out who'd have access to it."

"So the police are already investigating the case?"

"Yep. Hayes and Wilson are taking statements from all the Banned Book Club members. Hayes said he'd be around tomorrow morning to take one from you and your friend, the beautiful Quoth."

Shit. If the police needed to talk to Quoth, this was a big problem. Because his shifting was so erratic and he spent most of his time in his bird form, Quoth lived off-the-grid. If the police had cause to look into his background, they'd discover he didn't technically exist, and that could cause all kinds of problems. After all the effort we went to after Ashley's death to keep him out of things, he'd end up before the police anyway, and all because I'd encouraged him to come out of his shell.

That shell was what protected him, and I've gone and blown it to smithereens.

I excused myself, went to the ladies loo, and called Morrie. "We have a problem." I filled him in on Mrs. Scarlett's murder and the police investigation.

"Arsenic?" Morrie's voice perked up. "That's not exactly a common poison these days. Not quick or painless, either. I much prefer cyanide."

"I don't want to hear that. What are we going to do about Quoth? He helped me set up the book club meeting, and he stayed to serve tea to the ladies. They're all going to mention him in their statements, which means the police will want to interview him. It's all my fault! I never should have allowed him to stay at the meeting."

"Relax, gorgeous. We'll deal with it. As soon as you started your crazy campaign to get Quoth recognized as an artistic genius, I organized him some papers. As far as the police are concerned, tomorrow they'll be interviewing Mr. Allan Poe, an itinerant painter from Norwich with a passport, some dead parents, and his own Facebook profile. If Quoth can keep his feathers inside his skin, he'll be fine."

I let out the breath I didn't realize I'd been holding. "Thank you, Morrie."

"I know. I'm a genius. I'm already planning exactly how you

can thank me. It involves a blindfold and a flogger."

An ache spread between my legs. "What's a flogger?"

"One day soon, you're going to find out."

I rang off, my heart hammering for an entirely different reason.

After we finished our drinks, Jo offered me a lift home. She stood in front of her fancy new car, a Nissan Leaf, jangling the keys in her hand. Old, familiar shame welled up inside me. "It's fine. It's a nice night. I'd rather walk."

"You're not walking through *that* neighborhood in the dark on your own. I'm giving you a ride, and that's an order."

My breath hitched. "How do you know where I live?"

"You were the leading suspect in a murder investigation. I know far too much about you." Jo flung open the door. "Get in."

I glanced up. A black raven sat on the guttering opposite the pub, two beady brown eyes trained on mine. *I'll be watching you,* a silky voice reverberated in my head. Quoth took his duties seriously, but I couldn't tell Jo that.

Jo sighed. "If you get in the car, I'll let you know what I find out about the arsenic, as long as you promise not to pass on any information I tell you. Technically, I'm not supposed to be telling you details of an active murder investigation, but what good are friends if we can't dish the dirt to each other?"

My hands trembled, because I' already told Morrie about the arsenic. But I slid in beside her and pretended to zip my lips. "Exactly. Your secrets are safe with me."

Jo grinned. "Good. And I promise not to tell anyone you're a filthy polyamorous harlot."

"Deal." We shook on it. Jo pulled away from the curb and drove out of the village proper, onto the council estate. The quaint thatched cottages and pristine gardens gave way to shabby brownstones and brutalist concrete towers and streets littered with rubbish. A police siren wailed in the distance. My fingers dug into the armrest.

"It's fine," Jo said, breezing through the neighborhood. "I don't care where you come from, only who you are. Now, which one's your house?"

Numb, I pointed to the last door at the end of a block of tiny flats. A stack of crumpling wobbleator boxes leaned against the side of the fence. Mum's car sat in the driveway. Panic shot up my spine. *Please don't come outside and try to sell Jo animal dictionaries.*

"Cute place," Jo said. "I love the conservatory."

"That's my bedroom," I choked out, shoving the door open before Jo came to a stop. "No need to walk me up."

"Mina—"

"Talk to you tomorrow." I slid out of Jo's car and sprinted up the steps. On the porch, I fumbled with my keys, slipped through the door, and slammed it behind me. I watched through the faded curtain as Jo pulled away. When her taillights disappeared around the corner, I let out the breath I'd been holding.

Mum stood in the hallway, arms folded, a terrifying expression on her face. "What time do you call this?"

I glanced behind her at the clock on the microwave. "Mum, it's 8:15. *Eastenders* hasn't even started yet."

"You were at that bookshop all night again with that *gypsy.*"

"Mum, for the last time, *don't use that word.* It doesn't mean what you think it means. It's a derogatory term the Victorians invented because they thought the Romani people looked like Egyptians."

"I don't need a linguistics lesson, Wilhelmina. I need to know why you care more about those bookshop delinquents than you do about your own mother."

"Don't be so dramatic. You know that's not true."

"I needed you this evening. The local pet shop has agreed to stock some of my books, only the owner flicked through the cat one and she says it's filled with spelling errors. I can't understand it! The salesman says they'd been checked over by a best-selling author. Now I need you to check all the spelling and change it on the file—"

"Mum, I'm not spending my evenings helping you edit a cat dictionary. I have a job. I'm making friends. Actual friends who don't stab me in the back, like Ashley did." I winced at my choice of words as the image of the bloody knife in Ashley's back flashed before my eyes. "And if you must know, I wasn't with Heathcliff and Morrie and Quoth. I had a drink at the pub with my new girlfriend, Jo – not that I need to ask your permission. I'm an adult now. I lived for four years on my own in *New York City.* I can go out and see my friends if I want to."

"That was before you got your diagnosis. Mina, you're going *blind.* I understand you're upset and you want to rebel, but you have to be careful who you trust now, darling." Mum wrapped her arms around me. I stiffened under her touch. "I'm here to look after you, but you have to let me help you."

"Shouldn't the fact that *I* trust Heathcliff and Morrie and Quoth and Jo be enough for you?"

"Not when I haven't even met them. I need to know what sort of people my baby girl is hanging out with." Mum wiped a strand of hair out of my face. Her eyes widened with maternal care, and a lump rose in my throat. *Maybe I'm being too hard on her?* "Did you even ask the gyp— ask Mr. Heathcliff Earnshaw about stocking my dictionaries?"

I sighed and slid out of her grasp. *Nope, definitely not being too hard on her.* "I had a few other things on my mind today." In the kitchen, I filled the kettle and placed it on the stove. "A woman died in the shop."

"*Another* dead body? Oh, Mina, that place is dangerous—"

I sighed. I couldn't exactly argue with her. "I'm not giving up my job or my friends. What will make you feel better?"

She tapped her chin, her eyes glinting. *Great, I'm going to pay for this.*

"I want a dinner. You're going to invite these new friends over for a nice home-cooked meal. We'll sit down like adults and they can calm my fears with their own words."

I stared around our tiny kitchen, at the cracked linoleum and peeling paint on the cupboards, at the charity shop furniture and rickety shelves crammed with Mum's junk. It was bad enough that Jo and Quoth had seen the outside of the flat. It was bad enough they all knew I was poor and that I was going blind. If the boys saw inside this place, they'd realize that I wasn't this interesting person they thought they liked. They'd see all the secrets I'd tried to hide from them. I'd be wide open, exposed.

And Jo? She was a clever professional woman with an advanced degree and a mortgage and a electric car. She's been so deliberately trying to put me at ease when she dropped me off, that I knew the whole thing must've freaked her out. There was that familiar squint in her eye as she took in the dilapidated house and our delightful neighbors the drug dealers, the tilt of her lips into that look of pity.

People couldn't be friends with people they pitied. It upset the balance. My hand trembled as I poured the water into my tea. *I'm not having them over for dinner. I'm not losing the best people who'd ever happened to me.*

Now, how to convince Mum to drop it.

"They won't all fit around the table. We could go to the pub instead. My treat—"

"No, that won't do. If you can't invite them over here, then they're not close friends, and I don't think you should be spending so much time with them."

"You can't tell me what to do."

"Mina, can't you just let me meet them so I stop worrying about you?" Mum rubbed her eyes. "All this worrying is aging me horribly."

I swiped my hand across my eyes, hoping Mum chalked up the tears pooling in the corners as the result of one too many drinks. "Fine. I'll invite them."

CHAPTER NINE

"*I*'ll have four Cornish pasties, thanks, Greta, and my usual coffee order." I forced a smile for the tiny German girl across the counter.

Stop putting off the inevitable. Just get over to the bookshop and ask them. Make it sound so awful they'll have no choice but to refuse.

"Ja. The pasties are fresh out of the oven." Greta moved down the cabinet, placing my purchases into paper bags. "You are okay? You look upset."

I rubbed my eyes. "Just… stressed. You know, I moved back here from New York City. I thought Argleton would be slow, but between the boy problems and the dead bodies and that bloody mouse, I feel like I can't catch a break."

"Do not get me started on that mouse," Greta shook her head. "It ruined an entire batch of pumpernickel! But that is not your problem. I heard Gladys Scarlett was taken ill at your book club yesterday."

"Not taken ill," a distraught voice behind me cried. "She's dead!"

I whirled around. Mrs. Ellis stood in the doorway, her face

blotchy and streaked with tears. She clutched her carpet bag with white knuckles.

I rushed over and guided her to one of the tables by the window. Greta came around the front of the counter and placed a cup of coffee and a packet of tissues on the table. I nodded my thanks. She disappeared behind the counter again, leaving us to talk.

"The police came around to speak with me yesterday," Mrs. Ellis sobbed. "They asked me all these questions. Poor Gladys was poisoned."

Greta's head snapped up. "No, no. My food would not make her sick. I use only the freshest ingredients—"

"Not food poisoning, Greta," I said. "Actual poison. They said she'd ingested a fatal dose of arsenic."

As soon as I said it, I regretted it. Jo told me I wasn't supposed to tell anyone. It had barely been twelve hours and I'd already failed her.

Mrs. Ellis sobbed.

Greta paled. "That's horrible. Who would do such a thing?"

"The police believe it's someone in the Banned Book Club." Mrs. Ellis wrung her bag between her hands. "But I just can't believe it. I've known most of those ladies for decades. Well, except for Ginny Button, but she's a lovely girl, and so respected in the community. She works at the council."

"It must be so upsetting," I said. To Greta, I handed over a twenty-quid note. "Could you add one of Mrs. Ellis' favorite cream doughnuts to my order please?"

"They had better find the murderer soon," Greta said, speaking slowly and carefully, like she was trying to find the right words in English. "People will think my food is poisoned. They will not buy from the bakery, and I will go bankrupt and my brother and I will lose our home."

"That's not going to happen. Mrs. Ellis and I will tell everyone we see that it's not your fault," I assured her. Mrs. Ellis nodded unhappily.

While Greta went back behind the counter to finish my order, I leaned across the table and took Mrs. Ellis' shaking hands in mine. "You told me yesterday that Cynthia Lachlan was angry with Gladys because she blocked the King's Copse development."

"I don't know if Gladys actually blocked the application, but she blabbed Cynthia's secrets. That was wrong of her, but she felt it was her moral duty to let the committee know what kind of a man was trying to build at King's Copse."

"Did you tell that to the police?"

Mrs. Ellis shook her head.

"I know you don't want to speak ill of your friend, but it could be important. Mrs. Lachlan might've been the one who poisoned Gladys to get her out of the way!"

"I just can't believe that Cynthia would do such a thing. She and Gladys have been friends for so long. Gladys was her bridesmaid when she married Grey! Friends don't go around killing each other just because they have a falling out."

"I know they don't." That was exactly what happened with Ashley and I. When she turned up dead in the shop, the police assumed I was the murderer. "But the police really need to know all the information."

Greta slid my box of goodies across the table. I handed Mrs. Ellis a bag containing a delicious-looking cream doughnut dusted with icing sugar. She bit into it gratefully, smearing a dab of cream on the end of her nose. "You have to help us, Mina. You've got to find the real murderer."

I slid a napkin across to her. "Huh?"

Mrs. Ellis clutched my wrist, her eyes wide and earnest. "You're such a clever girl. You were one of the brightest students I ever taught. And you figured out who killed the Greer girl before the police even had a clue. I can't stand it if they take

Cynthia in without considering another theory. Please, help me find out who killed my friend!"

CHAPTER TEN

Still reeling from my discussion with Mrs. Ellis, I stopped by the charity shop on the corner to pick up a standing lamp I'd seen in the window yesterday. I emerged a few minutes later, three pounds poorer but with a large oak stand and cream lace shade under my arm. The lamp would go perfectly in the dark corner on the first floor beside the Folio Society shelves. I wondered how many lamps I could stash in the shop before Heathcliff noticed.

I set the lamp down to open the front door of the shop, flipping the sign around so it read 'OPEN'. Unlike the last murder, there wasn't a crowd of onlookers outside. It appeared news of Mrs. Scarlett's death hadn't made it around the village yet.

I left the lamp in the hallway and took Heathcliff his breakfast. "This coffee is cold," he muttered as I handed him the cup across his desk.

"Sorry. I was talking to Mrs. Ellis at the bakery." Quickly, I filled him in on how she begged me to help solve the murder.

"I told you that book club was going to be nothing but trouble," Heathcliff growled. "Don't have any more bright ideas about how to improve the shop. You attract murderers the way Grimalkin attracts fleas."

I thought of my lamp in the hallway and smiled. "It's fine. I'll do a little snooping for her. I want to see the killer brought to justice just as much as she does." I shuddered at the memory of Mrs. Scarlett's reddened face.

"Does this mean the bloody police are going to be poking around my shop again?"

"It certainly does, Mr. Earnshaw."

I whirled around. Inspector Hayes and DS Wilson stood in the doorway, coffee in hand. Behind them a small SOCO team pulled on protective gear.

"I bumped into Mrs. Ellis this morning and she told me Mrs. Scarlett was poisoned," I said quickly, to avoid getting Jo in trouble. "I'll show you the room, but I'm afraid we cleaned up after the meeting, so there might not be much of use."

"Thank you, Mrs. Wilde. It's a pleasure to see you again," Wilson's expression was stormy. She was still fuming after we solved the last murder before her.

I stood in the doorway of the World History room while Wilson and Hayes inspected the scene. "She was sitting in that red wingback chair when the mouse darted across the floor. She wheezed and heaved and clutched her stomach, and then she fell into the Victoria sponge cake."

Hayes inspected the surface of the table. "We'll get the team to go over this whole area. Did you vacuum the rug?"

"Yes. I'm sorry."

"It's not your fault. We're all shocked to discover this was a murder." Hayes inspected the windowsill while Wilson crouched to peer under the table.

"I can't believe any of the Book Club ladies would do something this malicious," I said quickly. "They seemed like such good friends—"

"My colleague and I will do the detecting this time, Miss Wilde."

"Found a feather," Wilson announced, holding up a black plume between a pair of tweezers.

"That's from Heathcliff's pet raven," I said. "He was watching the meeting, but when the mouse ran across the room he dived after it. He hit the bookshelf at one point, so you might find more feathers over there."

The SOCO team roped off the door with crime scene tape and started making a systematic grid to search the room. Hayes peeled off his gloves. "Where are the dishes you used for the food?"

"I'll show you the teacups upstairs. We washed them, though. The platters belonged to Greta from the bakery. I can also introduce you to Allan. He was helping me at the meeting."

Hayes and Wilson followed me upstairs. I showed them the rows of teacups and saucers lined up in on the drying rack. "Mrs. Scarlett had that one," I pointed to the cup covered with hyacinths. Wilson slipped it into an evidence bag.

I went to the stairs in the hall and called up. "Allan? The police are here. They want to talk to you about the Banned Book Club meeting."

A few moments later, a muffled voice called back, "I'll be right down."

"He has his art studio up there," I explained to DS Wilson, who was frowning at the steep steps. "He likes the solitude."

Quoth appeared at the top of the stairs, his hair streaming down his back in glorious waves. DS Wilson's eyes widened. Even she wasn't immune to his beauty. Under the dim hall light, his skin appeared to shimmer, and the paint splatters across his sharp cheekbones only enhanced his allure. Quoth gave a shy smile, which I knew covered his nerves. He'd have to get through the whole interview without shifting.

"If you'll come through to the living room, Mr. Poe, we can

corrupt the intercourse... I mean, conduct the interview." DS Wilson's skin burned a deep scarlet. She spun on her heel and stalked out. Quoth gave me a shaky smile and followed her.

"What's in this room?" Hayes asked, jiggling the locked door at the end of the hall.

My heart hammered. *Just a wormhole through space and time, no biggie.* "It's extra storage for the bookshop."

"Can I see?"

No, no you can't. I had no way of knowing what we'd be looking at when I opened the door. Would it be the dusty, empty room from our current time, or the Victorian master bedroom, or the Tudor reading room, or any of the other permutations of the shop's history?

I shook my head. "The floorboards are rotting. Heathcliff's under strict orders from the HSE inspector that he's not to allow anyone in there. You'll need to speak with him about it."

Hayes dropped the doorknob. "Mr. Earnshaw doesn't strike me as the conscientious type."

I shrugged. "He's been a fine employer. A little surly, but perfectly above board."

Except for that one time he kissed me. Hayes didn't need to know about that.

"Do you know anything about Mr. Earnshaw's history? He hasn't been very forthcoming."

"As far as I know, he was an orphan found on the streets of Liverpool, raised in a farmhouse in the North, and he's not aware of his own heritage beyond an Eastern-European origin. Ask around the village, people have all sorts of tall tales about him they'd love to impart." I forced a laugh. "Hell, I've even heard people say he's really the Heathcliff of *Wuthering Heights* come to life."

Hayes didn't even crack a smile as he scribbled notes. "Did Heathcliff enter the World History room at any time while you were setting up the meeting or while it was in progress?"

I shook my head. "No. Heathcliff didn't want anything to do with it."

"Why not? It's an event in his shop. I would think he would want everything to be in order."

"Hosting the meeting here was my idea. Heathcliff was against it. You've met him. He doesn't exactly like customers or anything that encourages more of them."

"Did you leave the room unattended at any time before or during the meeting?"

"No. Quoth and I arranged the furniture, and then Greta showed up with the food, and the ladies arrived after that – Mrs. Ellis first, then Mrs. Winstone, followed by Ginny Button, Sylvia Blume, Cynthia Lachlan, and Mrs. Scarlett was last."

"Who's Quoth?"

Shite. "Oh, that's what we call Allan. It's a nickname, because his last name is Poe and he's so goth."

Hayes made some more notes on his pad. "Thank you for your cooperation. We may return with further questions. In the meantime, if there's anything you remember about the meeting, no matter how unimportant it might seem, please give us a call."

He met Wilson in the living room, and they clattered back down the stairs. As soon as they were out of sight, Quoth fell into my arms. "That was scary," he said.

"I know. It's one of those times I'm glad Morrie is... who he is." I wiped a strand of hair from his face. "You did good. You didn't even sprout a single feather."

"I need to go do bird things for a while," Quoth ran a hand through his hair, which turned to feathers under his touch.

"Don't let me keep you. Go. Do what you have to do."

Quoth dived for the hallway. He grabbed the balustrade, his knuckles white as he half crawled, half hopped up the stairs.

"Quoth?"

He froze, his body stiffening. He turned back to me. Feathers stuck out of his cheeks. His nose had already fused to his upper lip as his beak formed.

"I'm so sorry I pushed you to show off your art and interact with people. It's my fault you had to go through that."

"Don't be sorry." His words rasped as his lips dried into a beak. "You are the best thing to happen to me since I arrived in this world."

"That's not true."

"It is." Quoth backed down the staircase until he could reach out and touch me. He wrapped his fingers around my arm, his skin hardened, the tips of his fingers already sharpened into talons. Sad brown eyes bore into mine. How was he so utterly perfect and yet so, so broken? "I thought hiding was the only way I'd be able to survive in this world. I thought at least as a bird I had some semblance of freedom. But now that I met you, I don't want to hide anymore."

"Good." I nuzzled my head against his feathered chest. "I don't want you to hide either."

Quoth let out a sad croak. The air between us sizzled. I listened through his chest at his heart beating, faster and faster. His feathers tickled my skin. He should have transformed by now, but something held him in this half human, half bird state.

Me.

"Quoth," Heathcliff's heavy footsteps clattered on the stairs. "There's a customer who wants to know if I've got any pop-up books on sex education. I need you to defecate on his head."

And just like that, the spell broke. Quoth drew away, his eyes sad. "Duty calls," he said, and *poof*, his clothes crumpled to the floor and a black raven disappeared down the stairs.

CHAPTER ELEVEN

*T*he SOCO team finished up their examination around lunchtime. Inspector Hayes even took our rubbish bin away for sorting (I pity the officer who got that job) and questioned me some more about the position of each of the women in the room, and if I knew anything else I thought might be important.

I hesitated, remembering Mrs. Ellis' horrified face as I mentioned telling the police about Mrs. Lachlan's grudge against Mrs. Scarlett for the lost development contract. But if someone in that room really *had* poisoned Mrs. Scarlett, the police needed to know. That didn't mean I couldn't keep looking for my own explanation.

"Cynthia Lachlan and Gladys Scarlett had a falling out," I blurted out. "It was over the King's Copse development. Mrs. Scarlett told the town planning committee about Cynthia's husband's old debts and she thought that swayed their decision to refuse his latest planning application."

Hayes scribbled this information down. "Thank you, Mina."

They left. People trickled into the shop. A forty-something man in a horrific sweater purchased two hundred pounds worth of railway books. One lady forgot her reading glasses and made me read the first chapter of *The Grapes of Wrath* out loud to see if she liked it, then refused to pay two-pounds-fifty for it and instead brought it on her e-reader right in front of me. Heathcliff got into another argument with The-Store-That-Shall-Not-Be-Named and karate-chopped the armadillo which, thankfully, survived. Morrie came home from another mysterious outing around three p.m. and pulled me into the storage room, bent me over a box of aviation magazines, and made me feel really, really good. Quoth pooped on two people who quoted 'The Raven.' Toward the end of the day, villagers crowded in to peer over the crime scene tape at the spot where Mrs. Scarlett had expired. Basically, it was a typical day.

We closed up at the usual time. I texted Jo and told her to come for dinner and a drink after she finished work, then walked over to the off-license and picked up a couple bottles of £2.99 wine. When I entered the living room of the upstairs flat, the fire had been lit, the curtains drawn, and the lights dimmed. Heathcliff settled in his armchair, his unruly hair falling over his eyes as he devoured a book. Grimalkin sat in his lap, her paws curled beneath her like a sphinx. Quoth set up an easel in the corner closest to the hall, adding rolling hills to a birds-eye-view landscape of the village.

Morrie frowned as he pulled the bottles out of the brown paper bag and lined them up on the mantelpiece.

"Can't you choose something *French*? I have my doubts as to the grape quality in the 'famous wine region of Suffolk.'"

"I'll get the fanciest wine they offer when Heathcliff gives me a raise."

"No," Heathcliff muttered from his chair, without looking up from his book.

"Look at this one." Morrie jabbed his finger at the label. "'Bouquet' is spelled wrong. That's it, gorgeous. I'm officially banning you from all alcoholic choices hereafter."

Morrie tossed my unopened bottles into the recycling and disappeared into the kitchen. A moment later, he returned with a dusty bottle bearing a label in what looked suspiciously like medieval Latin.

"This is more like it," he grinned, pouring five glasses and handing them around.

"This looks old." I sipped the wine. My mouth exploded with sensation – caramel, honey, almonds, and citrus compote blended together into a sweet, heady taste that clung to my throat. "Wow, it's amazing. Do I want to know where this came from?"

"You do not." Morrie lifted his glass at me and winked.

"It tastes like a musty old boot," Heathcliff glowered at his glass.

I whipped it out of his hand. "I'll have yours, then."

Heathcliff grunted, but I'd already slid down beside Quoth, sipping the delicious wine and watching his delicate brush-strokes. "Are you sure you're going to be okay down here with Jo?"

"I'm going to try," he said. "I can focus on my painting, and maybe my head won't go to the bad places it goes to before I shift."

"What bad places?"

Quoth's fingers pinched the brush so hard his knuckles turned white. "Not now. She'll be here any minute. Later."

I rested my head against his shoulder. His hair fell across my face – luminous strands of the deepest black, tinged with indigo and gold. *Quoth, what's going on inside that head of yours?*

Jo's face appeared in the doorway. "Hey. Hope you guys don't mind, but I picked up some fish and chips on the way over."

I leapt up to embrace her. Morrie joined our hug, and placed a wine glass in her hand. Jo nodded at Heathcliff as she set down the hot parcel of food, and strode up to Quoth and offered her hand.

I held my breath as she addressed him. "Nice to meet you, I'm Jo."

Quoth's face tightened with concentration as he shook Jo's hand. "Allan, but everyone calls me Quoth. You're the forensic pathologist."

"And you're the artist who painted those amazing pictures hung all over the shop. I want to buy the one with the *L'Inconnue de la Seine* hanging downstairs. If you'll take cash, I'll bring it home with me tonight."

Quoth's entire face lit up. "You really want my painting?"

Jo whipped out a leather purse and counted out a stack of notes. "Shut up and take my money. I must have that painting for my office. And I'm going to tell all my colleagues about you. Keep painting morbid scenes and you'll have your artwork in every mortuary in the UK."

Quoth's smile radiated through his whole body. His teeth glowed, his eyes dancing with flecks of orange fire. I slid back down next to him, and he reached behind my back and squeezed my hand.

"Which ugly painting is *The Unknown Woman of the Seine?*" Morrie asked, flawlessly translating the French phrase Jo spoke before.

"It's the one hanging behind Heathcliff's desk, of the woman staring with a serene expression through the dark water," I recalled.

"She was a real person," Jo explained. "An unknown drowning victim found in the Paris river in the 1800s. A pathologist in the city morgue became so smitten with her tranquil features and exquisite beauty that he made a plaster death mask, which was then copied and became a popular wall hanging in well-to-do homes from the 1900s onward. Her likeness was also used to create the face of the first ever CPR doll in 1958, and she's still used on all CPR dolls today."

"That's a cheery bedtime story." Heathcliff flipped open the edge of the paper and helped himself to a handful of hot chips. Grimalkin jumped down from his lap and put her paws on the edge of the table, her little black nose twitching in anticipation of a fishy treat.

Jo sank into my chair opposite Heathcliff. "I'm guessing you told the Scooby Doo gang here about the arsenic?" she asked. I nodded. "That's fine. I expected you to, but nothing I say leaves this room, right?"

We all nodded vigorously, diving into the hot food. I tore off a piece of fish for Grimalkin, who ate it with gusto, spreading bits of fish through the carpet fibers. Heathcliff placed a bookmark into his book and set it aside.

Jo turned to Quoth and I. "Hayes isn't looking seriously at either of you as suspects. He is digging into Heathcliff's background, but I think that's racial profiling more than any serious belief in his guilt. All the witnesses reported he was nowhere near the crime scene."

I glanced at Morrie in concern. Would his fake background documentation for Heathcliff stand up to police scrutiny? But Morrie seemed unperturbed. "Maybe if our resident anti-hero had a better customer service manner, he wouldn't find himself top of the suspect list."

Heathcliff growled. Jo leaned over and patted his arm. "I'd be the same if I had to deal with the living all day. They'll cross you off the suspect list as soon as they determine you barely knew Gladys Scarlett. This type of poisoning is *vicious*. The murderer is going to be someone who knew the victim."

"Poor Greta at the bakery is absolutely distraught," I said. "She thinks she's going to get a reputation for selling poisoned pastries and no one will buy from her again."

"Well, she can relax," Jo smiled, draping her boots over the arm of the chair. "I had the toxicology results back today. This was chronic arsenic poisoning, which changes everything."

Morrie's ears perked up. "Fascinating."

I leaned forward. "What do you mean by chronic poisoning?"

"There are two ways to kill a person with arsenic," Jo explained. "The first is with a single, lethal dose. That's how we assumed Mrs. Scarlett was dispatched, because that's what we'd normally expect to see in a modern arsenic case. But that wasn't true here. She was given continued smaller doses over a period of weeks or months. Over time the victims of chronic arsenic poisoning would experience nausea, headaches, vomiting, and other issues, until eventually the organs shut down."

"Mrs. Ellis said Gladys had been poorly for a while, with dizziness and stomach upsets," I remembered.

"Exactly. Mrs. Scarlett's doctor wouldn't have thought to look for arsenic, so he probably just assumed it was the normal kind of upsets older people experience regularly. Unfortunately, this means we can't narrow our suspect pool down to just the ladies at the Banned Book Club. Right now, anyone could have been the murderer. They would have to be close enough to her to administer a regular dose, so Inspector Hayes will focus his efforts on her family and friends."

"That's going to be a lot of people. According to Mrs. Ellis, she was on every committee in the village!"

"Lucky for him, that's his job." Jo sipped her wine. "Plus, hardly anyone has access to arsenic these days, so it's going to be easy to narrow the suspect pool."

"What's arsenic used for?" Quoth managed to ask, his brush poised in midair.

"Certain manufacturing and agricultural processes. Insecticides and pesticides. Wood preservation. One arsenic compound is used in laser diodes and LED lights."

"The Lachlans own a property development company, so they could probably get access to manufacturers who use arsenic," I said, turning this information over in my mind. "And Mrs. Lachlan would have ample opportunity to slip Mrs. Scarlett poison in all those planning meetings and village events."

"I believe she's been treated as a suspect, but there are other factors to consider. After all, arsenic could also be made in a lab if you knew what you were doing. The actual compound used as poison is called arsenic trioxide, and it—" Jo stopped. "Sorry, I was about to get terribly boring."

"I disagree," Morrie said. "Tell me more about how to make deadly poisons."

I glared at him across the room, but his face remained angelic.

"You and I can discuss chemistry later," Jo downed her glass and bit into a piece of fish while Grimalkin eyed her with wide-eyed jealousy. "I'm off the clock, so I want to know who's seen anything good on the telly?"

"We don't have a television," Morrie said. "Heathcliff doesn't approve of the noise."

"People need to read more books," Heathcliff growled.

"If you think that, why do you snap at every customer that comes in the door?"

"I don't want them to read *my* books."

"Meow," Grimalkin agreed, settling her head on top of her paws.

"Okay, so no one wants to dissect the latest *American Horror Story* series with me, that's fine. Anyone up to anything interesting over the weekend?" Jo asked, looking pointedly at Heathcliff. I glared at her. *What's she doing?*

"No." Heathcliff growled.

"You aren't going on a date with Mina?"

Heathcliff grunted, but didn't answer. Beside me, Quoth itched his neck. A black feather floated into my lap.

"My mum wants you all to come to dinner on Saturday," I blurted out, desperate to change the subject.

Heathcliff's head whipped around. "Does she, now?"

"Yep. I can't get out of it, so let's just get it over with."

"Food that doesn't come from a takeout container?" Morrie perked up. "I'm in. Can your mum make *coq au vin*?"

"Don't get excited. We're not... we live on the council estate. The menu will probably be cheese toasties and a Tesco's chocolate cake."

"I never knock a cheese toastie. My doctorate thesis was fueled by cheese toasties." Jo arranged chips on a slice of buttered bread, slathered it in tomato sauce, and took a bite. "Count me in."

"Okay, thanks."

"I'm not leaving the shop twice in one weekend," Heathcliff grumped.

"It's fine, you don't have to—"

Morrie kicked him in the shins. "We'll all be there," he promised.

"Yes." Quoth's finger traced a line along the edge of my hand.

"Are you sure?" My nerves fluttered. I'd half expected them to say no. *How are we going to keep Quoth in human form for so long? How are we going to make Heathcliff act like a human being for an evening? By Isis, how am I going to make* Mum *act like a human being?* "My mum's a little weird. She's going to try to sell you all dictionaries for cat language."

"Good." Morrie patted the cat's black head. "Grimalkin stands on my face in the middle of the night and makes this chirrup sound and I'd love to know why."

A lump rose in my throat. I swallowed hard. Why did their reactions affect me so much?

"When you consider what goes on in this shop," Quoth whispered, his soft lips brushing my ear, "how crazy could she be?"

A strangled laugh escaped my throat.

"Mina, you okay?" his face twisted with worry.

"No... I'm fine. It's just... Quoth wondered how crazy could she possibly be." I sighed. "You're about to find out."

CHAPTER TWELVE

When Jo drove me home, Mum wasn't there to give me the third degree. A note pinned to the fridge informed me she'd gone to the bridge tournament at the wrinkly village to sell her cat dictionaries. Apparently pensioners loved wasting their super payments on Mum's junk.

I sat down and made a list of all the information I knew about the case so far. I didn't want to disappoint Mrs. Ellis, but it seemed likely that Mrs. Lachlan or her husband were responsible – they certainly had the clearest motive. I did a quick online search through the Argleton Gazette for historical articles about Mrs. Scarlett to see if she was involved in any other town events that might breed resentment. Apart from coverage of heated planning committee meetings, the only other thing of interest was a letter to the editor from Mrs. Scarlett in defense of Sylvia Blume's aura readings and her right to open a witchcraft shop in the village.

I studied the letter with interest. It appeared that some members of Argleton Presbyterian had taken offense to the establishment of 'pagan rituals' in the village and Mrs. Scarlett had – quite rightly, in my opinion – taken them to task. In particular, she focused on one member of the committee who seemed to be leading the charge; the same Dorothy Ingram who had Mrs. Winstone banned as youth group leader.

I wonder if Mum remembers this. The article was from ten years ago, which was around the time Mum started offering tarot readings from Sylvia's shop. Asking Mum about her life would also make her happy. I saved the article to show her later.

I took a shower, changed into my pajamas, and crawled into bed with a vampire novel I'd borrowed from the shop. I jammed my headphones in my ears, stared up at the poster of the Misfits on the roof of my bedroom and all the photographs of me and Ashley, and thought about how I might never see a photograph again. When I went blind, would all my memories imprint in my mind? Would I remember the world before I could see? Would it fade over time, or would I be stuck forever looping visions I could no longer experience?

Fear rippled through me. All my life I'd known exactly what I was going to do – leave this stupid estate and this village and make it in the fashion industry. But now I was just as lost, just as stuck as the guys—

A weird blue light flashed and wiggled across my vision, like a neon sign in Times Square.

I bolted upright. *What's that?*

I rubbed my eye. The blue squiggle flashed again, then disappeared.

My body froze. *Don't panic. It could be anything.* A reflection from the street outside, a hallucination of my tired, wine-fueled brain.

But I *knew.* My ophthalmologist warned me that at some point my eye condition would advance, and I'd start to notice random explosions of color or colors swapping around as my brain tried to rewire itself to see again. They'd become more and more frequent and then, eventually, colors would fade to black and I wouldn't be able to see at all.

He told me I'd have years before I started noticing the lights. *Years.* But I hadn't mistaken the blue flare.

Sid Vicious screamed in my ears. I bit back my own urge to scream.

I grabbed my phone to text Morrie. I started typing a message. I got as far as, "I just saw a weird light in my eyes. Think I'm going blind. Need to talk to someone."

I stopped. My finger hovered over the SEND button.

Morrie wasn't the person to talk to about this. He was good for forgetting. But I needed… I didn't know what I needed. I flicked through my address book, my finger hovering over Quoth's name. I sent him a message. *Can you call me?*

I stared at the screen, willing the phone to ring. But it remained silent. *He's probably out, flying around the village. He can't exactly carry a phone under his wing—*

Something rapped at the window.

I threw myself off the bed, my heart pounding. I peered through the frosted glass. A black bird sat on the ledge, peering in at me with dark, soulful eyes.

My heart soared. I stood up and flung open the window. "Quoth?"

"Croak!" The bird fluttered inside and hopped across the bed. He nudged my hand with the top of his head. I stroked his soft feathers, and he swiveled his head and stared up at me with brown eyes filled with pain.

"You didn't have to come," I whispered.

He shifted, the black feathers retracting into his skin. A pair of muscular legs slid over the side of my bed, and a moment later a pale-skinned man with hair like a waterfall of midnight sat beside me.

He threw my bed sheet over his naked crotch and flashed me his brilliant smile. "Of course I came. You're upset."

"Have you been listening to my thoughts?"

Quoth shook his head. "I was painting and I saw your message. I thought… you needed me."

I turned away. Looking at his perfect face and his soft eyes and knowing that after everything he endured every day, he was still there for me, made shame bubble inside me. Losing my sight was nothing compared to what Quoth had gone through, was still going through – no memory of his past beyond a shadowed chamber and a dreary night, a body that betrayed him, a lonely and confined existence. A fat tear rolled down my cheek.

The corner of the room, where the light didn't reach, collapsed into a black hole of darkness. I'd been ignoring it lately, but my night blindness was getting worse, too. *I'm a mess. My whole life is a mess.*

"I feel so stupid," I said to the wall.

"You're not stupid."

"I can't ask you to come running every time…"

"Mina, tell me what happened."

In deep, halting breaths, I explained about the light, and what it meant. "I'm scared, so scared, Quoth. I thought I was getting better. After meeting you guys, I haven't been feeling so depressed and hopeless. But I'd convinced myself it was still years away, and now…"

Warm fingers brushed my hand. Quoth knitted his fingers into mine, squeezing tight. I squeezed back. "I'm not going to say that it will be okay," he said.

"Thank you."

"To quote some writer I've never heard of, your soul is 'with sorrow laden.' You're allowed to cry, or scream, or punch things. You will mourn your eyes the same way we all mourn things we've lost. But there will come a time when you don't want to mourn any longer. You will have other things to do. You are strong, Mina."

"I don't feel strong," I sniffed.

"You made me believe that there is more to this life than surviving. I don't doubt you'll believe that yourself again."

My heart did a squeezing, fluttering thing. Quoth's words hurt so good – with that velvet voice of his, he sung the stars and the rain. I leaned my head against his bare shoulder. The tear rolled out of my eye and fell on his chest, rolling over his alabaster skin to leave a salty slug trail.

"What happens now?" Quoth whispered, his voice tight. His lips brushed my forehead, sending flutters through my skin.

"I have to go to an ophthalmologist – that's a specialist eye doctor. They'll do some tests and tell me what's changed in my eyes. They'll give me an idea of how long I have and what I can expect next."

"I'll go with you, if you need me."

"Thank you." I knew what a promise like that meant to Quoth – every moment he risked exposing what he was. I squeezed his fingers. If I was crushing him, he gave no indication.

I flopped back on the bed, my eyes focusing on the bright circle of light from my single bulb, illuminating the Misfits poster and the outline of Quoth's head, his hair flowing down his back – a river of midnight.

Quoth lay down beside me, his head inches from mine. I watched our chests rising and falling in perfect synergy. My body buzzed with emotion. I itched to roll over and kiss him, but I held back. I didn't want my first kiss with Quoth to be with tears in my eyes and snot running out of my nose.

Here I am, talking about our first kiss as though it's inevitable.

"Quoth," I breathed. *Even his name is poetry.*

"Yes?"

"Don't tell the others about this yet. Please."

"Mina—"

"I just… I need time to process it, okay? Promise me you won't tell."

"I promise. But you should tell them."

"I will." I squeezed his hand, and my heart squeezed and tightened, too. I was supposed to have years left, but it might only be months before I went blind and so many pleasures were no longer open to me. Quoth's warm hand in mine steadied me about the darkness on the edges of my eyes and the darkness inside me that threatened to take over.

He was right, of course. I would mourn. I would mourn my motherfucking arse off. But now was not the time, not while I still had eyes to see. It *was* time I stopped giving a fuck about what other people thought of me and my life and my relationships. Maybe I needed to live to excess and indulge all my senses while I still had the use of them.

Maybe it was time I took Morrie's challenge to the next level.

CHAPTER THIRTEEN

"... *I* think the KT Strange werewolf rock band romance would be a great read for your Amalfi Coast holiday, and this book will make a lovely gift for your six-year-old niece," I finished, holding out a beautifully-illustrated story about an elephant and his balloon to the customer. "Just don't mix them up."

"Yes," she beamed. "That's perfect. You've been very helpful!"

Warmth flushed my cheeks from her praise. There was something satisfying for the soul about helping a customer find the perfect book. "I'm so glad you're pleased. I'll just ring these up for you, and—"

"Oh, no, no." She whipped out her phone and tapped the screen. "I'm buying them online. They're always so much cheaper. Thank you for the recommendations!"

Rage flared inside me as I watched her meander into the hall-way, tapping her way merrily through The-Store-That-Shall-Not-Be-Named. *Thanks for wasting half an hour of my time.* Heath-cliff's customer-ire was starting to make sense to me.

"Croak?" Quoth landed on the desk in front of me, tapping his beak against the till. He'd stayed with me all night last night, perched on the end of my bed while I slept, his superior avian vision scanning the darkness for danger. I told him again and again to go back to the flat, that I didn't need protecting, but he remained my solitary watchtower all night. We didn't do anything more than hug goodnight before he shifted into his raven form, but I'd never been more intimate with a person before. We'd both laid a piece of ourselves bare for each other.

"Go for it," I muttered.

Quoth fluttered out of the room and a moment later, a high-pitched squeal reverberated through the shop. I rushed to the archway and peered around in time to see the woman storm out, frantically dabbing at a stain on her shoulder with a lace hand-kerchief.

Gotcha.

The woman was so busy dealing with Quoth's present, she crashed into Mrs. Ellis coming up the steps.

"Where's the fire?" Mrs. Ellis called gaily after the woman, who sobbed in reply.

"Hello, Mrs. Ellis," I held the door open for her. Quoth fluttered down and landed on my shoulder, his talons digging into my collarbone. "Are you doing okay?"

"Oh, I'm surviving." Mrs. Ellis took off her gloves, her hands shaking. Her usual rosy-cheeked complexion was pallid and sallow. "Mina, I wanted to ask you something. We're having a little fete at the church after Gladys' funeral on Saturday. She was important to so many people and I know she'd want to bring the community together even in death. There will be no tears, just good old fashioned fun. We wondered if you'd like a book stall, maybe even some of your book artwork? Perhaps your friend with the beautiful black hair might like to paint a commemorative picture—"

"No." Heathcliff said without looking up.

Mrs. Ellis' lip quivered. "Oh, that's fine. I understand, of course. You're very busy, you must be run off your feet. I just thought I'd ask…"

"Ignore Heathcliff. We'd love to," I beamed.

"Oh, that's wonderful." Mrs. Ellis took an envelope out of her carpet bag and handed it to me. "Gladys would be so pleased. There's all the information you need in there. You're stall number twenty-three. We'll see you at nine thirty a.m. tomorrow."

"Great! I can't wait."

Mrs. Ellis leaned over and stage-whispered. "Have you made any progress on poor Gladys' case? The police have taken Cynthia and her husband in for questioning. She tells me they've applied for a warrant to search their house!"

If they're closing in on the Lachlans, then they probably know something I don't. And yet… "I don't want to get your hopes up, but I *did* find something yesterday." I explained about Mrs. Scarlett's article defending Miss Blume.

"Oh, yes, I remember something from many years ago… Dorothy hadn't been very friendly with Gladys since. It doesn't help that Gladys was always stirring the pot with the church committee. She attended service, of course, but she didn't abide all that fire and brimstone claptrap Dorothy's so fond of. She believed, as do I, that as long as it's not hurting people, what's the harm in a few astrology charts and a cream doughnut and a naughty magazine?"

"Did Dorothy say anything when Gladys started the Banned Book Club? She kicked Mrs. Winstone from the youth group just for being a member."

"Oh, she bent the vicar's ear, and we had to sit through a whole Sunday service dedicated to it!" Mrs. Ellis rolled her eyes, and I couldn't help but giggle. "Dorothy's a bible thumper if ever I met one, and without a good man in her life she spends far too much energy sticking her nose in where it isn't wanted. I have half a mind to believe she ran that digger through the town hall in an attempt to shut us down! Why... but you don't believe she could kill Gladys over the *book club?*"

"I don't know. It's just a hunch. Besides, I wouldn't know where she'd get the arsenic from, or how she'd administer it."

"Oh, Mina, I think you've cracked it! Dorothy works at the village pharmacy. Of course she'd know all about administering arsenic. I need to go to the police right now—"

"Hold on." I grabbed her arm. "We've got no evidence, only an old newspaper article and some wild ideas. If you go to the police now, they'll just think you're trying to draw their attention away from the Lachlans, and it'll make them look harder. They might even take you in for being in cahoots with them."

Mrs. Ellis paled. "You're right," she whispered. "What do we do?"

"Will Dorothy be at the funeral tomorrow?"

"Of course! She wouldn't miss the chance to lord it over the congregation, and gloating over Gladys' coffin will bring her added joy."

"Then I'll see if I can find out something while I'm there."

"Oh thank you, Mina. You're an angel." Mrs. Ellis kissed my cheek and shuffled off. My heart went out to her, losing a friend to poison, and being confronted with the fact it might've been another friend who did it. I still wasn't certain about my Dorothy Ingram theory, especially not with the police investigating the Lachlans, but it was worth checking up on for my favorite teacher.

Deep in thought, I turned to face a glowering Heathcliff.

"Why are you trying to ruin my life?" he growled.

I smiled sweetly. "I thought we were trying to sell books? Sometimes that means bringing the books to the people."

"We don't do church fetes or writers festival stalls or football club fundraisers." Heathcliff jabbed a finger at his desk. "We don't do anything that involves me having to leave this chair."

"Look, Duke of Grumpingham, I'm trying to figure out who

poisoned Mrs. Scarlett. Maybe you don't care, but Mrs. Ellis was the best teacher I ever had. She wants me to help, and *I* care. I think this Dorothy Ingram might've had something to do with it – she definitely had a grudge against Mrs. Scarlett. The funeral is the perfect time to observe Dorothy, as well as Mrs. Scarlett's other friends and relatives, and see who might be acting suspiciously."

Heathcliff studied me for a long moment, not saying anything. That intense look passed through his eyes, the same look he'd had when he kissed me – a wild turmoil of hunger and yearning and rage. The storm passed over, and he rested a hand on my shoulder. "You should take stock from the Theology and Children's Book sections, as well as your book artwork."

"You'll come help me run the stall?"

"No. That old bint's funeral is the perfect time to get a little bloody peace and quiet in this shop."

I stuck out my lip. "You're no fun. I'm going to talk to Morrie. Are we still on for dinner tonight?"

"Unless you changed your mind?" The words came out in a rush, as though Heathcliff feared my answer.

"Hell no." I smiled. "I've already made plans. And don't worry, no fancy clothes are required. Where we're going, even trousers are optional."

I hadn't meant that line to be flirtatious, but Heathcliff's eyes burned into mine, and heat crept up my neck.

I raced upstairs. "Morrie, want to help me run a stall at the church fete on Saturday—"

Morrie stood in the hall, staring into the open door of the master suite.

"Morrie." I stepped toward him, my hand raised, not sure what to do.

"Fascinating," was his only reply.

I peered around him and into the room. My eyes could only

make out a few dark shapes, but it was enough for me to tell that I wasn't staring at either of the rooms I'd seen earlier.

Dark bookshelves lined every wall. Instead of the spines of books, they held niches where rolled scrolls of parchment and paper sat in leather and silver holders. A large, rough oak desk stood in the center of the room. On top of the desk, an enormous book lay open, with tiny columns of text and ornate illuminated illustrations glittering in the dim candle-light. Behind the desk, the door to the pentagonal room was firmly shut. Curtains fluttered at the windows and the scent of wet ink stained the air, as if the room's occupant had just ducked out and would return at any moment.

I stepped toward the room and grabbed the handle to pull it open all the way. As I did, a white shape streaked between my legs and skidded into the room. The mouse dived under the desk and disappeared. I moved to go after it, but the door jerked from my fingers and slammed shut.

I jiggled the lock, but it was stuck tight, with the Terror of Argleton locked inside!

CHAPTER FOURTEEN

"What the hell are you doing?" Morrie's fingers dug into my arm. "You were trying to go in there. I thought we agreed none of us should enter that room."

"I was going to chase the mouse out. Now it's trapped in a wormhole in space and time. It's you who doesn't remember that conversation," I shot back. "You're the one who opened the door."

He made a face. "Do you believe I would disobey a direct order from Sir Angus McSurlybritches? I came out of the bathroom and here it was, door open, contents laid bare. As for the mouse, let him rot in the void between dimensions. The village will probably give you a medal in addition to that reward."

"What's going on?" Quoth appeared at the end of the hall, his naked body pale against the gloom.

"The door was open again." Morrie jiggled the lock and tapped the frame. "It slammed shut as soon as Mina tried to go in—"

Quoth's eyes widened. "You didn't go inside, did you?"

"It wouldn't let me!"

"What did you see?"

"It looked a bit like a printer's office or something. There were all these parchments in niches on the walls."

"Not a printer," Morrie said. "A book-binder and copier. I think we might've just seen Mr. Herman Strepel's 9th-century establishment."

My mind raced. *It's impossible. No way did we just open a doorway and see into a building that existed a thousand years ago.*

But then, it wasn't any more impossible than anything else that happened in this shop, like the fact that I was having a casual conversation about a wormhole into space-time with James Moriarty and Poe's raven.

"Say you're right." I faced the guys. "What does it mean? Have you ever seen that particular room before?"

Morrie shook his head. His eye sparkled with mischief, which, in his case, was a very bad sign. "Did you glimpse that enormous book on the desk?"

"It was hard to miss, even with my eyes."

"It looked to be a catalogue of all the texts for sale, and the different scripts, illuminations, and decorations available to order. That's exactly what you asked me to find for you. If we could get hold of it, we could see—"

I folded my arms. "No. You're not going in there and taking that book. You already took that empty book downstairs. For all we know, that's made the shop's magic more unstable."

"We don't have to take it. We could just sneak in, peek through, and run out before anything happens. You went into the Victorian bedroom and nothing bad happened."

I hesitated. Morrie was *technically* correct. I'd spent a good five minutes looking around the room and nothing bad happened.

"Mina," Quoth's silky voice warned. "Don't let Morrie tempt you. He's good at that."

I bit my lip. *Yes. Yes, he is.*

Heathcliff chose that moment to barrel up the stairs. "What's going on? There are customers downstairs asking questions and I need at least one of you to act as a buffer."

"Morrie wants to do something dangerous," Quoth said.

"And you've dissuaded him?"

"Not in the slightest."

I explained to Heathcliff what just happened. "This feels important, like it means something. Doesn't it seem odd that we learn books have been sold here ever since Herman Strepel's day, and then the room offers us a glimpse into his office? I think Morrie's right in that we should investigate—"

Wordlessly, Heathcliff shoved past Morrie. He drew a key from his pocket and shoved it into the lock. When he flung the door open, we all crowded around to see.

No candlelight shone to illuminate the gloom. From the square of light the hallway bulb and windows cast across the bare wood floor, I glimpsed a thick layer of dust, but nothing else.

"I can't see," I cried.

"Maybe you should move some ugly junk shop lamps up here too," Heathcliff grumbled.

"You wanker, how long have you known?"

"Since that weird one with the fringe appeared beside the Crime Fiction shelf. Suddenly I can see how dirty the shop is. Now I have to clean up all the dust and grime," he growled. "And it's all your fault."

"The room's empty, Mina," Quoth said, stretching his neck to peer inside. "There's nothing here."

Heathcliff slammed the door. "Are we all happy?"

"I'm happy that the Terror of Argleton has been blasted into the past," Morrie said. "But I'm not happy we lost our chance to peruse that book. Do you think if we open the door again, Master Strepel's office will return?"

"I think that standing around here isn't getting the rent paid or the dinner cooked." Heathcliff turned to me. "You're not being paid to investigate magical occurrences. Go downstairs and mind the shop."

"Why can't you do it?"

He threw me a withering look. "Because I've got to get in the shower before Morrie uses all the hot water. I need to look presentable for a bloody date tonight."

CHAPTER FIFTEEN

*A*fter closing the shop, I went over to Jo's apartment to use her shower and collect the date supplies I left there. Back at Nevermore, I paced along the hallway, heart pattering like a teen girl waiting for the football player to pick her up for the school formal. Above my head, footsteps thumped across the flat, and the sounds of swearing filtered down the stairs.

Why am I so nervous? I see Heathcliff every day.

Because I don't go on a date with my book crush and try to convince him to be part of a polyamorous relationship with his best friend every day, that's why.

Footsteps thundered down the stairs. I spun around, and my breath caught in my throat.

Heathcliff moved under the string of fairy lights I'd hung over the staircase, and his body revealed itself to me in glittering shafts of light. He wore a black shirt shot with golden threads that pulled across his broad shoulders in a way that made my mouth water. He'd rolled up the sleeves, revealing his tattoo of a gnarled tree and cursive script I'd never got close enough to read along one muscular forearm. He'd combed his hair back from his face, collecting it in a tie at the nape of his neck. Several recalcitrant curls had already worked their way free to spill over his face. Under the glow of the fairy lights his dark features softened, and his eyes sparkled with something that might have been excitement, if Heathcliff was capable of such a thing.

"Right. Let's get this over with," he grumbled, although his voice had none of its usual edge.

I'm going on a date with Heathcliff. The *Heathcliff.*

A big, stupid grin spread across my face. The corners of Heathcliff's mouth tugged upward. It wasn't quite a smile, but it was his and it was special.

"You look nice," he said.

I'd better. I followed Morrie's advice and worn my red jersey dress over a pair of black leggings. This dress hugged what little curves I possessed in all the right places. I teased out my hair with spiky fringe and applied a little smoky eyeliner. Combined with my wedge-heeled boots and a string of blood-red rosary beads I'd borrowed from Jo, I knew I looked *fierce.*

We pulled on our coats and scarves to ward against the winter chill. I held out my hand, and Heathcliff looped his arm around mine. "Where are we going?" he asked. "I hope it's not a movie. I hate all the people crunching popcorn and talking, and the music is always too loud—"

"Relax, Grandpa, it's like you think I don't know you." I grinned, hefting my tote bag over my shoulder. The objects inside clanked and rustled. "Trust me. This date is Heathcliff-friendly."

I led him across the green and down to the edge of the village, where the chocolate-box houses gave way to half-built new dwellings, and then rolling hills and a small, familiar wood. "This is King's Copse. Of course, when the King actually used to hunt here, the wood covered all the surrounding hills. But most of it was cleared during the 19th and 20th centuries, and only this small section remains."

"Doesn't this belong to the gent whose wife you reckon killed the old bint?" Heathcliff held my hand as I stepped over the style. "We're trespassing."

"Grey Lachlan? Yeah, he's the developer. But I'm not sure he did it. Mrs. Ellis believes the Lachlans are innocent, and I'm starting to agree. I mean, poisoning someone is a pretty extreme way to deal with a local planning committee, and killing Mrs. Scarlett isn't exactly going to change the rest of the committee's mind. I'm wondering about Dorothy Ingram – she's head of the church committee and believed the Banned Book Club was sinful. As for trespassing, it's a *wood*. It's not like it's got security guards. Kids from the village and the housing estate have been coming here for years. I used to spend a lot of warm summer evenings down by the stream."

"I hate to be the bearer of bad news," Heathcliff pulled the collar of his jacket tight around his face. "It's not a warm summer's evening."

"Hush. Man up." My teeth chattered, and puffs of steam formed in front of my lips. Heathcliff wasn't wrong about the temperature. "I want to show you something."

My excitement turned sour as soon as we started down the overgrown path. Away from the road, the darkness enclosed me. I couldn't make out anything – no outlines of branches arching over the path, no reflections in muddy puddles between the roots, no edges where one plant gave way to another. I flung my arms out and stumbled blindly down the path. Wet branches scraped my wool coat as I felt my way along the overgrown path. Tears of frustration prickled my eyes as my boots scuffed and tripped over roots and fallen debris.

"Mina," Heathcliff's voice growled in my ear. He grabbed my shoulders, bringing me to a halt. "Stop. You'll fall and hurt yourself."

"I know the way," I snapped. *It's not fair. This was supposed to be romantic. My stupid eyes ruin everything.*

"Of course you do." A hand looped in mine, huge, rough

fingers between my tiny ones, warm and reassuring. "But we can't have that fine dress of yours getting torn up. Let me follow the path; you tell me where to go."

I wiped the tears with the back of my hand, glad that in the gloom he couldn't see my mascara running. *This is stupid. Why did I think this would be a good date idea?*

But I didn't have a backup plan, or a torch, or even my mobile phone, so I let Heathcliff lead me down the path. I apologized every time I stepped on his heels or kicked his shins trying to avoid the roots. Ahead of me, behind me, below and above me – all the world was a deep, endless, terrifying void. *Is this what I'll see when I go blind?*

After a time, I stopped bothering to apologize or to avoid the obstacles in my path. I switched my grip to Heathcliff's elbow and glided along in his wake. Heathcliff was a force of nature, and I had no choice but to be swept up with him, letting go of control and trusting the darkness.

Trusting the darkness. Would I ever feel at home in this gloom?

"We've reached a fork," Heathcliff said after a little while. "Which way?"

"Left. We keep going until we reach a tiny stream."

We turned. Sounds reached my ears, close, but growing distant as we descended. Voices. Kids laughing. A rap song playing out of tinny USB speakers. And above it all – the bubbling water of the stream, rushing faster than I remembered as it swelled from the winter rains. The water grew louder, and the path widened out and became steeper, the trees loosening their oppressive weight on us. My feet slid over rocks and pebbles.

Heathcliff turned and gripped my sides, holding my weight easily as he helped me down the steep, rocky slope. At the bottom I stood upright, tugging Heathcliff's arm until he drew up against me. I pressed myself into the bulk of his body, and *listened*. I couldn't see the water, but I heard it, the sound bringing me back to my child-hood – reading books on a flat rock in this very spot, tucked away out of sight from the kids who hung out further up the stream.

My temples pounded from the effort of straining my eyes in the darkness, but I didn't care. Euphoria washed over me. *We got here in the end, and it's still the same.* It smelled and sounded exactly the way I remembered. So what if the date wasn't working out quite the way I hoped? I didn't need to see Heathcliff to know how fucking hot he looked, or how good his body felt pressed up against mine.

"You can't see this place from the road, and most people go the other way because there's a flat area that's nicer for sitting," I said. "Ashley and I used to skip school and walk out here. We'd listen to punk songs on an old Discman and draw fashion sketches. Once, we even went skinny-dipping in the stream."

Heathcliff grunted. Beside me, his body stiffened.

"Don't get excited – it was a *disaster.* Turns out, the stream's only knee deep, so we just waddled around in the buff. Then something bit Ashley's foot, and I got an ugly red rash from the weeds that didn't disappear for a *week*. I've never gone skinny-dipping since. Can you see a long, flat rock anywhere?"

"Over here." Heathcliff led me over to it. I felt around the edges with my hands, satisfied it was as I remembered and big enough for two. I unrolled a blanket from the top of my bag, spread it out on the rock, and sat down. A bitter chill rose off the water, blasting me in the face and drying my tears. The rock hugged me in familiar places – cool, reassuring, as much a part of me as the man who now sat down beside me, his thigh pressed against mine.

I opened my bag and laid out the food I'd brought earlier – a fresh loaf of bread from Greta's bakery, slices of chorizo and prosciutto, some fancy cheese, a bag of grapes, and two of Greta's amazing cream doughnuts. I handed Heathcliff a knife and ordered him to slice the bread and cheese while I poured us both a glass of wine.

"You thought of everything," he said as I unscrewed the lid of a jar of Mrs. Ellis' homemade strawberry preserve.

"I'm quite clever, you know." I handed him a plastic cup filled with champagne, and he slid a slice of bread loaded with cheese and chorizo into my open hand. I bit into it, savoring the spicy meat and sharp cheddar.

"Don't say that. You sound like Morrie. I don't want to think about Morrie tonight."

"Did I choose the perfect spot for our date?" I sipped my Champagne, the bubbles tickling my tongue.

"You did." Heathcliff's warm breath caressed my cheek as he leaned close to me. "I didn't even know about this wood. If I had, I'd probably come more often. I don't get out into nature as much as I should."

"Is it because it reminds you of Wuthering Heights?"

Heathcliff paused. "Probably. It's more that the England of my world doesn't exist here, not for me – the moors were the last true wild place, ethereal and menacing in equal measure. Their wild beauty hid danger and memory and a dream that withered into dust."

"The moors still exist, you know. You could go back there and be close to her memory." *Or her legend.* To him, they were the same thing.

"I cannot."

"Why not? Sell the shop. Buy a cottage in the middle of nowhere. You'd never have to see a customer again—"

"Don't say such things, Mina," Heathcliff growled. His plastic cup crinkled as he took a long sip of Champagne. "Don't think I haven't considered it."

"Then why do you stay? Surely one of the other fictional characters could run the shop, someone who's better with people. There's nothing to keep you here—"

"You're here."

Heat crept into my cheeks. "But I've only been here a few weeks. You could have gone before that."

"I have a duty," he said, stiffening.

"To Mr. Simson? But *why?*"

"Because of you!" he yelled, standing up and scattering food across the rocks. "Why must you ask so many bloody questions?"

"I don't know, why do you never give me a straight bloody answer? You can't just drop a bombshell like that and expect me not to ask more. Why because of me?"

Heathcliff breathed heavily. Tension rippled between us as the river roared in my ears. "Mr. Simson told me to wait for a girl to return to the shop. He said this girl was extremely important to all of us, and that she was in great danger, and we were to keep her safe. He described you. Or at least, we're pretty sure it was you. That blind codger's description wasn't exactly resplendent with visual detail. But when you walked into the shop and told that story about how you used to spend all your time there as a child, and Quoth realized you could hear his thoughts, we guessed he meant you."

I remembered something I'd overheard Quoth saying in his raven form, on the very first day I walked into the shop. *She's the one...* I'd assumed he meant, "she's the only one who'll put up with your bollocks," but this... I couldn't believe it.

"And that's why you gave me the job. Because Mr. Simson told you to. This is insane. Why would Mr. Simson ask you to wait for me?"

"I know as much as you do, which is nothing. Morrie's current assumption is that Mr. Simson used the master bedroom to travel into the bookshop's future and see that you were in danger. He's desperate to try it himself."

I narrowed my eyes. "Is this why Quoth is following me home every night and sitting on the end of my bed? Because you all

113

think I'm in *danger?* What kind of peril am I in that I can't handle myself?"

"He didn't elaborate."

"Well, you can stop bloody protecting me. I don't need it."

"Not going to happen," Heathcliff growled. "Danger follows you around like a curse. Not a single person died in Nevermore Bookshop until you showed up. We're not taking chances. One of us has been near you every moment from the time you walked into the shop. We take turns, making sure you're always safe."

They've been shadowing me, spying on me? I balled my hands into fists and shot to my feet. "You can't just spy on me without telling me!"

"I'm telling you now."

"You should have told me the *first day.* This is my life. I had a right to know."

"Not just your life," he snapped. "This danger will come down on all our heads."

"If I'm such a bloody danger to you all," I screamed into Heathcliff's face, "then why bother keeping me around?"

"*Mina.*" My name rumbled from Heathcliff's lips.

"Just fire me, Heathcliff. Rip off the Band-Aid. You don't even like me, anyway. You're just doing this out of some misguided sense of duty to Mr. Simson. Well, I'm not anyone's pity project. You'd be better off if I never came into your life. You'd be—"

"Oh, fuck it," Heathcliff growled. Something warm pressed against my lips.

Heathcliff.

All my protests flew from my head as Heathcliff devoured me, his tongue hot and demanding. He took no prisoners, wasted no time, not now that he'd declared what he wanted.

He wants me. Heathcliff wants me.

The rage inside me burned into hot passion, and I returned the kiss with everything I had. Heathcliff moaned as I sucked on his lower lip and met his ferocity with my own. Weeks of pent-up frustration flowed between us, as with hands and mouth and tongues we said all those things we'd tiptoed around for too long.

In the darkness, every sensation heightened. His kisses lit a line of fire straight through my body. Heathcliff's arms went around me, clutching me against him as he poured his passion and his rage into me, and I drank it up and threw it back.

Heathcliff's weight drove me back against the rock. His hands cupped my breasts, my ass, my cheeks, my hips. He explored with wild abandon, his hands everywhere at once, leaving me panting, breathless. My plastic cup of Champagne toppled over as I lay back on the blanket, splashing liquid over the blanket. *I don't care. Heathcliff's hands are on my body.*

"Mina," he growled, his hands sliding underneath me, tugging the jersey dress up over my hips. "Do you want me to stop?"

"Fuck no."

"Good." Heathcliff pulled the dress up, yanked down my leggings, and dived between my legs.

CHAPTER SIXTEEN

*H*eathcliff didn't waste time teasing me like Morrie did. His tongue found the perfect spot and he attacked it with all his wrath and fervor, wading in like some ancient warrior to render my body a helpless, quivering mess.

My back arched against the hard rock and tiny pinpricks of light penetrated the darkness – the stars twinkling in the night sky. A universe opening itself up to me as Heathcliff opened up my body, my heart.

He sucked my clit into his mouth and I was gone gone gone, tumbling wildly through the darkness, losing myself to the void of pleasure. My body shuddered as fire tore through my veins.

No sooner had a final shudder rolled through me then Heathcliff was back, cupping my cheek, pulling my face to his for another breathtaking kiss. He fumbled with his own clothing. Buttons pinged over the stones and plopped into the stream. I dug my fingers beneath Heathcliff's shirt, pressing my palms against his chest. His heart beat beneath my touch, alive and unburdened.

He yanked my legs around his waist, pulled a condom from somewhere and rolled it on, and fell against me like a man possessed, his fingers clawing at my skin as he leaned me back against the rock and entered me in a single deep thrust.

Yes, yes!

When Heathcliff drove himself inside me, a sliver of blue light arced across my eyes. I should have been terrified, but instead, I realized it was beautiful. My own personal fireworks display to match the fire in my veins.

If not for his arms pinning me in place, his powerful thrusts would've sent me sailing off the back of the rock. To him, my body was the battlefield where he waged a war against his own conscience.

In the moment, I didn't care, because his arms were around me and his cock was inside me and he felt so, so good.

The heat of our bodies clung to our skin, cocooning us in warmth against the frigid night. Heathcliff's kisses trailed across my face. His hand held my body, while he thrust and thrust and thrust, abandoning what little decorum he possessed and giving in to the wild, possessive man I'd fallen in love with between the pages of a book.

Heathcliff moaned as he thrust into me, his voice deep and tight with lust and pain. I rose up to meet him, grinding my thighs to push him deeper, to take his pain and make it mine. His fingers dug into my thigh, an exquisite sting that sent me closer to the edge.

I came again with the night cool against my face and a crackle of neon blue light streaking across my vision. Fireworks exploded in my body and behind my eyes. With a bellow, Heathcliff came too, his muscles tensing and releasing as his cock quivered inside me, a lion roaring his defiance into the night.

For a moment, for a single glorious moment while the frigid air brushed my body and Heathcliff clasped me to him, I thought it would be okay that I went blind. Because even when I couldn't see and crazy neon fireworks danced in my eyes, I could still *feel*.

In Heathcliff's hands, and Morrie's hands, there were *so many* good things to feel.

And then the moment faded, and the chill bit my bones, and the blue light kept dancing and I couldn't see the stars. I scrambled to pull on my dress and hide my face from Heathcliff, because even though *I* couldn't see, he might notice my tears and think they were because of him.

"Would you like to walk a while?" he asked, brushing dirt off my coat and winding my scarf around my neck. He picked up the rubbish from our picnic and slung the tote bag over his shoulder. "We could head through the wood to the fields, where it's brighter."

I wiped my face on the edge of my scarf. "I'd love that."

We linked arms again, and I gave over my trust to Heathcliff, allowing him to lift me up the steep bank and lead me back along the path. With every step his body straightened, his muscles remembering how to duck and run and ramble.

I itched to say something about what just happened. I desperately needed to know what Heathcliff was thinking about him and me, and me and Morrie. But Heathcliff wasn't Morrie. He didn't talk things to death and consider all the angles. He didn't have some grand scheme in mind. If I wanted to untangle Heathcliff, I'd have to parse his mind from the intelligible grunts he occasionally deemed to throw my way.

Further up the path, he diverged down another route, one that would carry us to the edge of the forest, where ramblers' paths were built-up by the Council and villagers walked their dogs or rode bikes in the weekends. Soon, we weren't walking on bare dirt and tree roots but a wooden boardwalk.

"Interesting," Heathcliff said.

"What?" I asked, my breath coming out in a rush. *Are we actually going to talk about what just happened?*

But no.

"Some of these trees have been cut down," Heathcliff said.

"There's an earthmover and some other equipment over there. It looks as if Gray Lachlan might have jumped the gun on starting work on clearing trees for his development."

I was disappointed, but also interested. If the Lachlans had started to push ahead with groundworks on the second stage of the development, before the committee tossed back their application again… I wondered if the police knew about this.

The oppressive weight of the trees lifted once more, and I knew we'd come to the edge of the forest, where a great wildflower meadow gave way to farmland further down the valley. Solar lights on sticks dotted the edges, giving me a faint glimpse at the tall wildflowers that surrounded me.

"I can see lights!" I cried. On the horizon, bright orbs arrested my vision, throwing up the dark shapes of buildings.

As we walked closer, the lights resolved themselves as windows and lanterns, casting shadows on stone walls and steep gables. A row of stone workers' cottages stood on the edge of the meadow, backing onto the open fields beyond. A copse of trees bent over them, the branches scraping against the crumbling stone and broken tiles as the wind twisted through them. Smoke billowed from ancient chimneys, and overgrown gardens spilled over low stone walls.

"Oh, I've never seen these houses before," I breathed. A puff of mist rose from my mouth, catching the light and floating into elegant curlicues. "They're beautiful."

"They're practically falling over." Heathcliff pointed to the house on the end of the row, where part of the roof had caved in. It was patched over with corrugated iron. "Isn't that one of your Banned Book Club biddies?"

I squinted where he pointed. In front of the cottage, an expensive-looking red sports car idled in the driveway, the headlights illuminating two white circles on the side of the house. A car door slammed, and a figure jogged through the headlight to the front door of the cottage. No matter how much I strained my eyes, I couldn't see the figure. "What does she look like? I can't see."

"Dark frizzy hair, tie-dyed dress under a vomit-colored trench coat—"

"Oh, that's Sylvia Blume. What's she doing?"

"She's got a key, and she's opening the front door. There's another person in the car, she's getting out…" Another door slammed. Heathcliff leaned forward. "This one is a snotty-looking woman wearing a king's ransom in diamonds. She's heavily pregnant. They're arguing."

Ginny Button!

What are they arguing about? Something in my gut told me this was important. Whispered words rushed past my ears, too quiet and too far away to be heard. Frustration welled inside me. How could I find out what was going on?

"What's happening now?" I hissed at Heathcliff.

"The pregnant one just leaned in real close, like she was threatening Frizzy-Hair. Now she's going back to her car, and—"

"You may think you're untouchable, Ginny Button!" Sylvia Blume's shouted words stabbed through the night. Her voice had risen an octave, the pitch betraying her fear. "But I know what you did. You're rotten, and you won't get away with it!"

"Oh, stop being so dramatic, Sylvia!" Ginny spat back, her posh voice thick with venom. The car door slammed again.

"Is something the matter?" A man's voice – deep, with a thick German accent – called out.

"Oh, look, it wouldn't be England without a nosy neighbor poking his head in," Heathcliff whispered.

Wheels spun and the red car backed into the shared driveway, then blew off up the gravel road, leaving a cloud of dust in its wake that obscured my vision even worse.

"It's fine, Helmut," Sylvia Blume called back, her voice wavering. "I just had a little argument with a friend, is all. I'm sorry for waking you."

"I understand. Goodnight."

"Goodnight." I strained to hear a door creaking open and shut again. A couple of the cottage lights popped off.

My heart pounding, I turned to Heathcliff. "What do you suppose that was about?"

"Pregnant Bitch took Frizzy-Hair for a drive to intimidate her," Heathcliff said matter-of-factly. "Then she brought her home and threatened her, but Frizzy Hair knows more than she's letting on."

"They were talking about Mrs. Scarlett's murder!"

"We don't know that for sure. Are these cottages part of the King's Copse development?" Heathcliff asked.

"I don't know, but I bet Morrie can find out. What are you thinking?"

"I'm thinking if you lived in a tiny stone cottage in the middle of nowhere, you wouldn't want a huge modern development going up next door."

"That's true. I read in one of the newspaper articles that there were some nearby residents whose houses would need to be bulldozed."

"It seems likely they're referring to these cottages. I'm also thinking that if you owned said cottage and you were annoyed at certain developers sniffing around, you might be feeding a certain neighborhood busybody information about any unto-ward earthworks or bad behavior, and that might make you a target."

"Are you suggesting that Mrs. Blume could be in danger, too?"

"If someone is desperate enough for this development to go ahead that they'd poison an old lady," Heathcliff said darkly, drawing me close to him and wrapping his arms tight around me, "then they'll do anything."

CHAPTER SEVENTEEN

"*D*o you have anything by David Copperfield?" an elderly man asked me as I carried boxes of stock out to the two shopping trolleys Morrie purloined from the market early this morning. It was the day of Mrs. Scarlett's funeral, and I'd arrived early to sort stock for the church fete.

And also to see Heathcliff and try to get some reading from him about last night, but that was bloody hopeless. The two grunts I'd received upon presenting him with coffee this morning could hardly be interpreted as *Mina is hot as fuck and I want more of her body.*

If Mum could come up with a Heathcliff-to-Human dictionary, I know at least one person who'd buy a copy.

"Ma'am?" The customer waved a hand in front of my face. "Where would I find the famous author David Copperfield?"

"Oh, sure. That way." I plastered a smile on my face and waved him in the general direction of the Literature section. Maybe he'd grow a brain by osmosis.

"Last night must've gone well," Morrie mused as we pushed the trolleys over to the church and found our table. "You're not correcting a customer's literary knowledge, and Heathcliff was singing in the shower this morning."

Despite myself, my stomach fluttered. "What was he singing?"

"I wouldn't take it personally, but 'You Give Love A Bad Name.'"

I punched Morrie in the arm. "Shame on you for being mean to me through Bon Jovi."

"You love it, gorgeous."

"If you must know, the date did go well." I leaned over our boxes to peck Morrie on the lips, too scared to do anything else lest I incur the wrath of one of the choir ladies bustling around the church car park. "How much are you wanting to know?"

"Give me every gory detail."

"I can't do that." My cheeks burned, and Morrie laughed. "But I can tell you that we discovered something interesting about King's Copse. There's a row of tiny stone cottages on the edge of the wood. From the looks of them, they're old workers' accommodations. I know there used to be an ancient wood mill out there. You can see some of the ruins in the wood if you're there during the daytime. I've never seen the cottages before, but they must be standing on the land Gray Lachlan needs for the development. *And* we saw Ginny Button drive up to one of the cottages with Sylvia Blume. Miss Blume got out of the car and went to the door. She had a key so she must live there. Ginny ran after her and was threatening her. Miss Blume yelled back that she knew what Ginny had done, and she wouldn't get away with it. It might not mean anything in relation to the murders, but..."

"It's another connection." Morrie nodded. "I'll find out everything I can about Sylvia Blume and her cottage, and about this Ginny Button."

Morrie lifted the boxes from the trolleys and I arranged the books across two trestle tables, careful to keep the religious books separate from the popular fiction. Beside us, a man draped a blue cloth over his own table and arranged iron pokers and wine racks in a pleasing display. As he turned to speak to a customer, I thought I recognized his deep voice and German accent. He was the man who spoke to Miss Blume from his window last night!

Maybe I don't even need Morrie doing an illegal search to find out what's going on. I stepped into the man's stall.

"These are beautiful." I picked up one of the wine racks. It was shaped like a dog, and when you inserted the wine bottle, it became the dog's body. I thought Mum would love it, but it was more than I could afford. "Did you make them all?"

"Ja," was the reply. "Thank you for compliment about my craft. I am blacksmith. I have a small forge on my property, and I even extract and smelt the ore myself."

"Is it difficult to do?"

"It is hard work for one person. In Germany, I worked with three other craftsmen, and we would travel around medieval markets and sell our work. But then my parents died and left us only with this small house here in England, where we used to come for holidays in happier times. My sister and I moved here a few years ago and I turned small outbuilding into my forge, so I have not the space to hire more craftsmen. But I do okay. I travel around the markets in the area, and I do commissions for people – gates and balustrades and such things."

"You live out by King's Copse, in one of the little cottages." His face twisted in surprise, and I added quickly. "I was walking with a friend there yesterday, and I noticed your truck. What do you think about that big development that's going in?"

"The new houses are very ugly and I will be sad to leave the wood. But they have offered a lot of money to buy our land and tear down the cottages. The money would build a bigger forge somewhere else, and maybe hire a team again." He glanced toward the church, where the Banned Book ladies bustled about, arranging flowers and setting out program baskets for the funeral. "I suppose with her dead now, the development might go ahead."

"You live next door to a woman in my book club, Sylvia Blume. She was the friend I was walking with."

"Yes, Sylvia. The fortune teller." It was hard to tell from his tone what he thought of her.

"How is she as a neighbor?" He frowned at my nosy question, and I thought quickly. "It's just that she's seemed a bit quiet and reserved lately, and I'm worried about her."

"She reads fortunes and forages for herbs. She had argument with other woman last night, but that's all I know. I don't like to gossip about neighbors. I just work in my forge. Not care about what happens around me."

"Helmut, ich habe dein Mittagessen mitgebracht." A familiar voice said behind me. Greta from the bakery held out a plate piled high with sandwiches and cakes, and the blacksmith – Helmut – accepted it with a smile. Greta nodded at me in her curt way. "Hallo, Mina."

"Hi, Greta. It was nice of you to come for the funeral. I know Mrs. Scarlett was a frequent customer of yours. She spoke so highly of your baking."

Greta nodded again. "Ja. It is very sad. Mrs. Ellis asked me to provide refreshments. I have a stall over there." I followed her finger to a table groaning under the weight of cakes and sausage rolls and pasties.

"It looks amazing. You're doing fine even with the Terror of Argleton still at large."

"That rotten mouse!" Her features reddened with anger. "He has been back to my kitchen many times. I see his little droppings everywhere, but he does not fall for my traps. Well, I will show him. I have nasty trap that not even clever mouse will escape."

Interesting, so he must have escaped from the past. "That's good. I really hope you catch him."

"Yes," Greta threw a look over her shoulder at her stall where a small crowd of people had already gathered. "I had better get back."

"Yes, me too." I noticed the man who asked about David Copperfield at the shop was now sifting through one of my boxes. "Customers always need so much help. Good luck today, Helmut. I hope you're able to move to a bigger forge soon!"

Helmut nodded his understanding. I returned to my stall just as a customer thrust a book under my nose.

"Why have you brought these books along to a church fete?" a female voice demanded.

I looked up and met the piercing eyes of a severe-looking middle-aged woman, her greying hair pulled so tight off her face it creased her forehead along the hairline. In one hand, she gripped the handle of an ornately-carved wooden walking stick. In the other, she held up *Of Mice and Men*, thrusting the cover under my nose.

"I've brought along a wide selection of titles," I explained. "This happens to be a book Mrs. Scarlett enjoyed—"

"*This* is a vulgar work," she jabbed at the cover with neat, unadorned fingers. "It has no place within the House of God."

Wow, taking puritanism to a whole new level. "We're not technically *in* the church."

"Young lady, don't answer me back!" The woman rapped her stick on the ground. "We are on sanctified ground, and God watches every move you make. He is not pleased that this filth is been sold on *His* land to corrupt *His* children. I *demand* you go through these books right now and remove anything that isn't wholesome."

Nothing made me angrier than censorship, except parents who abandoned their children and when Morrie chatted through a movie I really wanted to see. "You haven't read this book, have you? It has a powerful message about love and acceptance. I think every person here *should* read it, and I will not act as the censorship police."

Behind me, Morrie sniggered. I stepped back and stomped on his toe. *You might help me out here.*

The woman narrowed her eyes at me. "You're the girl who works in the bookstore run by that detestable gypsy. No wonder you have no sense of decency."

She did not *just say that.*

"Excuse me." My cheeks burned with anger. *I hope you're prepared for a war, lady.* "You use a racial slur against my employer – a perfectly decent member of this community who pays his taxes – and then lecture *me* about decency? I don't think so—"

Mrs. Ellis came running over, her carpet bag flapping against her side. She grasped the woman's arm. "Ladies, what's the matter here?"

"I expected when you organized this fiasco, Mabel, you would at least inform stallholders of our standards," the woman snapped back, rapping her stick for emphasis. "I want this vulgar bookstore and its rude employees gone before the funeral is over."

"Please, Dorothy," Mrs. Ellis' voice wheedled. "This is Gladys' funeral. The books are doing no harm."

So this is Dorothy Ingram? She was certainly fearsome. I could easily believe her getting kind Mrs. Winstone fired from the youth group.

"Doing no harm?" Dorothy sputtered. "These books will fill our innocent children's minds with evil, un-Christian ideas. It's bad enough that vile woman's funeral must be held in our fine church, but I've had just about enough of your book club being a corrupting influence in this village—"

Mrs. Ellis flapped her hands. "Yes, yes, but it's almost eleven. We'll be starting the service soon. If Mina leaves now, she'll interrupt the procession."

Dorothy shot me a dirty look, then nodded to Mrs. Ellis. "Very well. Pack up your books, girl, and prepare to leave as soon as the procession leaves for the cemetery. Mabel, I'll see you inside. I'll tell the organist to start the service." She stormed off, throwing me a final dirty look over her shoulder.

As soon as she was out of earshot, Mrs. Ellis made a rude gesture behind her back. I snorted a laugh.

"So that's Dorothy Ingram," I said.

"She's bursting with good Christian charity," Morrie grinned from behind me.

I glared at him. "You might've helped me deal with her."

"You looked like you were handling it. Besides, if I got too close to you, the steam coming out your ears would've flattened my hair." He ran a hand through his perfectly-styled close-cut locks.

"Don't you worry about Dorothy. She's all fire and brimstone, but it's just because she's got nothing in her life apart from the church. She's never been married, you know, unless you count being married to God, which to my mind offers none of the benefits of a husband—" Mrs. Ellis frowned. "That's odd."

I followed Mrs. Ellis' gaze. All around the church, mourners gathered in small groups, talking in hushed voices and glancing over the stalls as they waited for the service to begin. Standing apart from the crowd, on the steps at the back of the church, were Dorothy Ingram and Ginny Button. They bent their heads together in intense conversation.

"Dorothy would never associate with the likes of Ginny, a harlot bearing a child out of wedlock," Mrs. Ellis tapped her chin. "What could be going on?"

My heart plunged to my knees as several elements clicked into place. *What's going on is that Dorothy Ingram has it out for the immoral Banned Book Club, and especially their outspoken leader. If she wanted to hurt Mrs. Scarlett, she'd need someone on the inside to do it. Someone like Ginny.*

"Morrie, help the customers!" I cried, pushing my way through the crowd. I pressed myself up against the side of the church and peered at the ground, pretending to look for a lost piece of jewelry along the edge of the garden. I felt my way along the wall, creeping close to where the two ladies stood. I strained to hear what they were saying.

"... got her out of the way for you..." Dorothy said, casting a furtive glance around the church car park. She didn't sound so high and righteous now, and she leaned heavily on the stick, as if it were the only thing keeping her upright. "She's paid for her sins, and now you and I have no more business together."

"We're not done here," Ginny said. "There's something else you're going to do for me."

"I'm not your puppet, Miss Button. God detests a blackmailer."

"He also detests a *murderer*, Dorothy. I hope you're not threatening me, you self-righteous cow," Ginny made a big show of yawning and fondling her diamond-and-ruby necklace. "I don't care what God thinks of me. I only care about getting what I want. You do what I'm asking, or the whole village will know your filthy little secret."

"We'll see about that!" Dorothy huffed. She spun on her heels and stormed away.

Ginny as good as said that Dorothy's a murderer! I'd expected to hear Dorothy threaten Ginny to keep quiet, not the other way around. But there was no mistaking what I'd heard. Dorothy said, "I've taken care of her for you." The *her* was Mrs. Scarlett.

But how did she kill Gladys Scarlett with arsenic if they weren't close friends, and why did Ginny want her dead?

I rushed back to our table, desperate to tell Morrie what I'd heard, but he'd been surrounded by several teenage girls from the youth group. They batted their eyelids at him and gushed over his clothes and asked him all sorts of questions. He was lapping it up. Sighing, I left him to his adoring crowd and started packing the books back into boxes, watching as rows of mourners filed into the church. The other members of the Banned Book Club huddled together at the entrance, handing out programs and pulling handkerchiefs from their sleeves to blow their noses. Mrs. Winstone flashed me a kind smile as she dabbed at her eyes. Bells peeled across the village, and the sound of dreary hymns floated over the parking lot.

Forty-five minutes later, Morrie and I had sold a stack of vampire novels to the teenagers and a set of old bibles to the vicar's son, and packed all the boxes back into the trolleys. Beside us, Helmut was doing a roaring trade – he'd completely sold out of wine racks and was taking orders for more. *I guess it's okay to promote the evils of alcohol at the church fete, but not the perils of reading?*

With a final dreadful hymn, the service concluded. Mourners trickled out of the church, and the funeral procession made its way across the road to the cemetery. As the heavy mahogany coffin made its way through the carpark, I raised my hand and threw devil horns.

Rest in peace, Mrs. Scarlett. I hope you're up in heaven, causing all sorts of mayhem. I hope—

A piercing scream interrupted my thoughts. I whirled around. Mrs. Ellis raced from the church, her usually-red cheeks pale, her hands waving frantically. The procession stopped in its tracks and every face in the crowd swung around to gape at her.

"Come quick!" she screamed. "Oh, it's terrible!"

Morrie dropped the trolley handles and raced toward the church. I sprinted after him, shoving my way through the confused crowd of mourners at the entrance. Morrie poked his head into the church and withdrew, his mouth set in a firm line. He threw his arms in front of the door, blocking the way with his body. Mrs. Ellis fell into my arms, sobbing on my shoulder.

"I forgot my shawl. I just c-c-came back inside to collect it," she sobbed. "And I s-s-saw her."

'Saw what?" I scrambled toward the door. The conversation between Dorothy Ingram and Ginny Button playing over in my head. *What happened?*

Morrie threw out a hand to stop me. "Mina, don't—"

Ignoring him, I slipped under his arm and stepped into the church. Candles flickered from sconces beside the doors and on the altar, doing little to light up the dim space. I squinted into the gloom, trying to discern what had frightened Mrs. Ellis. I couldn't see anything amiss.

As I moved into the light cast by the stained glass windows, I noticed a crumpled pile of clothing at the bottom of the spiral staircase leading up to the bell tower.

Oh, no.

I stepped closer.

That's not clothes.

I took another step, peering down at the sprawled figure. Ginny Button lay at the bottom of the stairs, her dress torn. Blood pooled between her legs, and her neck was twisted at an impossible angle.

CHAPTER EIGHTEEN

*H*eart racing, I knelt down in front of Ginny Button and checked for a pulse. There was none. Her glassy eyes stared up at me, silent and accusing, as if I was the one who'd pushed her. I pulled out my phone and dialed an ambulance. Ginny might be gone, but if there was a chance her baby could be saved—

"Hi… we need an ambulance at the Argleton Presbyterian Church. A woman has fallen down the stairs." Morrie's hands wrapped around my body, and he pulled me against him. "She doesn't have a pulse, but she's pregnant. Yes… yes… thank you."

Morrie stroked my hair. "Oh look, another murder victim. Are you sure you're not cursed, gorgeous?"

"Not funny." *Please let Ginny's baby be all right.* "And this isn't murder. She tripped on the stairs."

"No, she didn't." Morrie pointed at her neck. Her bare neck. "Someone has stolen her necklace."

I shuddered. He was right. Ginny's expensive necklace was nowhere to be seen. And there was something else… a white object clutched in her hand. A piece of paper. I drew it from her fingers and read the message, flipping it over to check for a signature, but there was none. It read in a simple font:

> Meet me at the top of the bell tower after the ceremony. We have something important to discuss.

Morrie grabbed the note from me and held the paper by the corners, peering at it through the light. "Standard printer paper, inkjet. Not much to be gleaned from this except the threatening tone of the message."

I surveyed the crowd as they filtered into the church. *Any one of them could have done it.* Women screamed as they saw the body. The vicar and his son tried to push everyone back outside, but of course, you couldn't keep nosy villagers away from a body. Because of the chilly winter day, most of them wore gloves. There probably wouldn't be any fingerprints on the note.

"Someone lured her into the tower and killed her!" Mrs. Ellis cried, reading the note over my shoulder. People stared in horror at the body. Her words passed through the crowd, and heads bent to whisper accusations about who might've done it.

"We don't know that yet," I said to soothe Mrs. Ellis, so neither she nor anyone in the crowd would panic and flee. "Ginny probably tripped on her way up the stairs. They are slippery and uneven, and look at the shoes she's wearing." Ginny's stilettos were hardly adequate footwear for climbing ancient church steps.

"She was murdered, I know it! It's the same person who poisoned Gladys. Don't you see? Someone has it in for the Banned Book Club."

Dorothy Ingram's flared nostrils and twisted mouth flickered across my mind, as did the ominous words of her secret conversation with Ginny. *Maybe Mrs. Ellis is right.* "The police will look into every possibility. Did you see anyone else inside when you were looking for your shawl?"

"No. I went to the end of the row, and I noticed a lump at the bottom of the stairs leading up to the tower. I thought one of the flower arrangements had fallen over so I came to right it and... oh..."

I wrapped my arms around Mrs. Ellis' shoulders and tried to steer her away from the grisly scene. Outside, sirens wailed, growing closer. "I really think Ginny fell—"

"She didn't fall, she was pushed!" Mrs. Ellis gripped my shirt. "Ginny was as nimble as a mountain-goat in those shoes of hers. She'd not have fallen. And look, someone's taken her diamond necklace. That was her favorite, she never took it off. Oh, Mina, you have to help me."

"What are you talking about? You're not in danger."

"I am!" Mrs. Ellis' eyes bugged from her head. "Someone is killing off members of the Banned Book Club. And I could be next!"

CHAPTER NINETEEN

*A*fter we gave our statements to the police, I left Morrie to return the books to the shop and the trolley to the market, and helped Mrs. Ellis back to Nevermore Bookshop. Upstairs in the flat, she settled into Heathcliff's chair by the fire while I boiled the kettle and prepared the tea – the only appropriate English response to a terrible fright.

The more I thought about it, the more I realized she could be right about the Banned Book club being targeted. First Mrs. Scarlett, and now Ginny Button. The only thing those two ladies had in common was their membership to the book club and the fact that both of them had crossed Dorothy Ingram.

And then there was that strange conversation I'd seen between Dorothy and Ginny Button. From what Dorothy said, it was almost as if Ginny was blackmailing her. But what secret did a woman like Dorothy have, and what would she do to stop it being made public?

I handed Mrs. Ellis her tea, which she took in shaking fingers. "Mrs. Ellis, has Dorothy Ingram ever threatened anyone at the book club before?"

"Oh, yes. Every few months that nasty woman will get a bee in her bonnet about something in the village that doesn't meet her puritanical standards. She'll write letters to the *Gazette* and plaster the shops with flyers and work the church committee into a frenzy. She's got the vicar's ear, you know. But she could never get the best of Gladys. Every time Dorothy started a campaign against the Banned Book Club, Gladys found a way to make her look foolish and have people stop taking her seriously, and Dorothy found another group to terrify."

"I read a column in the *Gazette* where Gladys stood up for Sylvia Blume."

"Yes, that was a number of years ago, when Sylvia first wanted to open her crystal shop and offer her services. Dorothy tried to start a good old-fashioned witch hunt. Gladys couldn't stand to see bullies, so she let rip in the paper. Of course, Dorothy can't prevent a legitimate business from opening on the high street, and after Gladys' letter in the paper nothing Dorothy said would stop the villagers lining up to have their auras read, so she's mostly left Sylvia alone ever since."

Or has she? Ginny's visit to Sylvia Blume's home weighed on my mind. I was sure it was all connected, but I just didn't know how.

"I think you should tell the police what you've told me," I said. "It might go some way towards clearing the Lachlans of wrongdoing. After all, they can't have killed Ginny if they're still being held at the police station."

"Oh, I said as much in my statement at the church, but I don't think they believed me. And they haven't let Cynthia and her husband go. I'm so scared, Mina. It someone would push a pregnant lady down the stairs, think what they might do next! Won't you stay with me tonight?" Mrs. Ellis whimpered. "I'm terrified someone's coming to hurt me."

"Yes. Of course." Then I remembered. "Oh, no, I can't. I'm having dinner with my mother."

And my three male... boyfriends.

"I'll come too!" Mrs. Ellis perked up. "I promise I won't be a bother. I'll even bring along my world-famous cottage pie. I've got one stashed in the freezer for just such an occasion."

What in Astarte's name am I supposed to say to that?

"Um… I don't know if there'll be enough room. Heathcliff and Morrie and Quoth are coming, and Jo, the forensic pathologist. My mum's house is very small—"

"Nonsense. With such a fine crowd, you won't notice one more. And I might be able to wrangle some useful information out of that pathologist to help you solve the case."

I sighed. As if this night couldn't be any more of a disaster. "Sure. I guess you can come."

~

*A*fter finishing her cup of tea, Mrs. Ellis perked up a bit. Grimalkin curled up on her lap and I didn't have the heart to remind them Heathcliff didn't want anyone on his chair. I brought her a stack of steamy romance books and a block of chocolate and she was back to her old self in no time.

Downstairs, I gathered Heathcliff, Morrie, and the raven, and filled them in on what happened at the church and on the conversation I'd overheard between Ginny Button and Dorothy Ingram.

"Mrs. Ellis believes this is about the Banned Book Club, and after today, so do I."

"If this witch tries to hurt you, I'll make her swallow a bloody crucifix," Heathcliff growled.

"If Dorothy Ingram is behind this, I doubt she's after me. I've only been to that one meeting."

"You did bring all those corrupting books to the church," Morrie pointed out.

"True, but I think whatever this is goes back much further. Ginny spoke about Dorothy's 'ugly little secret.' That could be what Dorothy is killing to protect. The only thing that doesn't make sense is the conversation between Ginny and Dorothy."

"Agreed," Morrie rubbed his chin. "You made it sound as if Dorothy killed Mrs. Scarlett on *Ginny's* orders so Ginny wouldn't reveal a secret about her. But Ginny wanted Dorothy to do more of her dirty work. Dorothy pushed her down the stairs in order to stop the blackmail."

"Maybe that means she won't kill again?"

"I wouldn't count on it. We don't know who else knows this dirty little secret. We already know Gladys is the type to blab a secret all over the village. Isn't that what she did to the Lachlans?"

I nodded.

"In that case, all we need to do is figure out why Ginny Button would have wanted Mrs. Scarlett dead, and what dirt she had on Dorothy Ingram." Morrie grinned. "Uptight bint like her? I bet it's absolutely *filthy*."

"I'd rather not find out, if it's all the same to you," Heathcliff muttered.

"You mean you're not in the least bit curious?" Morrie looked scandalized. "I confess that I'll never understand you, Heathcliff. I do *so* love a juicy secret."

He did at that. James Moriarty already had a lifetime of my secrets stored within the vast vaults of his mind. I wondered again if Morrie had any juicy secrets of his own. He played the easy-going, devil-may-care villain too well. But I suspected underneath that act was a man hiding a whole ocean of pain.

Or… maybe underneath the act was just the Devil himself. It was one or the other.

"I'll look into Dorothy's background. I've already done a thorough background check on all the ladies in the Banned Book Club, and nothing popped for Ginny, except for the fact that she insured that diamond and ruby necklace for twenty thousand pounds. The only old biddy with a record is Mrs. Ellis, who flashed her tits at a police officer in an attempt to get off a parking ticket."

"Go Mrs. Ellis!" I grinned. "I knew she'd had a wild youth."

"Youth? This incident occurred last year."

Heathcliff choked on his doughnut.

Quoth fluttered down from his perch on the chandelier to sit on my shoulder. He bowed his head, his wide brown eyes tinged with concern. I patted his head.

I'm worried for you, he said inside my head. *Why are you meddling in another murder? Shouldn't the police be trusted to solve the case?*

"I agree with the bird," Heathcliff added. "We've got enough to concern ourselves with, given the shop's penchant for opening doors and throwing surprises, and our continued feud with The-Store-That-Shall-Not-Be-Named. Solving murders isn't part of your job description."

I stared them all down, meeting fierce black eyes, calculating blue, and kind brown. "It is now. The police are still trying to pin Mrs. Scarlett's death on the Lachlans. They think Ginny Button fell down those stairs. If Dorothy Ingram is behind this, we've got to get to the bottom of this before anyone else dies." I winced. "*After* we endure a dinner with my mother."

CHAPTER TWENTY

"**W**hy do we have to take a taxi?" Heathcliff grumbled. "It's a waste of money. Your little church fete stall didn't exactly rake in the millions."

"Cheer up, Lord Crotchety-Goo," I grinned. Heathcliff hated it when we made up noble names for him. "We're taking a taxi because it's a long way for Mrs. Ellis to walk, especially while there's a murderer on the loose. And that's the last complaint I'm hearing about it, or we're staying for a game of after-dinner charades."

Heathcliff snapped his mouth shut as the taxi pulled up. The five of us piled in – Mrs. Ellis in the front seat, her sequined shawl pulled up around her ample shoulders. Me in the middle between Heathcliff and Morrie. Quoth in a fold-down seat in the back. Jo had called earlier to excuse herself – she had to conduct the autopsy on Ginny Button. She'd also given me the good news that the child – a little boy – had survived and was in stable condition at the hospital.

Morrie and Mrs. Ellis kept up a steady stream of chatter as we drove through the council estate. I stared out the window, cringing at every detail. Heathcliff's huge fingers clamped on my knee and wouldn't let go. I thought he was just trying to reassure me, but when I looked at his face, his features were drawn. *He's nervous, too.*

I didn't know what to make of that.

We turned the final corner and slowed down in front of our row of flats. The next-door neighbors were having some kind of party. People spilled out their door onto the rickety deck and the overgrown lawn, and out into the street. Our driver swore as he swerved around a large sofa that had been set on fire in the middle of the road. People laughed and shouted as they tossed beer cans into the blaze.

"Well," Mrs. Ellis said with fake brightness as she slid out of the taxi and clutched her purse against her chest. "This is *lovely.* Very festive."

"At least they're staying warm," Morrie's teeth chattered. He'd worn one of his tailored jackets over grey slacks and a thin white shirt and black silk waistcoat. He looked delicious, but not exactly dressed for a British winter evening.

Mum threw open the front door, beaming down at us. She wore an apron and a chef's hat made of rolled-up newspaper. "Come on in!"

No, mum, no. She acted like a complete fool, trying to pretend she was super fancy, whenever I brought anyone around to the house, which I hadn't done since the first time Ashley came over for dinner and Mum tried to smoke her own salmon in her Gore-Met Kitchen Whiz (another get-rich-quick-scheme) and gave Ashley food poisoning.

I gritted my teeth. *Just get this over with and she'll stop hassling me about the shop.* "Hi, Mum, we're all here." The guys followed me inside, Mrs. Ellis trailing behind. As we filed into the living room, I peeked at the kitchenette table. Mum had cleared away the boxes of crap that usually littered the surface, and set placemats (colored cardboard) and all our best crockery and glassware (all mismatched, chosen because they were the pieces with the smallest chips). Two bowls sat in the middle of the table, lids on tight. I shuddered to think what might be inside. A stack of pet dictionaries had been artfully fanned across the table.

This is going to be a disaster.

"Well, here we are." Mum clasped her hands to her chest. "I'm so pleased to finally be meeting Mina's new friends."

Morrie stepped forward and held out his hand. "James Moriarty, although my friends call me Morrie. It's a pleasure to meet you, Miss Wilde. I've chosen a wine for the occasion – it's a sparkling wine, so it will need to be kept chilled at ideally six degrees. Do you have an ice bucket?"

Mum didn't register the significance of Morrie's name. She wasn't exactly a big reader. "Thank you, Morrie. No ice bucket, I'm afraid, but you could stick it in the freezer for a bit? My, you're tall."

"Yes, I am. Apart from my dashing wit, it's one of my finest features." Morrie went into the kitchen to fuss over the wine situation.

Heathcliff stepped forward and offered his hand. His frame loomed large in our tiny flat, and under the fluorescent light, his black eyes and wild hair gave him a menacing air. "Heathcliff," he muttered.

Mum hesitated a moment before shaking his hand. "Do you have a last name, there, Heathcliff?"

"Just Heathcliff."

"It's Earnshaw," I shot Heathcliff a withering look. In his world, he'd had only the one name, but ours demanded a surname.

"Heathcliff Earnshaw." Those words sound so wrong on my mother's tongue. "That's a very English sounding name. But you're not English, are you?"

I glared at her, but she pretended not to notice.

Heathcliff shrugged. "That depends on your definition."

"Well, *Heathcliff*, I'd say that a real Englishman would be—"

"I'm Allan Poe," Quoth stepped around Heathcliff's bulk and stuck out his hand.

Thank you, my beautiful raven.

As Mum turned from Heathcliff to greet Quoth, she jumped a little, and her eyes glazed over. Whatever horrendous thing she was about to say to Heathcliff slipped from her lips. Quoth's beauty had that effect on people.

"It's a pleasure, Allan," Mum breathed, her eyes flickering over Quoth's porcelain skin and deep fire-ringed eyes and black hair that fell like a midnight waterfall down his back.

"And I'm Mabel Ellis. I used to teach Mina at school." Mrs. Ellis wrapped my mother in a warm hug. "It's so nice of you to have me. Here. I've brought a cottage pie."

"That's lovely, thank you. Well, let's not stand around. Please, take a seat. I've made spicy chicken starters." We perched on the threadbare sofas and chipped plastic dining chairs while Mum handed around a plate containing chicken nuggets sprinkled with chili flakes, skewered on toothpicks.

"Sure." Morrie folded his long body into the sofa and popped two nuggets in his mouth. I stifled a giggle as his eyes bugged out and he fanned his face with his hand. Mum must've really gone all out with the chili.

"I'll pass," I grinned.

Heathcliff and Quoth passed also. Mrs. Ellis took one, but wiped the chili off down the edge of the sofa while Mum had her back turned. Mum came back with a tray of drinks and passed around plastic cups filled with Morrie's expensive wine, and we did an awkward toast.

"So, Heathcliff, you're not local to Argleton?" Mum asked, trying again to corner Heathcliff into a conversation where he would admit to being a gypsy.

"I live in the shop."

"But you didn't grow up here, did you?"

"I think Mum's asking where you come from," I said, glaring at Mum. She smiled sweetly, chewing on a chicken nugget.

"I was raised at a farmhouse on the Yorkshire Moors," he said. "Although that is not where I was born. My parents abandoned me on the streets of Liverpool, and I was found and raised by the Earnshaw family. I do not know my true origin, and I don't care to know."

"Why, I should think you of the Romani people, judging by your coloring," Mum said.

"It has been suggested," Heathcliff said tersely.

"Morrie's from London," I announced, eager to change the subject.

Mum made a face. "London is so big and noisy. We must seem like such country bumpkins after living in the big city."

"Argleton is a slower pace of life, but it's not without its charms." Morrie trailed a finger down my thigh, and a shiver ran through my body. "But yes, London has always been my stomping ground. Barring a brief stint at Oxford where I obtained my degree, I've always been in the city, and I may yet return."

"Oxford?" Mum's ears perked up. "Did you hear that, Mina?"

"Yes, Mum. I heard. I was thinking about going to Oxford myself, if you recall."

"But you never had a head for that kind of fancy learning. You're too creative. Morrie here has got the brain smarts. What are you, Morrie? A doctor? A lawyer? A tech entrepreneur?" Her eyes sparkled. I could practically see her spending Morrie's money on a garish footballer's mansion and a kidney-shaped pool.

"I have some medical experience, but I am primarily a mathematician."

"Oh," Mum's face froze. "And how much does a mathematician earn?"

"Mum, you shouldn't ask people what they earn!"

"I don't mind," Morrie grinned. "It all depends on the type of mathematics you perform. My line of work is exceptionally lucrative."

"Oh, well, that's wonderful." Mum gave me a pointed look, and I knew she was picturing what my wedding dress would look like when I married Morrie the handsome and rich mathematician. *Floor, please swallow me now.* "And what about you, Allan? Where were you born?"

"Richmond, in the United States," Quoth replied.

"Is that where your accent is from? You don't sound American."

"Don't I?" Quoth tilted his head to the side. His hair flowed over his shoulder. I couldn't resist the urge and reached over to tuck it behind his ear. He jumped as my fingers grazed his skin. *He's worried.*

"He certainly sounds exotic with that sexy husky voice," Mrs. Ellis piped up. Beside her, Heathcliff choked on his wine.

Mum didn't know how to respond to that. She gulped back her drink, thankfully forgetting to ask Quoth what he did for a living. Instead, she turned back to Heathcliff. "So does anything interesting happen at the shop apart from people being murdered?"

"Mum!"

"What, honey? I'm just *asking*. Surely Mr. Heathcliff meets interesting customers."

"No," Heathcliff muttered into his glass.

"We've had an appearance by the Terror of Argleton," Morrie said, shuddering at the memory of the mouse in his pants.

"The mouse in the paper?" Mum's ears pricked up. "Did you get a picture?"

"Hardly. The bloody thing is too fast for us. Not even the shop cat Grimalkin has been able to catch him."

"I know!" Mum rummaged through the stack of books on the

table. She pulled one out and thrust it into Heathcliff's lap. "You need this!"

I glanced at the title. *Mouse Language for Humans*. "Mum, no—"

"Yes, it's perfect! You can translate his squeaks, figure out what he wants, and then use that to trap him."

Heathcliff's jaw worked up and down. I thought he was pissed, but then I noticed the sparkle in his eye as he struggled to hold back laughter.

Morrie rubbed his chin. "It's worth a shot. At this stage, I'll do anything to get rid of that foul creature. How much do I owe you for the book?"

"Keep that one for free. When you capture the mouse, the paper will do a story on you and you can tell them all about how my book helped you. We can work together to improve our PR!"

"An excellent plan." Morrie patted Heathcliff's knee. "Heathcliff definitely needs some help with his PR."

Heathcliff slipped the book into his jacket. "Thank you," he managed to choke out.

"Mum, there actually is something we want to ask you. Has Sylvia Blume had any recent run-ins with Dorothy Ingram lately? Or Ginny Button?"

"Oh, Mina, you're not meddling in that murder, are you?" Mum frowned. "You'll make the police suspect you again."

"I'm not, Mum. I swear." I thought quickly. "I'm just found this old article in the paper while I was helping Mrs. Ellis write the obituary."

I whipped out my phone and showed her the article. She skimmed through it, her mouth turning into a smile at Mrs.Scarlett's barbed words.

"Sylvia's nasty business with Dorothy Ingram was over many years ago. As far as I know, Dorothy has never set foot in the shop nor said another word about Sylvia being a witch. Ginny Button came in all the time laden in diamonds to have her fortune read. Weirdly, she never seemed to pay for her readings. I didn't like her very much – she said such snide things about my outfits." Mum smoothed down the front of the mustard-colored cocktail dress she'd scored from the charity shop. "I suppose she won't be saying anything now."

"Did you ever see Ginny with Mrs. Scarlett?"

"Oh, all the time! Those two were heavily involved in the historical society, who've been working on that big project at the old Argleton hospital, you know, sorting through the records, etc, before it's torn down. They'd pop back to town for coffee and come in to gossip with Sylvia. Of course," she frowned, "that hasn't been happening recently."

"Why not?"

"I don't know, honey. All Sylvia said was that she wasn't happy with the way Gladys was running the planning committee. But I don't pay any attention to that political stuff."

The buzzer went off in the kitchen. Mum stood up. "Oh, that's dinner. Mina, if you could seat everyone at the table and make sure the glasses are full."

I pulled out chairs and everyone sat down. Mum bustled back from the kitchen, carrying a large tray of something that looked suspiciously like meatball stack.

It is *meatball stack. What is she thinking?*

I'd practically been raised on meatball stack. It consisted of layers of hash browns, boiled eggs, and cheap sausages chopped up into pieces and cooked in canned pasta sauce, and all finished off with a layer of cheese.

My cheeks reddened. To Mum, this was her signature dish, but to anyone else, it was a horrifying wobbly, greasy mess. It was almost, *almost* worth seeing gourmet Morrie's face twitch as she set the dish down in front of him and started cutting through the cheesy hash brown crust.

"Is this enough for you, Morrie?" she said brightly, serving him a huge dollop. The tomato sauce glowed a lurid red under the fluorescent lights in our kitchen.

"Oh, yes, that will be lovely." Morrie grabbed his wine and drained it, then reached for the bottle on the counter and filled his glass right to the brim.

"Mina, pass around the salad," Mum ordered, as she dumped an even bigger slice on Heathcliff's plate.

Gingerly, I lifted the lids off the two dishes on the table, revealing a Tesco's potato salad and some sad-looking dinner rolls. Beside my mother's food, Mrs. Ellis' golden brown cottage pie looked like Michelin star fare.

Heathcliff dug in as soon as Mum handed him his plate. Mum beamed as if it was a compliment to her culinary skills. It wasn't – the moors must have addled Heathcliff's tastebuds because he'd eat *anything*. I once saw him chew on a licorice rope so old it had *fossilized*. I picked at my food, too mortified to taste a single mouthful.

"This is delicious, Helen." Morrie winked at me as he forced down another bite. "Is this what you cook every time Mina brings a boyfriend home?"

"Mina's never brought home a boy before," Mum said, beaming at her words. I wondered if she'd already chosen the wedding flowers. "She doesn't like me to be involved in that part of her life, do you, darling?"

I wonder why that might be, Mother?

"I'm surprised," Morrie said, building a wall with his hash browns in an attempt to make it look as though he'd eaten more. "Mina's so beautiful and devastatingly clever. I imagine the only reason she hasn't had more boyfriends is the fact that dead bodies stack up in her wake."

Heathcliff snorted. Beside me, Quoth squirmed in his seat. He raised his hand to his cheek as a black feather shot through his skin. *Shit, shit.*

"Mina is *too* clever. That's her big problem. I keep telling her boys don't like clever girls, unless they're mathematicians, of course. Is one of you Mina's boyfriend?" Mum glared around the table, her smile hopeful as she landed on Morrie.

Oh Mum, if only you knew...

"I don't know if she could pick just one of us," Morrie said smoothly, sliding his meatball stack onto Heathcliff's plate.

"I have to go to the bathroom," Quoth breathed.

"Certainly, Allan. It's right through—" Quoth threw me a desperate look before disappearing into the hall. Mum shot me a look which I pointedly ignored.

"Actually, Mum, I just need to... freshen up my face," I gasped.

"But Mina, I want to know who you're dating!"

"Morrie's right. I couldn't possibly choose. I'll be right back." I dashed into the hall. The bathroom door was still open, but my bedroom door was shut. I rapped on the wood. "Quoth?"

"Croak!"

I pushed the door open. Clothes littered the floor of my room. A raven scrambled against the window, his talons scrabbling for purchase as he tried to maneuver the lever open.

"Oh, no you don't." I grabbed the latch and pulled it shut. Quoth hopped angrily on the bed. I knelt down beside him, meeting his frightened stare with one of my own. "If I have to endure this torture, then so do you. I've seen you over the last couple of weeks – you're learning to control your shifts. You just have to *want* to control it. If you won't do it for yourself, do it for me."

"Croak!" Quoth flapped his wings and hopped from foot to foot.

Mina, I can't do this. I can't! Tell your mother I was feeling ill and I had to go home—

I stood up. "No. I'm not making excuses for you. I'll see you outside. Don't leave me alone out there with Morrie and Heathcliff and *my mother.*"

I left the door open a crack and returned to my seat. Morrie and my mother had their heads bent together and were whispering furtively. Mrs. Ellis had finished her wine and had started on mine, while Heathcliff was polishing off Quoth's food.

"What did I miss?" I said brightly, plastering a fake smile on my face.

"Oh, Mina. Morrie was just telling me all your clever ideas for the shop," Mum beamed. "Running book clubs and author talks and hanging work by local artists and starting social media. And you've also been brightening up that dreary place with lamps and lanterns!"

'Oh yes, Mina has all sorts of plans for *my* shop," Heathcliff muttered.

"You do know what else is a really clever idea?" Mum held up one of her dictionaries. "A display of pet-dictionaries on the counter! There are so many pet owners in Argleton and—"

"Mum, *no.*"

"You've got hundreds of books in that junky old shop no one will buy. I don't see why adding a few more is any problem." Mum beamed. "Especially with your business skills, Mina. You could come up with a clever marketing plan and—"

Outside, there was a loud bang in the street as one of the neighbors let off his air rifle. Something thumped against the hallway wall, followed by a faint, "croak?"

I sighed and pushed my chair back. "I'll go see what that is. Maybe the bathroom door got stuck—"

"Croak!" Quoth crashed into the room, his eyes wide as saucers. He barreled across the table, flinging plates and cutlery across the room. He skidded off the edge and crashed to the floor.

"Quoth?" I reached out to him, but in his panic, he didn't see me. He scrambled up the couch and launched himself into the air, flying in circles around the room and letting out frightened croaks.

"Argh, what's that bird doing in here!" Mum grabbed for the broom and swung it at Quoth. "Shoo, shoo!"

I tried to go out the window! Quoth yelled inside my head. *Your neighbors shot a gun at me!*

"You're okay. It's just an air rifle," I cried, lunging for him. But adrenaline must've been crashing through Quoth's tiny body, filling him with the instinct to flee. He dived between my arms and sailed back toward the table.

"Hit it with the wine bottle!" Mum cried.

"No, Mum, it's okay. He's… um, he's Quoth, our shop bird." I tried to coax Quoth out from under the table. "He's a bit possessive, so he must have followed us all the way here. I think the neighbors scared him."

"Well, get it out of here."

I tried to shoo Quoth back into the hallway, but he wasn't having that. He skidded across the kitchen floor and squeezed his body into the gap between the counter and Mum's dictionary boxes. The stack of boxes teetered, and the top one slid off and crashed on the floor.

"Oh, Mina," Mum cried. "Stop him!"

As I scrambled over the furniture after a panicking Quoth, a sharp ringing accompanied his cries. Morrie raised his phone to his ear and made to leave the room. I clamped a hand over his knee. "You cannot leave me here."

"Sorry, gorgeous, I can't hear a thing over Quoth's caterwauling. Besides, you seem to have everything under control." Morrie winked.

"Tell them to call you back. I *need* you."

"I won't be long." Morrie slipped away. Heathcliff hadn't even got up from the table, although his eyes followed me with an intense stare.

"Well, this is fun!" Mrs. Ellis beamed, helping herself to Morrie's wine as Quoth shot out from behind the boxes and made a beeline for the sofa. I dived across the room and wrapped my arms around him.

"Gotcha!" I held up his quivering body. Poor thing, he was really terrified. I held Quoth against my chest and cooed to him.

Mina, Mina, they shot a gun at me!

I know. Shhh. It's okay now.

"Is it safe for you to hold that bird like that?" Mum frowned. "What if he carries disease?"

"No, he's fine. We give him shots." Quoth nestled his head into my shoulder. I frantically searched for some way to salvage this situation. "I'll just keep him like this, and he'll behave, I promise. Did I see some kind of meringue in the kitchen?"

"Oh, yes!" Mum dashed off to fix dessert. I slumped down next to Heathcliff, Quoth in my arms. "Do you keep anything stronger than wine in your desk at the shop?"

"I have booze stashed all over the shop. It's the only way I can tolerate customers. Why?"

"After tonight, I'm going to need to drink it all. Every last drop."

"Not if I get there first." Heathcliff's dark eyes twinkled, and the corners of his lips tugged upward, almost reaching a smile. A weird, fluttering feeling tugged at my chest as I clasped my hand in his.

"Here we go!" Mum entered the room with a large tray. She frowned as she saw Heathcliff and I sitting together. "Where is everyone? Is Allan not back from the bathroom yet?"

"He said he was constipated," Heathcliff mumbled.

I slammed my foot down on Heathcliff's boot. He winced, but didn't retract his statement.

"Morrie just had to duck out for a phone call." I stared down at the dessert in horror. "Mum, what *is* that?"

"I call it 'Helen's mess.' It's like Eton mess, except instead of strawberry puree, I've used strawberry ice cream sauce and licorice allsorts." She pointed at the giant pile of lollies. "And I've put some Cadbury chocolates all over the top. I thought we could have something fancy to celebrate your friends coming to visit."

"It looks delicious." I let her spoon a huge portion into a bowl for me. "Thank you."

Morrie barreled into the room, waving his phone. "I'm sorry, Helen. We're not able to stay for dessert." He slid the phone back into his pocket. "That was Jo. Mrs. Winstone has been admitted to the hospital. Someone tried to kill her."

CHAPTER TWENTY-ONE

"*O*h, I'm perfectly *fine*," Mrs. Winstone croaked. "The doctors say I'll be out tomorrow."

She didn't look fine. A splotchy purple bruise covered half her face, and there were more bruises on her arms. She clicked the button on her bed to raise her head up to face us, and the twist of her jaw revealed how the jerking movement pained her.

I can't believe someone tried to kill this sweet lady. It didn't seem real.

"Pffft. What do doctors know? They're even worse than those incompetent detectives," Mrs. Ellis scoffed, gripping her cousin's hand. "Brenda, our book club is being picked off one by one, and they're *still* holding Gray and Cynthia. Why, the Lachlans couldn't have attacked you, because they're behind lock and key!"

"I just spoke with Inspector Hayes," Mrs. Winstone said, annoyance flickering across her features. "That silly bobby doesn't believe Gladys' death was related to my attack."

"Bah! Then he's an even bigger fool than I first thought." Mrs. Ellis rubbed Mrs. Winstone's fingers. "Now, don't you worry. Mina is going to help us catch the person who attacked you."

Mrs. Winstone's eyes widened. "Mina, is that true? Oh, you really are a treasure."

"I'm going to try," I promised, because that was what you did when a person in a hospital bed looked at you with such a hopeful expression. "But you've got to remember that I'm not a police officer, so I don't—"

"Oh, I don't trust that Inspector Hayes as far as I could throw him, even though he is very handsome with that mustache." Mrs. Ellis sighed. "Do you have a suspect in mind?"

"A couple," I thought of Miss Blume speaking with Ginny at her cottage, and Dorothy Ingram's angry face at the church. "I'm starting to put things together. Can you tell me what happened?"

"I was at the library, speaking with the librarians about running a children's craft and story hour. They're very enthusiastic, especially after they'd heard such good things about my management of the youth group. Apparently, all those lovely children are begging me to come back." She smiled wistfully. "On the way home, I stopped at the market and picked up some groceries. I was setting the bags on the front stoop and hunting in my purse for the keys when someone leapt out behind me and hit me across the face with something hard." She winced as she raised her arm. "I remember thinking, 'you're not going to get me the way you got poor Gladys!' I lunged at the assailant, grabbing their arm and wrestling with them. I managed to seize the object they struck me with – it was long and round and wooden – but they wrenched it free and kicked me and I fell and hit my head on the stoop. They hit me a few more times," she gestured to the bruises on her arms. "They must've thought I was a goner because they scarpered without finishing the job."

A long wooden object, like Dorothy Ingram's walking stick.

"Did you get a good look at the person who attacked you? What can you tell us about them?"

"It was a slight person, maybe a woman, but I couldn't say." Mrs. Winstone wrung her hands. "They wore a veil over their face and dark clothing. It had just started to go dark when I got out of the car, and the bulb over the door is broken, so I'm afraid I can't say more than that for certain."

"And did you mention to anyone at the library that you planned to go to the shops?"

"Well… yes. A couple of ladies from church were in front of the library, handing out leaflets listing church-approved reading material. I stopped to chat. Cassandra Irons and Dorothy Ingram agreed with me about the dismal vegetable selection at the market. Dorothy told me they got in fresh carrots from the Ingles farm that morning and if I got in quick I'd be able to procure some for dinner."

"So Dorothy knew you were going to the market?"

Mrs. Winstone nodded.

"And what about cars on your street as you drove home? What about your husband – where was he? Did he notice anything unusual?"

"Oh, Harold's out of town on business, chasing down some old archives to do with the old hospital project. He's been gone for a few days now, and he said not to expect him back for at least three weeks."

"And he can't drop it to see you in the hospital?" I was starting to believe what Mrs. Ellis had said about Harold Winstone, famous historian.

"Oh no, I told him not to worry about me," she beamed. "I'm fine, and Harold is so wrapped up in his work. I don't want to disturb him. As for what else I remember, there was a grey car parked on the corner as I turned in. I recall it distinctly, as it was parked on the street outside my neighbor Gillian Appleby's place and that's very unusual. Gillian's visitors always park in her driveway, but I happened to notice her curtains were closed. It didn't even look like she was home."

I turned to Mrs. Ellis. "Do you know what kind of car Mrs. Ingram drives?"

"Why, I believe it's a grey Nissan," Mrs. Ellis said. "Mina, what are you suggesting?"

I turned to Mrs. Ellis. "Dorothy Ingram had opportunity – she knew Mrs. Winstone was going to the market, which gave her enough time to drive over there and hide in the garden. She owns a grey car *and* uses a walking stick that might've been the weapon. *And* she had motive – she wanted to end the Banned Book Club. I think she's responsible not just for Brenda's attack, but for the other murders."

Mrs. Ellis gasped. "Surely that's not reason enough to murder poor Gladys and Ginny and nearly kill Ginny's baby, too!"

"If I've learned one thing from the hundreds of murder mysteries I've read over the years, it's that people have all sorts of motives that can't be explained. Both Mrs. Scarlett and Ginny Button incurred Dorothy's wrath for their so-called sinful behavior. Gladys for starting the book club, and Ginny for having a baby out of wedlock, and I also believe she was blackmailing Dorothy Ingram." I patted Mrs. Winstone's arm. "And *you* were trying to corrupt the minds of innocent children through unsanctioned books. It all fits. We have to go to the police."

"I already told them everything I just told you," Mrs. Winstone said. "Even with that note in her hands and the missing necklace, they think poor Ginny's death was just an accident. Hayes said one of the mourners pocketed the diamonds during the kerfuffle, and he thinks I was hit over the head by some young hoodlum trying to snatch my purse. But when I came to my purse was on the ground next to me!"

"What can we do if the police refuse to listen!" Mrs. Ellis cried.

"We need to find some more compelling evidence. If it's okay with you, Brenda, I'd like to take a look around your garden."

"Of course." Brenda's fingers closed around mine. "If Dorothy is behind this, I want to see her in jail for what she nearly did to poor Ginny's baby. To hurt a child is the most horrible thing. We are so blessed the child survived."

That poor baby. "What will happen to it now? Will it go to its father?"

"No, no. If Ginny even knew who the father was, she didn't make that information known," Mrs Ellis said. "Brenda is going to adopt the child just as soon as she's able to, isn't that wonderful?"

Brenda beamed. "I always wanted a child of my own. If there is to be a silver lining in this tragedy, it's that I can give that child a happy home."

A nurse came in and shooed us away so Mrs. Winstone could rest. In the hall, Mrs. Ellis shivered. "Whatever am I going to do? If Dorothy really is killing members of the Banned Book Club, then I could be next!"

"I'm not going to let that happen." I thought of the Terror of Argleton, and the elaborate traps concocted by Greta and the other shop owners in the village. "I have an idea. We're going to set a trap."

CHAPTER TWENTY-TWO

"*H*ow exactly are you planning to turn my shop into a trap, *again?*" Heathcliff growled.

"It's simple. I've left notes in Mrs. Ellis' and Miss Blume's mailboxes inviting them to a special sleepover meeting of the Banned Book Club to honor the passing of their dear friends and to talk about a recruitment drive to get more young people reading banned books. It will be held right here in the shop. Mrs. Ellis is going to make sure she mentions it to every gossiping old biddy she knows, which is basically all of them. We'll make sure word gets back to Dorothy Ingram. Tonight, the ladies camp out in the World History room, and no food or object will be allowed past the door unless any of us have personally acquired or inspected it. And then we wait. Quoth will follow Dorothy and see what she does."

"I have a problem with this plan," Heathcliff announced.

"Only one?" Morrie piped up, tapping on his phone. "I have at least seventeen, starting with the fact that you're sleeping downstairs with the old biddies and not upstairs in my bed."

"I'm not exactly going to be *sleeping* with a murderer on the loose," I pointed out.

"You wouldn't be sleeping in my bed, either, gorgeous."

"What I want to know is why do all the bloody traps have to involve my shop?" Heathcliff grumbled. "And why do you have to put yourself in danger?"

"Because if something happened to Mrs. Ellis, I couldn't live with myself knowing I could have done something. That's my final word."

I left the boys to secure the windows and stage a booby trap in the doorway of the World History room, then went across to Greta's bakery and ordered a big stack of food, which I watched her prepare and hand to me. I couldn't afford to take any chances. Then, I went to the off-license and chose a few bottles of wine. I checked the lids thoroughly to ensure they were still sealed. At Mrs. Ellis' flat, I pulled sheets and duvets off the bed and carried them next door to set up for the sleepover.

Quoth met me in the doorway and relieved me of my burden. "This place almost looks cozy now."

I had to agree. They'd shifted all the furniture to the side, the same as I'd done for the Banned Book Club meeting. Morrie had hooked a projector up to one of his hard drives and was already rolling the 1939 version of *Wuthering Heights,* with Laurence Olivier doing his best smoldering Heathcliff.

"If I wasn't fearful for my life, this would be quite fun!" Mrs. Ellis swiped a cream doughnut from the top of the stack and stretched out across the chaise lounge. "You should run events like this in the bookshop more often. I'm sure Brenda would love to bring the youth group."

My mind raced, thinking of book-themed movie nights with the projector, and maybe lectures on local history or book launches. "I'm trying to convince Heathcliff."

"No," said Heathcliff from behind his desk in the other room.

"You didn't even hear what I said."

"You want to turn the shop into an attractive place people want to come, and I said no."

I stuck my tongue out at him. "You're no fun."

"That's not what you were saying on Friday night."

Mrs. Ellis bolted upright, her eyes dancing. "What was Friday night, dearie?"

My face flushed. "Go back to your movie, Mrs. Ellis. I need to speak to Heathcliff *privately*."

She squeezed my hand, pulling me closer so she could whisper something so filthy it made me blush from head to toe.

How did this woman teach innocent children for forty years?

I slipped out of the room and sat on the edge of Heathcliff's desk. "They're all set up, snug as two bugs in rugs."

"That's a terrible saying. A bug wouldn't need a rug, barely even a handkerchief." He turned a page in his book. "Morrie wants you upstairs."

"He does? You don't want me to—"

"No." Heathcliff's fingers slipped between the pages. His mouth twisted up into a smirk. "I'll take first watch."

"You sure?"

He leaned back in his chair, folded his ankles over each other, and patted the stack of books beside him. "I'm happy."

"Okay. Set your alarm and come get Morrie in two hours."

"If you say so."

I slipped upstairs. I'd strung even more fairy lights around the staircase. Morrie had left them on for me. As I made my way through the twinkling lights up to the second story flat, I felt like I was ascending into a magical world. Which, in a way, I was.

"Morrie?" I pushed open the door to the flat, expecting to see the glow of his computer screen from the alcove he used as an office. Instead, the living room was cast in shadow, the only light coming from the hallway that led to the bathroom and bedrooms.

"Oh gorgeous," a sugary voice called to me from the depths of the flat. "Won't you come and find me?"

I stepped into the hall, my heart pounding with delicious

anticipation. Morrie's door was open a crack. I pushed it with my foot and peered into the gloom. "What?"

"I have a surprise for you," he whispered, his words dripping with lust.

"Yes?" All thoughts of catching the murderer fled as excitement shuddered down my spine. I stepped into the room. Morrie's bedside lamp was on, the beam trained up toward the ceiling, where a pair of leather and steel cuffs hung from the hook above the bed.

"Surprise," Morrie whispered in my ear, as he drew up behind me and lowered a blindfold over my eyes. "Tonight, you are mine."

CHAPTER TWENTY-THREE

*A*s the material slid over my eyes, a faint flicker of panic flared in my stomach. I reached up and grabbed his wrist. "Morrie, what is this?"

He lowered the blindfold and stepped out of the shadows so I could see him. He wore a beautiful blue shirt that brought out the ice in his eyes, and a wicked grin – a grin that turned my limbs to jelly. He nodded to the handcuffs hanging from the ceiling.

"I've been thinking about you, Mina, about how you fear the darkness. Not just the darkness that may eventually become your world, but also the darkness you see inside me." Morrie paused. "Inside Heathcliff and Quoth, too. But you fear your own darkness most of all."

I gulped, staring at that blindfold. I thought back to the blue lights that had flickered across my vision that so far only Quoth knew about. "I sound like a real scaredy cat."

"You're not. You're the bravest person I've ever met." Morrie leaned forward, pressing his lips against my forehead. He lingered there, the heat of his lips searing through my doubts. "Maybe if you learn that the darkness is nothing to fear, then you'll be able to unleash all that Mina fury I know is hidden inside."

"I don't know…"

"The other day, you said you wanted to try this. Do you retract that statement?"

"No, I just…"

"You kept up your end of the bargain with Heathcliff, so I've decided to reward you. Do you trust me?" Morrie asked.

Did I? Academically, I shouldn't. I had to keep reminding myself that the sexy computer hacker I thought of as Morrie was really James Moriarty, the 'Napoleon of Crime' who was Sherlock Holmes' ultimate arch-nemesis. And yet, even though I'd seen Morrie perform any number of illegal acts during the course of hunting out Ashley's true killer and trying to get to the bottom of the Banned Book Club murders, I knew there was more to him than that. I *knew* that if I fell, he'd be there to catch me.

"I trust you."

Morrie slipped the blindfold over my eyes. Darkness enveloped me, sweeping over my body like a cold wave. The panic flickered again.

Morrie's mouth pressed against mine, his tongue searching, enjoying. His fingertips trailed down my arms, and the flickers of panic became shivers of desire.

I want this. I crave this. But Dorothy Ingram… everyone downstairs…

"Morrie, we can't do this now."

"We can do anything you want," he murmured against my lips. "I cleared it with Heathcliff. That's why he's taking the first watch. No one will disturb us unless there's an emergency."

"You *told* Heathcliff…"

"Of course," Morrie grabbed my neck, forcing my chin upward as he deepened this kiss. "Quoth, too. I couldn't very well have either of them flying up here every time you screamed."

It was on the tip of my tongue to ask what Heathcliff had said about me and Morrie and *this*, but then Morrie's lips left mine. I leaned forward, searching, bereft of his touch. He chuckled as he darted away, shuffling behind me. His skin slid against mine – the featherlight touch doing all sorts of exciting things inside me.

Morrie's fingers danced over my shoulder, sliding underneath the fabric, pushing my blouse down. His lips grazed my neck. His teeth... *oh, oh.*

I moaned as Morrie kissed and caressed my neck, my ears, my collarbone. In the darkness, every touch lit up my body, every inch of skin tingling with the anticipation of his next move. I didn't even notice that he'd unbuttoned my blouse and tossed it away. His fingers slid under my bra strap, unhooking it with ease.

Morrie wrapped his arms around me and helped me up onto the bed. "Arms above your head," he whispered, his authoritative voice strained with desire.

I raised my hands obediently. How easily I'd slipped into the role, trusting him with my body. It was just like in King's Copse with Heathcliff. I'd had to trust him, too. But really, it was about trusting myself – that if I fell into the darkness and these guys didn't catch me, I'd be able to catch myself. I'd never really believed that until I came home to Nevermore Bookshop.

Morrie slid my wrists into the cuffs and locked them. I gave them a tug. I was held fast. Morrie's fingers grazed my ankles as he placed my feet shoulder-width apart on the end of the bed.

"Normally, I'd use a spreader bar on your ankles to keep you like this," he said, kissing a trail up my leg until I moaned. "But I want to keep things simple for your first time."

Spreader bar? My mind whirled. *How does Morrie even know about this stuff? There weren't any spreader bars in* The Final Problem.

Air whistled over my naked skin. Morrie withdrew his hands. I stood naked, waiting for him to touch me. The room came alive with sound. Morrie's breathing, slow and heavy. The rustle of clothing or fabric or… the clink of a glass… Faint voices from the movie floating upstairs… *but where's Morrie? Why won't he touch me…*

I jumped as fierce cold traveled down between my breasts, the edges bright with wet heat. *An ice cube,* I realized. Morrie had an ice cube in his mouth.

Oh.

He trailed the ice in a circle on my belly, and my skin danced from the shock of it, chased by the heat of his lips and tongue. I tried to keep my body still, focusing on the sensations as Morrie drew intricate circles on my skin.

I whimpered as Morrie withdrew the ice. He responded by pressing the cube to my nipple. I gasped as cold, stabbing pain shot through my body. Morrie thrust a finger inside me as he held the ice cube still, and I writhed and gulped and cried out because it hurt but it was so good and *why why why.*

If this was what he'd meant by embracing the darkness, then maybe I could get used to it.

"Careful, gorgeous. Your cries have attracted a little birdie."

"Quoth?" I whispered.

"I didn't mean—" his husky voice croaked from the doorway. "I only heard the scream and I—"

"I told you what I was doing in here. Aren't you supposed to be running surveillance on our murder suspect?"

"I was just heading out. I thought you were hurting Mina." Quoth's voice tightened.

"Does she look like she's hurting?" Morrie sounded amused.

"No." Quoth whispered. So much emotion poured through that one word, my heart opened for him. I'd have put my arms around him if they weren't currently tied above my head.

Why am I not totally mortified right now? Why do I care more about Quoth's feelings than the fact he's seeing me naked and strung-up above Morrie's bed?

Why does the thought of Quoth seeing me naked and strung-up make my toes curl and my stomach flip like this?

"Why don't you come over here and help me, little birdie?" Morrie said. "That is, if it's okay by Mina."

"It's okay," I said.

What? What did I just say?

My heart pounded as the bed creaked, and another presence stood behind me. "Are you sure about this, Mina?" Quoth's breath tickled my neck.

"I'm sure."

"Good. Because you look so fucking beautiful." Quoth sighed as he pressed his lips against my skin.

CHAPTER TWENTY-FOUR

I moaned as Quoth's lips touched my skin, my body shivering all over – from nerves, from fear, from desire.

Quoth's lips remained against that one spot, heat from his kiss spreading right through my skin. The bed creaked again, and I knew Morrie now stood in front of me. I gasped as he cupped my breasts in his hands, teasing the nipples with his fingers – the tips still cold from handling the ice.

The only parts of them that touched me were Morrie's fingers and Quoth's lips. And yet, my body responded. Every sense kicked into overdrive. Their scents mingled in the air around me – Morrie's zesty grapefruit and vanilla, Quoth's crisp air and sunshine and fresh-cut grass. I wet my lips with my tongue, longing to taste one of them, *both* of them. The air shifted around me as they moved on the bed, their bodies close, so close, but untouchable. Oh, how I itched to touch. Electric currents leapt from their skin and crackled against mine, drawing them closer, closer…

Quoth moved his lips in feathery kisses along my collarbone.

His fingers twined in my hair as he kissed down my spine and over my shoulders, each touch standing my hairs on end. I leaned back into the cuffs, testing my weight against them, trying to press myself against Quoth's body. But he stayed just out of reach.

"She's keen," Morrie chuckled. His hands skimmed my sides, teasing my thighs, circling between my legs, so close to where all my aches converged, but never touching, never giving me what I wanted.

"Please…" I murmured.

"Since you asked so nicely…" Morrie surged forward. One hand cupped my cheek, his tongue plunging between my lips. His other hand dived between my legs, battering against my clit. I reeled under his sudden force, and my back slammed against Quoth. I moaned as he wrapped his body around me, enveloping me in his protective warmth.

The two of them pinned me in place, exactly where I wanted to be. Four hands caressed my body, exploring every part of me, circling my breasts, rolling and pinching my nipples, stroking and rubbing my clit. I lost myself in the sensations of it, giving up on the need to know who was who and what they were doing, and reveled in the hedonism of being worshipped by the two of them.

Under their relentless caresses, I was gone. The ache inside me became a roaring fire, an inferno, that swept through my veins and swallowed me whole. I bellowed into Morrie's lips as I came.

Blue light exploded across the darkness. My legs collapsed from under me. The handcuffs scraped my wrists as they caught my weight.

"Oh, no, gorgeous. We're not done with you yet." Morrie whispered something to Quoth. I strained to hear what they were planning. But then their hands were on me again, touching and diving and caressing.

The bed creaked as someone knelt on the edge. Two hands wrapped around my thighs, swinging me forward. A tongue slid down me, parting my lips, lapping at me. *Morrie. That has to be Morrie with his cool, controlled rhythm...*

Behind me, a condom wrapper crunched. A finger touched my cheek, light as a feather, turning my head to the side. Quoth's lips brushed mine, soft, cautious. I parted them with my own, slipping my tongue over his, drawing him closer, deeper.

"Mina," he whispered, his voice choked with need. "Do you want me?"

"I wanted you from the moment I saw you," I whispered back.

Quoth moaned, folding his body against my back. His cock pressed between my legs, hard and ready. I spread my thighs wider. He slid in.

Oh, yes.

Quoth felt so good, so perfect, filling me completely. He sighed against my lips as he moved slowly, drawing himself out and thrusting in again. And all the while Morrie's strong hands gripped my legs, his tongue lapping at me.

This is... I can't...

The intensity of it blew me away. I came again, howling against Quoth's lips as my body lost control. Morrie's grip and Quoth's cock held me upright. Quoth's nails dug into my thighs as he rode through my orgasm, moaning as my walls closed around his cock.

They didn't stop. My clit hummed with fire as Morrie continued his relentless rhythm. Quoth thrust inside me, burying himself so deep, and this time I screamed as another orgasm slammed into me. Bright stars of blue and purple light exploded across my eyes.

Wow. Okay... wow...

I faded into a wobbling mess of nerve endings, coming again as Quoth buried his teeth into my shoulder. Pain surged from the bite as his muscles tightened and his cock twitched and he came.

"My turn," Morrie cried happily.

"I can't…" I gasped.

"Sure you can." Quoth's body fell back. Morrie slid behind me and rolled on a condom. Quoth must've positioned himself in front of me, because his body pressed against my chest and his lips sought mine.

Morrie parted my legs again and pushed his way inside me. My body tightened and ached, adjusting to his size. While Morrie thrust with his regular, controlled rhythm, Quoth kissed me, his tongue fluttering against mine, his lips releasing all the things he couldn't say to me. His soul he did outpour in a kiss that stole my breath and broke my heart at the same time.

Everything about this moment was so perfect. Quoth released his hopes into me as Morrie released all his desire for control. Morrie's body tensed, and his teeth scraped along the same spot on my shoulder as he too came, in that one nanosecond where he allowed his own chaos to reign.

Morrie slumped against me. Sweat clung to my skin, and I could no longer feel my wrists. Quoth pressed his lips to my forehead. "Thank you," he whispered.

I tried to say that he was welcome, which was kind of a weird thing to say after one's first threesome, but my lips had gone numb and I couldn't make words happen.

"Lean against me, gorgeous." Morrie's strong arms wrapped around me. He reached up and unhooked the cuffs. My body slumped against his. I couldn't hold myself up.

He lifted the blindfold off my eyes. The face that stared back at me wasn't the confident master criminal I usually encountered. Morrie's icy eyes pooled with concern, his features drawn. Sweat dripped down his forehead. He gave me a lopsided smile. "Are you okay?"

"I—" I struggled to find the words. "That was amazing."

"Good." Morrie broke out into one of his self-satisfied grins, and just like that, his mask slipped back on. He scooped me up and deposited me in the bed. "Quoth is going to cuddle with you for a bit."

"But you—"

"I need to be elsewhere." Morrie slunk away into the darkness. I reached out a hand to him, but the door slammed shut. He was gone.

My lip trembled. *What just happened?* Morrie had just orchestrated the best sex of my life. He'd just somehow convinced me to have a threesome, and I had absolutely zero regrets. And then he takes one look at me with the blindfold off and runs away?

My mind swam. There *was* something going on in Morrie's head behind all that swagger and bravado. Had I just caught a glimpse of it? Was that why he ran, because he didn't want to be vulnerable in front of me and Quoth?

Speaking of vulnerable...

Quoth lifted the edge of the sheet. I smiled, beckoning him in. He slid in beside me, wrapping his arms around my body and pulling me against him, tangling his legs in mine. I rested my head on his bicep and gazed into his eyes, watching the ring of orange flare around the outside of those deep brown orbs.

"He should be here," Quoth said, his fingers trailing over my face and across my shoulders, raising trails of goosepimples.

"It's okay. I have you." I nestled my head into his shoulder, placing my hand on his chest, over his beating heart.

He sighed. "Mina, how did this happen? How did I get so lucky?"

"Thank Morrie later. I half wonder if he planned it to be this way. Did you know he told me I had to sleep with you and Heathcliff? He suspected you and I would dance around each other for months unless he thrust us together."

"If that's the case, I take back every bad thing I've ever said about him." Quoth's eyes crinkled, and he smiled. *Oh, Isis, that smile...*

"Don't take back that time you called him the Neapolitan Ice Cream of Crime, because that was hilarious."

He laughed, hugging me tighter. "Never."

"Quoth," I whispered into his chest. "I'm sorry if I tried to force you out of your shift at my mum's house. I really thought you just needed a hard word, but I was wrong. You were so terrified." My heart broke all over again remembered how his raven body had trembled in my arms.

"It's okay."

"I'm not sure it is. I thought I was helping, but I don't understand what it is to be you, what goes on in your body, or in your mind."

"I'm a grim, ungainly, ghastly, gaunt, and ominous bird of yore," Quoth said. "You know everything you need to know."

"You shouldn't talk about yourself like that, even if Poe did. You are so much more to me. Please, don't let me push you into going outside and doing things if you can't—"

"I *want* to be a human, Mina," Quoth's voice quivered with venom. "I *want* to be able to be in the world with you. I want to be able to help you when—" he stopped.

"Finish the sentence. You want to help me when I go blind." I didn't trip over the word, the way I normally did. "I appreciate that, but I'm starting to realize that's not your job. It's mine."

"I swore that I'd protect you," he insisted.

"You did, and that's very noble, if a little odd. But if I don't at least do some of the protecting for myself, then I'll never be able to look my poster of Sid Vicious in the eye again." I laughed. "Actually, that might be a real problem soon."

"You saw the colored lights again?"

"Yes." I gave him a squeeze. "I'm still scared, but I feel like with you and Heathcliff and Morrie by my side, I can conquer the fear. And I want to be there for you while you conquer your fear. But I don't want to force you, because that's not how we roll, all right?"

"You could never force me," Quoth said, his voice fierce.

"Good. And you'll be so kind as to tell me if I'm being a right cow in the future."

He laughed again. "Be quiet and close your eyes, Mina Wilde. Or your words shall be our sign of parting."

CHAPTER TWENTY-FIVE

*Q*uoth and I lay together, fading in and out of consciousness, our lips and hands exploring each other's bodies in a strange world between waking and sleep. Heavy boots clomped up the stairs, startling me out of my reverie. I sat up just as Heathcliff called my name.

I slid from under Quoth's arm and gathered Morrie's quilt around me like a gown, then swept out into the hall.

Heathcliff stood in front of the fireplace, his eyes blazing. Tension rose off his body in waves. I stood my ground, unsure if he was about to start yelling and throwing things, or if he was going to throw me against the wall and fuck me. I was hoping for the latter.

"Morrie's driving me crazy. I came up to..." Heathcliff's words died on his lips as he stepped toward me, lowering his eyes to my shoulder. I followed his gaze and noticed a line of purple bruises across my skin. Bite marks.

"Morrie's handiwork," he whispered, pressing his finger into my skin. The hickey turned white, then darkened to pink again.

"And Quoth's," I said.

Heathcliff raised an eyebrow. "So it's going to be like that, is it?"

"I don't know. I have no idea what I'm doing. All I know is, it felt good. You all feel good."

"You feel amazing." Heathcliff closed the gap between us, brushing his lips against mine, and then his hands tangled in my hair and I dropped the sheet and pressed my body against his.

Tension rippled down his arms as his hands explored my body, lifting me and smashing me against him, as though we couldn't get close enough until we had crawled into each other. My languid senses leapt to life, relishing the possessiveness of his touch.

Heathcliff spun me around and slammed my back against the wall, devouring my mouth with his. I managed to squeeze my hand between his legs and unzip his fly. As I wrapped my hand around his cock, he moaned against my lips.

He yanked a condom from his pocket, tearing the wrapper between his teeth. Heathcliff rolled it on and I wrapped my legs around him. Heathcliff held me easily, his huge hands cupping my arse, his cock entering me in one slick motion.

My back slammed against the wall as he took me, pushing into me again and again, deeper and harder than he'd ever done before. His wild eyes bore into mine, and I drowned in their black depths.

Heathcliff drove faster. I arched my back, digging my nails into his shoulders as the ache inside me bubbled over and an orgasm slammed into me.

Wow. Wowowowowow.

I'd never come just from penetrative sex before. But something about the angle and the way Heathcliff's smoldering eyes burned into mine had sent me over the edge. Behind his head, two flame-ringed eyes glowed from the darkness. Quoth, sitting on his perch, watching us, always watching, always making sure no one was hurting me.

Heathcliff cried out as he came, the sound like a release of something ancient and primal. Inside me, his cock twitched and released. He slumped against me, still holding me tight.

My mind reeled with a million disjointed thoughts. *I just had a threesome. I just slept with three guys on the same night.*

And they're okay with it. And I... I might be okay with it, too.

We could hash out the details later, when we weren't trying to solve a murder. But right now, as Heathcliff slumped into his chair and pulled me onto his lap, wrapping his arms around me, and Quoth's watchful eyes burned through the gloom, right now I wasn't scared at all.

CHAPTER TWENTY-SIX

"*W*akey wakey, sleepyheads."

Heathcliff leapt to his feet, dropping me on the floor. "Get away from her, or I'll gut you like a fish!" he yelled, brandishing a fire poker into the darkness.

"Relax," a voice I recognized as Morrie chuckled. "You're not in any imminent danger."

"Shite." I rubbed my eyes. "What time is it? Is it time for my watch?"

"It's seven a.m. I came up to see if you wanted me to cook breakfast. I was thinking a little *boule de pain—*"

"You didn't wake us?" Heathcliff growled. "What happened? Did Quoth even go out to follow the suspect?"

"Relax, everything's fine. I tried to wake you, but Mina looked too cute and you growled at me, and I didn't want to risk my neck. I watched the biddies. Quoth spent the night watching Dorothy Ingram through her window. Apparently, she knitted a hideous scarf and cried her way through *An Affair to Remember.*"

"I didn't growl at you!" Heathcliff yelled.

"I assure you that you did, kind of like you're doing now."

"I couldn't have. I was asleep."

"Then you growl in your sleep, like a giant cuddly teddy bear." Morrie ducked out of the way as Heathcliff swung a fist at him.

"Guys, can we focus, *please?* Mrs. Ellis, Miss Blume, are they okay?"

"Yes, perfectly safe and in fine form. I've just delivered their tea. Miss Blume dumped hers out the window in order to 'divine the leaves.' On my way out, Mrs. Ellis pinched my bum."

I smiled. They were definitely fine. "What does it mean that Dorothy didn't show up?"

"Probably nothing," Morrie said. "Maybe your killer didn't get the message about the slumber party, or perhaps she suspected a trap, or your screams of ecstasy echoed across the village and gave the whole game away."

My cheeks burned. I scrambled to my feet. "I'll go talk to them," I mumbled as I headed for the stairs.

Mrs. Ellis winked at me as I walked into the World History room. *Great, so she'd heard me, too.* This was going to be all over the village before sunset.

And oh Hathor, Miss Blume works with Mum. This is very, very not good.

"Did you guys sleep well?" I managed to choke out.

"Oh, as well as could be expected," Mrs. Ellis grinned. My whole face burned. "We were up all night, listening for the sound of our killer coming for us."

"We heard all sorts of creaks and moans," Miss Blume added. "This old building certainly is *lively.*"

Astarte, kill me now.

"Right, well," I cleared my throat. "Obviously you were perfectly safe. Will you be okay staying here in the shop today? Morrie and I are going to inspect Mrs. Winstone's garden."

Mrs. Ellis folded up her duvet. "Oh, no, we can't stay here. We need to visit Brenda at the hospital, and Sylvia has clients booked—"

"Very well, Quoth— er, *Allan* will go with you to the hospital."

"Mina," Quoth whispered from behind me. "Can I talk to you in private for a moment?"

Mrs Ellis' eyes bugged out of her head as she leaned forward to peer around the corner at a shirtless Quoth, who shrank back into the shadows.

"Sure." I followed him across the hallway and into the Children's room. Quoth encircled my wrist in his long fingers.

"Didn't you just say you were going to stop pushing me?" Fire flared in his eyes.

"Didn't you say that you wanted to be pushed?" I shot back.

"You sound far too much like Morrie. Watching an old lady through her window was one thing, but you saw what happened at your mum's. If I mess this up, Mina... if I shift in front of someone in the village—"

I squeezed his hand, losing myself in the deep brown of his eyes. "You're just nervous, is all. The others have filled your head with all kinds of nonsense. You deserve a real life, Quoth. I want to walk hand-in-hand with you through the village and watch people's heads turn. I want to take you to a punk concert so you can feel the way the music cuts you inside and forces all the bad stuff out. I want us to go to the National Gallery, and the Tate Modern, and maybe even one day we could take a trip to Paris and see the Louvre and all the amazing paintings that will fill you with joy. That could be your life, and I could share it with you, and it'll be amazing. But if you want that life, you have to take Mrs. Ellis and Miss Blume to the hospital. Okay?"

In response, Quoth raised my hand to his lips, pressing them against my skin. A jolt of electricity shot through my body. Too soon, he pulled away, turning to leave.

"Where are you going?" I tried to tug him back, but he slipped from my grasp.

Quoth's brilliant smile lit up the room better than any junk store lamp. "If I'm to visit the hospital, I should put on a shirt."

I grinned as I collected Morrie and we went out to snoop. On the way, we stopped at the bakery for coffee. As we turned to leave, clutching our cups and cream doughnuts, Dorothy Ingram entered with two other ladies from the church. She gave me a dirty look as she hobbled past, her walking stick clutched tight in her hand. I shot her an evil glare back, resisting the urge to stick my foot out and trip her up.

Morrie kept up a steady stream of chatter on the way. I tried to ask him about last night, about why he'd run away, but I couldn't get the words out. I still couldn't believe it had happened.

The Winstones lived in a lovely cottage down a small lane on the opposite side of the town green, overlooking a picturesque meadow. Even though it was the middle of winter, the garden burst with color and texture. Morrie took out a pocket magnifying glass and went around the low stone wall, while I bent to examine the front stoop where she'd been attacked. A tall hedge of wisteria stood along one side. It would certainly give enough cover to an assailant lying in wait.

I bent down to examine the hedge. There were a few broken twigs at the front, but not as many as I'd have expected from the kind of tussle Mrs. Winstone described. *Either this would-be killer was careful, or she snuck up the path instead of hiding in the bushes.* I pictured Dorothy Ingram with her stick and limp. She wouldn't be sneaking up on anyone. I peered closer at the hedge. The ground didn't appear to be trampled. *Of course, Dorothy is a small woman so she wouldn't need as much space as a big man.*

I shifted the dead leaves, hunting for more broken branches. Maybe I could find where she'd crouched down in wait. My hand brushed something hard and smooth. I wrapped my fingers around it, dragged it out of the bed, and held it up into the light.

A wooden walking stick.

The killer must have dropped it as they were making their getaway. I studied the shaft, noticing spots of dried blood around the ornately-carved handle.

My mind reeled. *Dorothy had her stick with her when we saw her at the bakery. Which means this can't be hers.*

Unless she has a bunch of them. But that seems unlikely. It's a very distinct stick, and it looks expensive.

"Morrie!" I called out. "I found something."

He came running over and inspected the stick, trailing his fingers along its shaft and studying the dried blood near the handle. "This was definitely the weapon that attacked Mrs. Winstone."

"But Dorothy had her stick with her." I pointed to the handle. "I think this one's different. Dorothy's has flowers carved around the handle. This one has these half-moon shapes."

"This is the phases of the moon, mixed with sacred geometric shapes. It's an occult design." Morrie made a face. "You're right. Our religious fanatic wouldn't use this."

I stared at the walking stick in my hands, hardly able to believe what I saw. This stick blew a huge hole in our theory. Dorothy Ingram had every motive and opportunity for killing off the members of the Banned Book Club. But if it wasn't Dorothy's stick, then whose was it?

CHAPTER TWENTY-SEVEN

*M*orrie and I sat down on the curb and finished off our now-cold coffee. Morrie made me recount the evidence we'd collected so far, especially the conversation I overheard between Dorothy and Ginny Button.

"Dorothy seemed afraid of Ginny," I recalled, trying to remember the exact words I overheard. "She said, 'I got her out of the way for you. She's paid for her sins, and now you and I have no more business together.' Only Ginny wanted her to do something else, so she said that God detests a blackmailer. Then Ginny said she hoped Dorothy wasn't threatening her, because she'd hate for anyone to discover her secret."

"Her filthy secret," Morrie corrected, with an undue amount of relish.

"Yes, of course. Her *filthy* secret. And she called Dorothy a murderer. Then Dorothy got angry and stormed off. And the next thing, Ginny's lying dead at the bottom of the stairs."

"And it was the night before when you saw Sylvia and Ginny?"

"Yes. Ginny was saying something that scared Sylvia, and as Ginny stalked back to her car, Sylvia yelled, 'You may think you're untouchable, but I know what you did. You're rotten and you won't get away with it!'"

"So Ginny could have killed Mrs. Scarlett," Morrie mused. "Or she could have got Dorothy to do it. But what if Sylvia found out about it? She could have pushed Ginny. She was at the funeral. But then if Ginny's dead, who attacked Mrs. Winstone?"

"Why did you run away last night?" I blurted out.

"Heathcliff needed me downstairs. We were waiting to trap a murderer, if you recall."

"That's not the reason. You orchestrated that whole evening for me, including sending Heathcliff upstairs. So why didn't you stay?"

"It's simple. You'd just had an intense sexual experience. You needed someone to take care of you, bring your emotions back to a normal, happy place. You needed cuddles and sweet kisses and poetry. That's not what I do." Morrie flashed me a grin that wavered at the edges. "Quoth yearns for cuddles, so you were in good hands. This is the beauty of our arrangement, gorgeous. You get all the benefits."

"And you don't have to do any emotional work, right?" I demanded. "You get to remain aloof and in control and above it all?"

Morrie bit his lip. "I wouldn't attempt to armchair psychoanalyze me, Sigmund Wilde. The last person who did went over the edge of a waterfall with me, or so I'm told. Talking about feelings defeats the purpose of having them. I don't want my mind to become a spectator sport. Keep your eye on the prize – we're trying to catch a murderer here."

Nice change of subject there, Morrie. Don't think this is over. If I have to face up to my own reality, then so do you.

"I still think it's Dorothy," I said. "It doesn't make sense for it to be Sylvia if pushing Ginny was all about getting her to stop whatever she was doing. Maybe Dorothy purchased another walking stick in order to throw off the authorities."

Morrie shrugged. "Possible. I think we confront Dorothy, see if we can shake her up a bit. I overheard her conversation in the bakery. She said she was going to the church to do some cleaning. With any luck, we'll find her there, alone."

We raced over to the church. Sure enough, there was only one car in the parking lot – a grey Nissan. The wooden door to the church was open a crack. Morrie and I peered inside, but without the candles lit, I could barely see a thing.

Morrie stepped inside and slammed the door behind him. *BANG.* The sound reverberated through the towering nave.

"Who are you? What do you want?" A voice snapped from the altar. "Can't you see I'm busy?"

"Dorothy Ingram, it's a pleasure," Morrie purred. "We're a couple of concerned citizens come to speak with you about recent crimes in the village. Namely, two murders and one assault on members of the Banned Book Club."

Dorothy straightened up, dusting her hands on a white apron she wore over her severe black dress. "Police officers, are you?"

"In a manner of speaking," Morrie said, sliding his phone from his pocket and tapping at the screen.

"Don't lie in God's house," she snapped. Even in the dark, I could feel her eyes staring daggers through my chest. "The two of you work in that heathen bookshop. I see no reason to speak to you and don't see how I could be of interest. I hardly knew those unfortunate ladies."

"That's not true, though, is it?" I said. "I overheard you talking to Ginny before Mrs. Scarlett's funeral. She was blackmailing you. She wanted you to do something for her, or she would tell everyone about your *filthy little secret.*"

"That's preposterous." Fear cut through Dorothy's bluster.

"Is it? You hated Mrs. Scarlett because of her influence in the community. She kept stepping on your plans to make the village more wholesome and God-fearing. You considered the Banned Book Club a personal affront."

"Even if I did, I didn't lay a finger on her. Killing is against God's Commandments! I would never commit such a despicable act."

"And just where does aborting your unborn child sit on God's moral scale?" Morrie asked, still concentrating on his phone.

Dorothy's face paled. "Wha... what are you talking about?"

Morrie held up his phone. On the screen was a scan of a printed form. "While we've been talking, I hacked your mobile phone, and what was the first message Ginny Button sent you? This in-patient form for an abortion clinic... with your name on it."

"That's not mine. It's been doctored!" Dorothy shrieked.

"I don't think so," Morrie grinned, slipping his phone back into his pocket. "You were only nineteen, and an unwed woman. Whatever would God think? Tell me, was it a single night of unbridled passion, or did you have a long-term lover? Was he hung like a donkey? Did he make you scream? Did he stick it in your arse—"

"Get away from me, you vulgar man!" Dorothy screeched, swinging the broom at Morrie.

She's really upset. I reached out to stop Morrie, but he was on a roll. He wrenched the broom from her hand and broke it over his knee like it was nothing. She sobbed and cowered behind the altar, and all the while he just kept talking in his calm, cheerful tone. "So you had the abortion, and no one ever had to know. Except Ginny Button came across this old file somehow, and she used it to make you do her bidding. She made you poison Gladys Scarlett, and then you threw her down the stairs in order to stop her blackmail. I know you work in the village pharmacy. You would have access to the equipment needed to make arsenic. You had no love for Gladys Scarlett. But what I *don't* know, what I desperately want to know, is why Ginny wanted Mrs. Scarlett dead?"

Dorothy peered over the top of the altar, laughing like a

hyena. "What a load of cockaninny! Ginny didn't ask me to kill Gladys Scarlett. She wanted me to use my position on the church committee to remove Brenda Winstone from the youth group. I was only too happy to do it because Gladys' corrupting influence had tainted Brenda's sweet nature. But then, the day of the funeral, Ginny said it wasn't enough. She wanted Brenda to *suffer*. She wanted me to accuse Brenda of touching a child inappropriately so that Brenda would never be able to be near children again."

I thought about how Brenda had lit up when she chased the children around the shop, and how her voice faltered when she said her husband didn't want kids. *What an evil thing to do. It would destroy Brenda.*

"So you wrote that note and had Ginny meet you after the service," Morrie said. "Perhaps you tried to reason with her, but she wouldn't back down. And so you pushed her."

"No! I didn't see Ginny after the service. I stood at the door to offer a basket of flowers to the mourners so they might place them on that ungodly woman's grave. Cassandra Irons can attest I was in that position until Mrs. Ellis screamed, and she has no love for me."

"Why did Ginny want to hurt Mrs. Winstone?" I piped up.

"She never revealed that to me, and I didn't ask. I do not care about the petty squabbles between harlots and heathens." Mrs. Ingram rose from the altar and waved her arms. "If that is all your questions, I'd be thankful if you left me in peace. If you have any kindness in your hearts, do not reveal my secret in the village."

"Oh, don't worry." Morrie crossed himself furtively. "I love to keep secrets. They're much more valuable that way. We must be off. Say hi to Jesus for me. Toodles!"

"*Toodles?*" I punched him in the arm as we exited the church.

"I was just been friendly. So, Mina the clever detective, do you believe her?"

"I… I'm not sure. I find it harder to believe she had an abortion, honestly. But if she's telling the truth, that puts us right back to square one again. If Dorothy Ingram didn't kill either of them or attack Mrs. Winstone, then who did?"

"Perhaps when Miss Blume said, 'I know what you've done' to Ginny, she meant getting Mrs. Winstone kicked off the youth group. In which case, Ginny's motivations may be unrelated." Morrie held up his phone. "I think we need to figure out if Ginny Button was blackmailing anyone else."

"How are we going to figure that out?"

"I haven't found anything in her emails. She's been very careful. But even the most careful blackmailers leave evidence. We need to see if she has incriminating documents on anyone else."

"How do we do that? The police will have her phone."

"A smart girl like Ginny will have her evidence stored in hard copy." Morrie tapped his phone to bring up a map, zeroing in on a house in the village. "The only way we're going to get answers is to do a spot of breaking and entering."

CHAPTER TWENTY-EIGHT

$\mathcal{G}$inny Button lived in one half of a Tudor residence on one of the most picturesque streets in the village. Planter boxes hung from the windows, filled with herbs and winter blooms, and the pink front door had recently had a fresh coat of paint. The same sporty red convertible that had dropped off Sylvia Blume sat in the carport. Appearances had clearly been important to her – she had spent time perfecting her home in the same way she had perfected her image. I wondered where all her money had come from – she hadn't been married, and I knew from Mrs. Ellis that she was an administrative assistant at the council, which couldn't have paid much.

Quoth dug his talons into my arm. We'd swung by the shop on the way and picked him up, with a promise to return him in twenty minutes so the ladies could visit the hospital. I learned from Ashley's case just how useful it was to have a raven when one was breaking and entering.

"We'll have to be quick," Morrie said as he led us around the side of the house and through a tidy garden. "I don't want to leave Heathcliff alone with the old biddies any longer than necessary."

"That's sensible." I nuzzled Quoth's soft feathers as Morrie scanned the facade for an entry point.

Mrs. Ellis pinched his bum this morning, Quoth said inside my head. *He told her that was against the rules. She said there were no rules, so he wrote a list and nailed it to the wall.*

"Of course he did." I shuddered to think what rules Heathcliff might include on what was sure to be an exhaustive list.

"Ah." Morrie pointed to an open window on the second floor. "There's our way in."

You owe me for this, Quoth's voice echoed between my ears as he took off. He soared up and cleared the window, landing inside with a faint *plop*.

A few moments later, the back door unlatched, and a naked Quoth ushered us inside. I peered around the tiny, immaculate kitchen, admiring how Ginny had modernized the old home with distressed furniture and industrial fittings. Bitch or not, the woman had impeccable taste.

"There's a study in here," Morrie whispered, creeping through the living room into a small alcove. He set down his bag of computer gadgets. "I'll search here. You two take the bedrooms. Don't rub your naked arse on anything, little birdie."

I followed Quoth up the steep staircase, my heart pounding. From somewhere in the house, a faint *scritch-scritch* of something scraping against wood jumped my nerves into overdrive. *It's just the old house, nothing to worry about.*

Photographs hung from every wall – a young Ginny smiling as she hung off the arms of important-looking men. There was a different man in each picture, and I recognized some of their faces as minor celebrities and football players. A bunch of glamour shots and magazine covers featuring Ginny on the landing revealed that at some point in her past, she'd been a model.

I wonder if that's how she made her money. It might explain why she's now in Argleton, instead of up in London. Ginny was still beautiful, but she was definitely past her prime in terms of modeling and attracting footballers, and I had the feeling she wouldn't have wasted time hanging around a scene where she wasn't the center of attention.

The first bedroom was a guest room, containing a bed worthy of a boutique hotel covered in a mountain of pillows. I pulled out the drawers in the dressing table – they were filled with clothing, but no secret blackmailing notes. Quoth opened the wardrobe and inspected rows of shoes. "Why does one person need so many shoes?" he asked.

"That's one of life's eternal mysteries."

Scritch-scritch. There was the sound again.

We moved on to the master suite. Quoth started on the drawers while I pulled boxes out from under the bed. In a battered shoebox, I found stacks of love letters – real filthy stuff – between Ginny and a man who was simply called 'H'.

"Look at this," I held up one of the letters. "This 'H' must have been the father of Ginny's baby. She kept copies of all the letters she sent him, and this letter was dated two weeks ago. Ginny wanted H to leave his wife and marry her."

Quoth leaned over my shoulder, his hair tickling my skin. "Is there a response?"

I riffled through the stack of letters. "Not that I can see. But I'm guessing it didn't happen, otherwise she'd have had a ring on her finger."

Scritch-scritch. Scritch-scritch.

"Quoth, can you hear that?" I glanced around the room. It was even louder in here.

"Termites," Quoth said. "In an old house like this, there must be all sorts of bugs in the wood." He licked his lip hungrily, as if the thought of gross wood bugs excited him.

"Squeak!" whispered an unknown voice.

"Do termites usually make a squeaking noise?"

"That's just a hinge… no, wait, I smell something…" Quoth

muttered, sniffing as he bent down to pull another box from under the bed. Sometimes, it was easy to forget that Quoth *was* part bird. It was especially hard when he crouched beside me, completely naked, his long thigh brushing against mine.

Scritch-scritch, scritch-scritch, creeeeeak...

"That scratching is coming from the wardrobe," I cried.

I'd barely got the words out when the wardrobe door burst open and a tiny ball of white fur barreled toward me, squeaking with jubilation. The mouse streaked across the room and under the curtains. As its hind legs disappeared up the fabric, I noticed an all-too-familiar brown patch above its hind leg.

"It's the Terror of Argleton! Oh, Quoth, I wonder how he got stuck in Ginny's wardrobe—"

"Croak!"

Raven feathers exploded across the room as Quoth's animal instincts kicked in. He dived for the window, forgetting he'd closed it earlier. I cried out as he smashed against the glass and collapsed in a heap on the floor.

"Quoth!" I scrambled toward him, touching the corner of his wing just as he picked himself up and shook out his head, his eyes rolling.

The Terror of Argleton took that moment to streak past Quoth again, squeaking with glee as it rocketed up the dresser and along the picture rail. Quoth lurched after it, his body wobbling and crashing as he chased it around the room.

"No, guys, stop!" I scrambled after them. Something smashed downstairs. Morrie swore.

"Morrie, help!" I scrambled up on the bed to shoo Quoth down before he tore out the chandelier. I couldn't see where the mouse had got to, but from the way Quoth scratched at the top of the wardrobe, I could hazard a guess.

I threw the window open again and after flapping my arms around madly, managed to get Quoth to fly outside. I sank to the floor to catch my breath.

What was I just *thinking about having a raven around making things easier?*

Morrie's head appeared around the door. "Time to fly, gorgeous. We've already been here too long. Hey, where's the little birdie?"

I held out a hand and he helped me up. "You shouldn't call him that. And he's outside. The Terror of Argleton showed up and he went Full Metal Raven on us."

Morrie shuddered as he yanked me to my feet. I noticed a stack of papers under his arm. "If that mouse is here, we're leaving *now.*"

He dragged me downstairs and out the open back door, locking it and pulling it closed behind him. We raced down the side of the yard, where Quoth fluttered down from a nearby tree and perched on my shoulder, his talons digging into my skin.

Morrie didn't stop running until we reached the corner of the street. He checked the legs of his trousers for any resident mice before straightening up again.

"Croak," Quoth said, his head bobbing up and down as if he was laughing.

"Yeah, well, you didn't fare any better, did you? Smartarse. While you two were making new friends, I found something actually useful." Morrie held up his stack of papers. "Records of Dorothy Ingram's abortion, as well as this doctor's report of a mysterious death. And an official name-change application. According to these articles and papers, a Mr. Wesley Bayliss died in the old hospital after ingesting hemlock. Shortly afterward, his wife – Sally Bayliss – changed her name and moved from a nearby village into Argleton. Want to guess what her name is now?"

"What is it?"

Morrie grinned. "Miss Sylvia Blume. Which means, Ginny Button was blackmailing our spirit medium."

CHAPTER TWENTY-NINE

I stared at the paper in Morrie's hand, a sick feeling pooling in my stomach. "Miss Blume said she'd never been married."

"She lied," he said.

Hands shaking, I pulled out my phone and dialed Jo's number.

"Hey, Mina. I hope you're calling to tell me how your date with Heathcliff went."

"It went… well." I blushed as Quoth nudged my hand with his head and Morrie brushed his finger over the welt around my wrist, and I remembered what happened last night. *I have a lot to catch Jo up on*. "But I can't talk about that now. I need to ask you about hemlock."

"That's the poison that killed Socrates. What about it?"

"Do you know anything about it, like how someone might use it to kill?" I paused, trying to think of a plausible reason I might be asking about hemlock. "I'm trying to win an argument with Morrie."

Jo laughed. "I'm happy to help with such a noble cause. Hemlock is from the *Apiaceae* family, the same as carrots and parsnips. It's been used in small amounts in herbal remedies for centuries. It acts as a neurotoxin. Numbness creeps through the body from the feet to the chest. The victim remains lucid through the whole process, as Plato reported Socrates speaking with his pupils right up until the moment the poison reached his heart. As far as forensic records go, no one has been murdered with hemlock since ancient times. We do see a lot of hemlock deaths, but they're always accidental – usually, foragers who think they're found a choice crop of wild parsnips, or rich nobles in Italy dining on songbirds, which become carriers of the poison when they consume hemlock seeds. Although, of course, it's always difficult to say. There might be many poisoners who've gotten away with using hemlock over the years."

I can think of one. "Thanks, Jo. I appreciate it."

"Hang on, don't keep me in suspense. Did you win?"

Morrie's hand stole under my shirt, his fingers stroking my nipple through the fabric of my shirt. "Yup," my voice strained. "I absolutely, definitely won."

I rang off, pushing Morrie away even as my body screamed for more. "None of that. We might've left Mrs. Ellis alone with her murderer."

"She's not alone." Morrie kissed along my neck, his hands roaming freely down my body. "She's got Heathcliff to protect her."

I shoved him away, harder this time. "Maybe *you're* not worried about your friends being fed hemlock or arsenic by some crazy fortune teller, but I am. We've got to get back to the shop!"

I tore myself from Morrie and fled across the village toward Nevermore Bookshop, Quoth flapping along behind me. Morrie's expensive brogues pounded on the footpath. "Mina, wait up!"

Something's wrong. I can feel it.

I shoved the door open. "Heathcliff? Mrs. Ellis?" I cried. "Are you in here?"

"Oh, Mina darling, you're back!" Sylvia called. "We're right here where you left us, just *dying* to get out."

Heart pounding, I picked my way around the stacks of books and found the three of them in the World History room. To my surprise, Heathcliff sat across the table from Mrs. Ellis, Grimalkin curled asleep in his lap and a game of Scrabble spread out in front of him. He wore a pained expression and clutched a teacup in his hand. Behind him, Miss Blume stood beside the tea trolley, pouring another cup.

"She forced me to play this insipid game," Heathcliff muttered, glaring at Mrs. Ellis. "And then she dances around the room when she wins. There are bloody shawls and carpet bags flying everywhere. It's all fun and games until someone loses an I—"

The tea! Of course. Sylvia makes her own tea, which she served at the Banned Book Club. I bet she added arsenic to Mrs. Scarlett's cup!

I snatched the teacup from Heathcliff's hands and held it out of reach. He glanced at me in concern. "It wasn't that bad a joke. Hers have been much worse, take my word for it."

"Take my word for it! Ha ha!" Mrs. Ellis hooted in delight, but her face creased with concern when she noticed me. "Are you all right, honey? You're looking a little pale."

"Perhaps your chakras need aligning," Sylvia put in. "I'd be happy to help."

My mind whirled. All I could think about was getting Sylvia away from the bookshop, away from tea and liquids and things she could use to hurt my friends.

"I'm fine, thank you," I gasped. "Didn't you want to go to work today?"

"Yes," Sylvia glanced at her watch. "I have two appointments this afternoon."

"Well, Morrie and I will happily accompany you if you're ready to leave now."

"Oh, yes, I suppose so, if you really don't want me to take a look at your chakras?" Her puzzled expression turned my stomach. "I have to pick up some things from my cottage."

"That's fine. We'll walk you there. It would be good to check if the killer has been to your home."

"That would be a relief, thank you." Sylvia bent down to hand the tea to Mrs. Ellis, but I whipped it out of her hand. "Sorry, Mrs. Ellis. I just saw a spider fall into the tea. It's not drinkable."

"Croak!" added Quoth from my shoulder.

Heathcliff stood up and followed me into the main room. I shoved both cups into his hands. "Take those upstairs and leave them on Morrie's desk. Don't let anyone drink or eat anything Sylvia has touched."

Heathcliff's dark eyes studied me. "I can assume from this erratic behavior that you have a new suspect?"

"You assume correctly."

"And you're about to run off into the woods with her," he growled.

"Morrie will be with me. I'm not in any danger." I leaned up and pecked his cheek. "I promise."

Heathcliff grumbled under his breath as he shuffled up the stairs. Grimalkin trotted around his ankles, assuming if he was heading up to the kitchen, it would be to offer her a treat.

Quoth stayed behind to accompany Mrs. Ellis to the hospital. Morrie and I flanked Sylvia as she gathered her tote bags and left the shop. Glass jars and bottles clanked inside. What horrors she had hidden in the depths of those bags, I couldn't fathom.

She poisoned her husband and started a new life. And now she's doing it all over again. But why?

Miss Blume kept up a steady stream of chatter as we walked out of the village and along the road toward King's Copse. Morrie's hand hovered over his pocket, and I knew without asking he had some kind of weapon stored inside. That made me feel better, and I hated myself for that. *I should not be looking to James Moriarty for protection.*

We passed the narrow path where Heathcliff and I had entered the wood. Another half-mile down the road, a dirt driveway curved through the trees. We followed it into the wood, down to the half-circle of cottages.

In the daylight, the homes looked small and drab. Chimney pots collapsed against dilapidated roofs. Piles of rubbish were stacked along the stone walls. The boardwalk leading into the wood where Heathcliff and I had stood appeared to sink into the ground around it, boards broken and collapsing in several places.

"Here's my humble abode." At the last house, Miss Blume pulled a jangle of keys from her flowing skirts and inserted one into the lock. She shoved open the door, revealing a gaping blackness within.

I followed Morrie inside, waiting for the grey light from the windows to illuminate squares of the internal space. Inside, Miss Blume's home resembled a cross between a prepper's bunker and a witch's lair. Narrow shelves lined every wall, crammed with cans of preserves and large bags of flour and sugar, along with hundreds of medicine bottles and jars of herbs. My stomach tightened as I noticed several bottles labeled with a black skull and crossbones. *She's got poisons everywhere in this house.* Stacks of lopsided onions and dirty vegetables lined the benches in the tiny kitchen, while sprigs hung from large drying racks under the largest window.

"What's all this?" I asked, scanning the carefully-lettered labels on the jars.

"Herbs. I forage and dry all of them myself." Sylvia pointed to square wooden molds and cutting tools on the kitchen table. "I make herbal soaps and skin creams, as well as remedies, tea blends, and spell kits for my shop. The wood gives me such a bountiful harvest."

I spied a round drum in the corner. When I bent to inspect its contents, my stomach tightened. Inside were several carved wooden walking sticks, all of different lengths and designs. I

STEFFANIE HOLMES

fished through the drum and found one identical in style to Dorothy Ingram's floral design, and another that matched the one we found in Mrs. Winstone's bushes.

Behind my shoulder, Morrie's expression hardened.

"These are beautiful walking sticks," I said, plastering a smile on my face as I held the moon-phase one out to her.

"Ah, trust Mina the artist to find those," Miss Blume beamed. "I'm very proud of that particular design. Wood-turning and carving are hobbies of mine. I make ritual bowls and statues for the shop. I carved all those walking sticks by hand, and they're some of my best sellers. I use only fallen trees and branches I find in the wood. Would you like to see the studio?"

No. I'd like to get out of here and go straight to the police. "Very much so."

Sylvia led us through the tiny cottage and out a rickety back door. As I stepped outside, I noticed buckets spread across the floor to catch drips from the leaking roof. I shivered in the damp conditions. These cottages really weren't habitable.

Outside, an overgrown path led down to a small corrugated iron structure. Sylvia opened a narrow door and gestured for me to go inside. I glanced at Morrie and he nodded, leaning against the doorframe.

She can't hurt me while Morrie's here.

My nerves jittering, I stepped into the shed, casting my eyes around the shelves of carved bowls and trays and wooden clocks. In the corner, several more walking sticks stuck out of an umbrella holder.

"Most of the cottages have workshops attached. Lots of artists live here because the houses were so cheap. I stock a lot of their artwork in my shop, and we swap supplies and overstock where we can. We have our own wee community." Miss Blume pointed across the low fence to another shed. "That's Helmut's shed. He's a talented blacksmith, and I sell many of his magical knives and

208

other implements in my shop. He lives with his sister, who bakes the most amazing treats."

"Greta. I know her." I forced a smile.

"Yes, she's lovely. I've been working closely with her and her brother these past few months as we've made submissions to the planning committee to get the housing development expedited."

"You… you wanted the housing development to go ahead!"

"Of course! They needed this land for the new houses, and they were going to pay each of us a huge sum of money, much more than these old shacks are really worth. Helmut was going to build a proper forge, and I planned to buy my shop outright and live upstairs." Sylvia rolled her eyes toward the roof, where rust had eaten large holes in the iron. Water dripped onto the cold stone floor. "Oh, to live in a warm, dry, home, I cannot even imagine the luxury! Of course, with all the hullabaloo over the planning application, we haven't got our payout yet. And if the Lachlans go away for dear Gladys' murder, I'm not sure we ever will."

Sylvia wanted the development to go ahead! Mrs. Scarlett's protest was getting in her way!

"Thank you so much for showing me your workshop, Sylvia. If you collect the things you need, we can walk you to your shop."

"Of course. Thank you very much. Mabel and I really appreciate everything you're doing. The police have been less than helpful. They still believe the Lachlans poisoned Gladys, can you believe it?"

No, I really can't.

As Sylvia bustled around, filling two more tote bags with soaps and crystals and jars of weird leaves, Morrie and I pretended to hunt for signs of the killer's presence while I carried out a hushed conversation.

"There are more poisons in this room than in Lucrezia Borgia's parlor," Morrie said.

"Agreed. And did you see all that chemistry equipment next to the soap-making molds? Miss Blume has the tools and the skills to isolate arsenic. I think she gave Mrs. Scarlett some of her tea laced with arsenic. And the walking sticks…"

"The evidence is certainly pointing toward one person. *And* we have a motive for the first old lady's murder. If Mrs. Scarlett managed to sway the committee against the development, none of the cottage owners would get their payout." Morrie shuddered as he wiped at a wet stain on his shoulder. "With all this damp and misery, having the money to buy a warm, dry, home would be worth killing for."

"Quick, she's coming back!" We straightened up just as Sylvia arrived, laden down with tote bags.

"Shall we be on our way?" she grinned. "Thank you again for helping me and checking for the murderer. Last night was fun, but I'm *dying* to get back to work."

CHAPTER THIRTY

"You've just outlined a Machiavellian plot worthy of an Agatha Christie novel," Heathcliff muttered as I filled him in on what we discovered at Sylvia's cottage.

"I know that, but it happens to be *true*. I'm telling you that we've found the murderer. We have to go to the police before Sylvia kills Mrs. Ellis, too!"

"But what evidence do you have apart from a wooden walking stick that anyone could have purchased from her shop?" Heathcliff demanded. "It's not even the same poison she used on her husband, if that even *is* what happened."

"It shows she has a knowledge of different poison types! And Morrie searched the geotechnical reports conducted in King's Copse and they show arsenic deposits in the soil and ore leftover from the old mines."

"But it doesn't explain the other two murders, or the assault. Even if she did kill the old bint and the posh bitch who was blackmailing her, why attack that third woman?"

I had to admit I was in the dark about that, too, but I was sure we'd find a connection if we looked deep enough. "You're supposed to be the brooding, passionate bad boy. Since when were you such a slave to *evidence*?"

"Since the police insisted you stop meddling in their cases, else you're liable to end up in custody again," Heathcliff shot back.

"Well, if you're so clever, who do you think killed Mrs. Scarlett and Ginny Button and attacked Mrs. Winstone—"

"Wait, hold on!" Morrie rubbed his chin. "We've been looking at this all wrong."

I twisted around. "What do you mean?"

"I mean, it's just occurred to me – although it should have occurred to me sooner, which is a concern – that we've got three different crimes, yes? A malicious poisoning, a shove down some stairs with a stolen necklace, and a brutal beating with a wooden walking stick. What does this tell you?"

"That the killer has a thing about the Banned Book Club?"

"No! Think about it. Why go to all the trouble of slowly poisoning Mrs. Scarlett in a way that all but ensures you'd never get caught, if you then just shove Ginny Button down the stairs, nick her jewels, and beat up Mrs. Winstone with a walking stick in broad daylight?"

Morrie's protests dawned on me. "You think we're dealing with different murderers."

"I do." Morrie grabbed his phone and started doodling on a notes app with his finger. "Ginny's death and the attempted murder of Mrs. Winstone – if it even *was* attempted murder – are the acts of desperate people. Mrs. Scarlett's death was clever and insidious because of the amount of planning involved. Which means we're either dealing with two different killers, or your suspect's situation is becoming precarious."

"We need to figure out if Mrs. Winstone—" My phone buzzed. I pressed it to my ear.

"Wonderful news," Mrs. Ellis chirped on the other end. "Brenda's been released from the hospital. I'm helping her with the paperwork now, and then I'll take her back to her house and get her settled. She's still in a lot of pain, but the doctors said she can recover at home."

"What about her husband, Harold? Wouldn't he want to take her home himself?"

There was a pause on the other end before Mrs. Ellis said, "Dear Harold is still out of town on business. Will you come, Mina? Your beautiful friend came with us, but he seems to have disappeared somewhere. I hate to think of who might be waiting for us at Brenda's home."

"Of course we'll come." I hung up the phone and filled in Heathcliff and Morrie on what Mrs. Ellis had said. "Quoth must've had trouble holding his human form. I'm going to go round to the Winstones to check out the house. Maybe Brenda could tell us why Sylvia would want to kill her."

"I'm coming with you." Morrie grabbed for his jacket.

"No need. Quoth will follow the ladies in his bird form, so I'll be protected. I need you to go to Sylvia Blume's shop and make sure she doesn't leave. And if my mother's there, don't let her eat or drink anything Sylvia offers."

"What about me?" Heathcliff barked.

"Stay here. Mind the shop and be your usual charming self. I'll call you if I need you."

I bolted from the shop and across the green, panting as I reached Mrs. Winstone's house. There was no car in the driveway, but I assumed they'd taken a ride share. Mrs. Ellis didn't have a license because she loved to flirt with the drivers. As I'd predicted, Quoth perched on a branch above the door. His gaze flicking from the front window to survey the street. I waved at him, and he nodded at me.

I haven't let them out of my sight. No one followed them here, he said inside my head.

Thank you. I knocked on the door.

"Just a minute." Mrs. Winstone shuffled through the house.

"Oh, do sit down, Brenda. I'll get it." Mrs. Ellis flung open the door. "Mina, I'm so pleased to see you. Your friend dashed off unexpectedly in the hospital and left some of his clothes behind. I don't know where he got to in the buff, but I do hope we see him soon. Do come in and help me get Brenda settled."

I followed Mrs. Ellis through the front hall into a comfortable sitting room. On every surface, photographs had been flipped down or leaned backward against the wall. As I walked past the hall table, my dress caught the edge of a frame and it slid onto the rug. I bent down to pick it up. It had flipped over, revealing an image of a young Mrs. Winstone, beaming from ear-to-ear as she embraced a man.

"My husband, Harold." Mrs. Winstone said, her voice rising in pitch. She sat in a reclining chair beside the window, her feet up on a sheepskin footstool. Mrs. Ellis fussed with a coffee table beside her. "Isn't he handsome?"

"Oh yes." The man in the photograph did exude a sort of slick charm. "Mrs. Ellis said he was away on business. Whereabouts did he go?"

"Lord only knows," she spat, her tone suddenly bitter. "Twenty-six years of marriage, and he's left me."

Poor Mrs. Winstone. I placed the photograph back on the table, feeling stupid. Of course, that was why she'd turned all the photographs the wrong way around, and why he wouldn't come to the hospital to see her. "I'm so sorry."

"He was always a rotten bastard. You're better off without him, dear." Mrs. Ellis knew to say the right things, the things girl-friends said to each other the world over after some man broke another heart.

"He was *wonderful,*" Mrs. Winstone sighed. Her eyes swung to the ceiling, a thousand miles away. "He was so handsome and clever. I never really understood what he saw in me. I did every-thing right, everything a good wife is supposed to do. I begged him for children, but he said he could never take time away from his work. I gave up my dream of being a mother for him, and he left me!"

"There, there. I'll get the kettle on," Mrs. Ellis stacked another pillow behind Mrs. Winstone, standing back to admire her work. "I've bought some groceries. Mina, will you help me in the kitchen? The paramedics put all Brenda's food on the countertop and some of it's gone off."

"I'll wash my hands and I'll be right out." I spied a bathroom at the end of the hall.

As I passed the kitchen door and linen cupboard, a foul smell rose up to meet me – a whiff of rot. *It'll just be that food Mrs. Ellis was referring to. It's what happens when you're taken to the hospital suddenly.*

The bathroom decor was exactly what I expected of Mrs. Winstone – fluffy towels and a plastic shower curtain covered in a pattern of prancing cats. I did my business and washed my hands with soap shaped like a conch shell.

Mrs. Winstone is looking a little pale. It was a lot to deal with, your husband leaving you and then being beaten up all in the same week. *I wonder if she has anything in her medicine cabinet that might help.*

I opened the mirror door, peering into shelves of cosmetics and perfumes and soaps. As I pulled a bottle of ibuprofen off the shelf, something slid out and clattered into the sink. A necklace. Something about it seemed familiar, a nagging sense that it was important.

I picked up the necklace and held it up to the light. Stones sparkled in elaborate drops – deep red rubies surrounded by diamond clusters. My hand trembled.

Diamonds and rubies.

I remembered where I'd seen the necklace before.

Around Ginny Button's neck.

"Harold gave that to her, you know."

I whirled around. Mrs. Winstone stood in the doorway, her bruised face twisted in an expression of quiet rage.

Danger prickled at the edges of my conscience. "Your husband gave a necklace to Ginny Button?"

"That's the sort of thing men like Harold do for their mistresses."

Her words took a moment to sink in. Harold Winstone. The 'H' in Ginny's love letters, the man who'd fathered her baby, who she wanted to marry… he was Mrs. Winstone's husband.

Oh no.

Mrs. Winstone nodded, her eyes sad. "Harold had plenty of women over the years. It was expected, a man as handsome as him, traveling for work. He did get so lonely. I put up with it because I knew that one day he'd give me a child and I'd never feel lonely again."

I cast my gaze over Mrs. Winstone's shoulder to the hall beyond, hunting for an escape. *She's weak from the attack. I could shove my way past her and run outside. Quoth could transform and help me tackle her.* "Why do you have this necklace, Mrs. Winstone?"

"I took it from the trollop, and I am taking her child. It's mine by right. He's *my* husband."

"But how…"

My mouth fell open. The necklace slipped from my fingers, clattering against the tiles.

Mrs. Winstone *killed* Ginny Button.

Mrs. Winstone laughed. "There, you see, dearie. I knew you'd understand. I ripped it from her before I pushed her down the stairs. The crunch as her neck snapped was like choir music – so beautiful, so righteous. It had to be done. Thank heavens the doctors were able to save the child. *My child.*"

"You killed Ginny?"

"She brought it on herself. She shouldn't have been sleeping with my husband or having his baby, the baby that should have been *mine*. She wanted to rub it in my face; that's why she joined the Banned Book Club, so that I'd have to look across the teacups and see Harold's baby growing inside her. That's why she had Dorothy Ingram kick me off the youth group, so I'd have nothing, so I'd be so humiliated that I'd just fade away and she'd become the new Mrs. Harold Winstone." Mrs. Winstone gave a sad shake of her head. "But one can only deal with so much before one bites back."

"But if you killed Ginny, then who attacked you?"

"Oh, I knew that I'd be the first person suspected if Ginny was killed and it was discovered Harold was the father of her child. I figured she kept copies of her letters, in case she needed to blackmail me or Harold at a later date." Mrs. Winstone's eyes turned glassy. Mrs. Ellis came up behind her, a tea towel over her shoulder and a pursed expression as she listened to her cousin's confession. "Ginny loved to use blackmail to get what she wanted – that's why she had herself assigned as the assistant at Harold's old hospital history project in the first place – she had access to all kinds of fascinating records. She had something on Dorothy Ingram, of that I'm certain.

"Anyway, gossip in this town works much faster than the police. And I needed everyone to look elsewhere for a murderer. So I set up my own attack, staged it perfectly, with just the right clues to lead the police to the other truly guilty person. I was saving the necklace to plant in Dorothy's car as soon as I got out of the hospital. It's the perfect way to ensure all involved get their just punishment." Mrs. Winstone pointed to her bruises. "It hurt terribly, but not as much as Harold's betrayal."

"The other truly guilty person… you mean Dorothy Ingram?"

"Dorothy railed against me because of the Book Club, and yet she allowed that harlot to steer the church committee to fire me? It was not fair. The youth group was my one pleasure in life, and Dorothy took it away from me. With dear Gladys gone and me in the hospital, I was certain she'd be blamed because of her hatred of the book club, but the police are so incompetent, they want to make out that Ginny's death was an accident!"

"Oh, Brenda," Mrs. Ellis cooed, rubbing her cousin's shoulder.

"I even left the walking stick in the bushes so they'd find it! But only you were clever enough to suspect Dorothy," Mrs. Winstone said, tears pooling in her eyes. My stomach churned to think that I'd very nearly helped her frame an innocent woman. "All I ever wanted was a baby all of my own. Harold was going to have one with *her*. I couldn't abide it. I just couldn't. That child should have been mine." She sank to her knees.

"There, there," Mrs. Ellis patted her shoulder. As she did so, she drew her mobile phone from her carpet bag and tossed it to me, motioning for me to head outside with it. I marvelled at how calmly Mrs. Ellis was dealing with her own cousin's murder confession. "Mina and I are going to help you. We'll make sure that the police understand why you did what you did."

"I wanted them all to suffer for what they did to me. Dorothy and Ginny and Harold are the ones who did wrong!"

But if you punished Ginny and Dorothy, then why not Harold? She must have loved him something fierce.

"We'll make sure the police know that," Mrs. Ellis cooed. Her eyes widened as she made a dialing motion at me behind her cousin's back. "But you'll have to come with us and tell the whole story, so they understand."

"Yes, I suppose they should know everything," Mrs. Winstone agreed.

My finger hovered over the keypad. A couple of things still didn't add up. "What about Mrs. Scarlett? Why did you poison her? What part did she have to play in this?"

Mrs. Winstone tsked. "No, no. I never hurt Gladys. She was the one who told me about Ginny and Harold in the first place. Her unfortunate death gave me the perfect opportunity to ensure Dorothy would pay, but it was not my doing."

CHAPTER THIRTY-ONE

*A*fter making the call, I had to wait with Mrs. Winstone and Mrs. Ellis for the police to arrive. Every second stretched for eternity while I turned the question of Mrs. Scarlett's murder over in my mind. If Mrs. Winstone hadn't killed her, did that mean it was Sylvia Blume?

Quoth, if you can hear me, go back to the bookshop and tell Morrie and Heathcliff what happened.

I'm not leaving you until the police get here, Mina, was his only reply. Brown eyes ringed with fire peered in through the window, shadowing my nervous pacing across the sitting room.

Mrs. Winstone sat in her chair and rocked and rocked. She occasionally spoke to tell me more about Harold and how wonderful he was. Again, I wondered at how she could brutally murder an adulteress, frame another woman, and yet let her husband go on with his work like they were still the perfect couple.

I tried to ask her about Harold, but Mrs. Ellis shushed me. *I guess it can wait for the police. It's better not to aggravate her.*

An eternity later, the doorbell rang. Inspector Hayes and Detective Sergeant Wilson stood on the stoop. Jo was behind them, carrying her crime scene kit. In the tree behind them, Quoth took off, soaring over the village in the direction of the shop.

"Mina Wilde," Hayes said. "I thought I said that I never again wanted to see you mixed up in a murder investigation."

"You did, and I agreed. I promise this is my last one." I opened the door. "Come in. Brenda is in the living room. She has much to tell you."

The officers sat on the floral sofa and started their formal interview. Mrs. Ellis held Mrs. Winstone's hand while she poured out the sad tale again. Jo pulled me into the hallway.

"Well done on figuring this out and getting a confession out of the old lady. Are you sure you aren't interested in becoming a police detective? The work is hard and the pay is shite, but we could work together."

I smiled. "I think I'll leave all the dead bodies to you, if you don't mind. Besides, I wouldn't have gotten this far if it wasn't for you answering all my odd questions, and Morrie and Quoth and Heathcliff being their usual selves."

"Speaking of a team effort, what have you got to tell me about the guys?" Jo's eyes twinkled with mischief.

"Morrie said something, didn't he?"

"He might've let a few details slip." Jo elbowed me in the ribs. "Go on, spill."

"Um, don't you have a scene to investigate?"

"Oh, right, that." Jo held up her bag. "First, I hunt for evidence to convict this nice old lady. Then we talk about the handcuffs."

Another whiff of rot wafted past my nose, worse than before. I gagged. "Can you smell that?" I sniffed again. *Yup, definitely rot.*

"Don't try and change the subject—" Jo's face wrinkled. "You're right. There's definitely something putrid in here. In fact, it smells distinctly like a dead body."

A dead body... oh no.

Mrs. Winstone must've seen us from the living room. "You two, stop snooping in my house!" she cried out.

Suspicion flickered in Jo's eyes. I spun around, searching the hallway for something Mrs. Winstone didn't want us to see. My gaze landed on the linen cupboard. I leaned close to the doorframe and sniffed.

"Oooh," I pinched my nose. "That smell is *definitely* coming from here."

Mrs. Winstone leapt to her feet. "No. Don't open that—"

I flung the door open. Something heavy slid from the gloom and tumbled across the floor. A cold arm flopped against my boots.

Even though he was older now and one side of his head was smashed in, I recognized the features from Mrs. Winstone's photograph. I was looking at the dead body of her husband, the famous historian Harold Winstone.

CHAPTER THIRTY-TWO

"Guys," I banged the shop door open so hard it hit the bookshelf on the other side, rattling one of Quoth's rat trophies off its tiny wall hook. "You won't believe what just happened. Mrs. Winstone admitted to killing Ginny Button and hurting herself in order to frame Dorothy Ingram. And she had the body of her husband Harold stuffed in her linen cupboard. She's just turned herself in to the police. But she says she didn't kill Mrs. Scarlett so we—"

I stopped short. Heathcliff and Morrie stood in the middle of the hallway, staring at something on the floor. Heathcliff held a squabbling Grimalkin in his arms.

"What's going on?"

"Nature has triumphed where we have failed," Morrie declared. Quoth and I rushed over, and I followed his gaze down to the tiny shape on the carpet.

It was the little white mouse with the brown spot on his leg. The Terror of Argleton. Only it wouldn't be terrorizing anyone again. It lay on its back, tiny feet turned toward the ceiling, completely dead.

I slapped Quoth on the shoulder. "Took you long enough."

"Don't look at me," Quoth said. "I came inside and found him like this."

"Grimalkin didn't do it either," Heathcliff growled as the cat slashed at his eyeballs. He dropped her and she lunged for the mouse. He shoved her away again. "I don't want her to touch that animal. It looks like it's been poisoned."

Poisoned. A nagging feeling tugged at my mind, a connection between the mouse and the murders. It was the same sensation I'd had when I picked up Ginny's necklace. I bent down and peered closely at the mouse. I caught a faint whiff of something in the air.

Garlic.

Grimalkin shoved her way past me and tapped the mouse with her paw. I scooped her up and stumbled away. "Heathcliff's right. Don't touch it, girl. None of you touch it."

"Hallelujah," Heathcliff muttered. "I'm right. Someone acknowledges my genius."

I tossed Grimalkin into the Children's room and slammed the door shut. Next, I went to Heathcliff's desk and pulled out a plastic sleeve – we kept a stack of them for protecting Quoth's art prints. I held it over the mouse and scooped the tiny body inside.

"Mina, what are you doing?" Morrie's eyes bugged out of his head.

"Can't you smell that?" I held the bag open and sniffed again. *No, I'm definitely not imagining it.* The faintest whiff of garlic, the same smell I'd caught on Mrs. Scarlett's breath before she died. I held the bag out to him, but he wrinkled his nose and backed away.

"I've taken some interesting drugs in my time, but no way is my nose getting anywhere near that bag."

I sighed. "Fine. I'll tell you that it smells like garlic. I think this mouse has eaten arsenic."

"That's the poison that killed the old bint," Heathcliff glared at me.

"Exactly. I think our little friend Terror here has had a nibble of the same supply. Which means I know who killed Mrs. Scarlett."

CHAPTER THIRTY-THREE

"*C*an I help you?" Greta looked up as I entered the bakery.

"Hi, Greta. I just wanted to tell you that we got the mouse," I said. "The Terror of Argleton won't be troubling you again."

"*Danke.* That rotten creature chewed a hole in one of my flour bags. It made a mess everywhere!" Greta beamed over the display. "I was afraid the health authorities would have stern words for me. Please, could I offer you a treat? It will be free for you."

"Oh, no, that's okay. I have somewhere I need to get to."

"Please. I insist."

"Oh, well..." My tastebuds watered as I took in the cakes and slices in the display cabinet. *No, Mina, be strong.* "Sure. One cream doughnut, please."

Greta picked up the tongs and expertly slid one of the creamy treats into a paper bag. "Anything else?"

"Yes, actually. I was wondering, do you have any of those special gluten-free doughnuts you gave Mrs. Scarlett? I'm visiting a friend who's a health food nut and I know she'd appreciate it."

Greta shook her head. "*Nein.* I have stopped making them.

They were so expensive, all those special flours! Now that Mrs. Scarlett has passed away, no one wants them any longer."

"Fair enough. You sure treat your customers well, going above and beyond to make food everyone can enjoy. Every morning Mrs. Ellis and Mrs. Scarlett came in and bought their doughnuts. Mrs. Ellis said you even put their treats aside for them to make sure they didn't sell out before they got there."

"It is what you should do for loyal customers."

"Really?" I leaned forward and glared at her. "You should poison them with arsenic?"

Greta's smile drooped a little. "What did you say?"

I held up the doughnut. "Every morning you dusted Mrs. Scarlett's doughnut with arsenic. It would have looked exactly like icing sugar. A little bit every day, not enough to raise suspicion. And eventually, she'd drop dead."

"I did not do this thing," Greta scowled. "How *dare* you accuse me without proof."

"I have all the proof I need," I held up the bag containing the dead mouse. "The Terror of Argleton was brought down by the same poison that killed Mrs. Scarlett. You told me the other day that you put out poison to trap the mouse. Your mistake was using the *same* poison."

"Nonsense. I would not know the first thing about arsenic."

"That's a lie, too. Your brother Helmut extracts and smelts his own ore in his forge behind King's Copse. I know that the ore around that area contains a high quantity of arsenic deposits. The arsenic would dry in the chimney of Helmut's forge, where you could easily scrape off the powder."

Greta's mouth wavered. I drew the bag containing the Terror of Argleton from my purse and waved the mouse in her face.

"This mouse smells of garlic, *exactly* as Mrs. Scarlett smelled in the days leading up to her death. I'm taking it to the lab now, where a simple test will confirm if arsenic was the poison that killed him, and the source of that arsenic. The only thing I can't figure out is *why*. Apart from as a customer, you hardly knew Mrs. Scarlett."

"She is rotten woman!" Greta yelled. "She holds up the development because of her petty vendettas. My brother and I, we have been waiting to build our new home for four years! She wants to make us miserable because she hates the Germans. Well, I showed her. I did!"

Of course. It's about the money Greta and Helmut would get for their tiny cottage from the developers.

"You did show her. You poisoned her." I held up the mouse's body. "And I've all the evidence I need to convict you right here."

"Give me that mouse!" Greta lunged across the counter, grabbing a knife from the rack. I backed toward the door, but she was faster. She flung her body between me and the door and raised the knife, her eyes glinting with malicious purpose.

"You know the truth. You will go to the police. I must kill you."

CHAPTER THIRTY-FOUR

"Greta, no." I held up my hands. "It's over. You're only going to make things worse for yourself."

"Give me the mouse, Mina." Greta stepped toward me.

"No."

I stumbled backward as Greta lunged with the knife. My thigh crashed into the edge of a table. I tossed a chair into the room, trying to put obstacles between me and Greta. *This is my life now, avoiding stabbings.*

A dark figure came out of the kitchen. "Sister, what are you doing?"

Greta froze, knife held aloft. "Helmut?"

Helmut set down a dish on the counter and rushed around to the front. "You are threatening this woman with knife?"

"She sure is," I piped up, inching toward the door.

"She's going to go to the police," Greta spat. "She will take me away from you."

"I heard everything, your whole conversation. She says you are a murderer, but this is not true. This cannot be true." Helmut stepped toward his sister, holding out his hand. "Give me the knife, Greta."

"That nasty woman was ruining us! She did it deliberately because we are German. And she had the nerve to come in here and demand doughnuts made for her stupid diet!"

"I know." Helmut shuffled closer, his eyes fixed on her. His hand didn't waver as he reached for the knife handle. Greta's wrist jerked, but she didn't lower the weapon, only continued to stare at her brother with those flint eyes.

"I scraped the arsenic from the chimney in your forge," she whispered. "I thought, a little bit on her doughnuts every day, it will make her sick, and maybe she will see reason."

"Oh, Greta." Helmut wrapped his arms around his sister. I backed through the door, coming to stand beside Morrie, who had his phone pressed against his ear, talking to the police.

"At this rate, we're going to need to keep Inspector Hayes on speed dial," I mused.

"Not if I can help it," Morrie sighed, ringing off the call and sliding his phone back into his pocket. "I'd prefer if in the future you could keep the police as far from my affairs as possible."

I grinned up at him. "Are these pesky murders putting the kibosh on your criminal plans?"

"It's disgraceful," Morrie agreed, pulling me into his chest and crushing me in his embrace. "It's no time to be the Napoleon of Crime. I shall have to settle for being Mina Wilde's most handsome and clever boyfriend instead."

CHAPTER THIRTY-FIVE

"*A*re you saying that with this dictionary, you were able to figure out the mouse had a particular fondness for Havarti cheese, and by using that particular cheese with the poison, you finally ended his reign of terror?" The reporter's eyebrow rose so far up her face it practically slid off her forehead.

"I said it the first time," Heathcliff growled, slamming *Mouse Language for Humans* down on the desk. "Can we take the photograph now?"

"Just one more question. What are you going to do with the reward money?"

"It's going into a fund to help with baby Button's care and adoption," Mum said, tossing her hair over her shoulder like a movie star. "That was my idea, of course. I'm very community-minded. Can you take the picture from this side? Sylvia Blume tells me this is my best side."

"Of course." The photographer made a final adjustment to his setup and clicked the shutter. Mum beamed from over Heathcliff's shoulder as the photographer snapped the picture. On the desk in front of them stood stacks of pet language dictionaries, with a handwritten sign proudly displaying the price (which I noted Mum had raised by two quid because of her new 'social proof').

"This is going in tomorrow's paper, under a big headline, 'The Terror of Argleton Is No More,'" the journalist said, snapping her notebook shut. "Thank you so much for your time."

"Do you have any of those books for dogs?" the photographer asked, pawing through the stack. "I'd love to know what my little Binky is barking about."

"Of course." Mum handed him the dictionary, elbowing Heathcliff out of the way in her haste to get to the register. "Now, will that be cash or credit card?"

Heathcliff rolled his eyes. I stifled a laugh as I watched the scene. Of course Mum got her way in the end. She'd weaseled into life at Nevermore Bookshop.

Like someone else I know, Quoth teased inside my head. I glanced over to where he sat on top of the armadillo, and shook my fist at him.

It was two days after Helmut convinced Greta to turn herself in to the police. A quick talk with Sylvia Blume had cleared up the remaining threads of the mystery. Her husband *had* died from eating hemlock, but it was a terrible accident. They'd foraged for wild celery, which they'd both eaten in a stew that evening. The next day, numbness crept from her husband's toes through his body, eventually reaching his heart. Sylvia hadn't eaten as much of the stew, and she'd recovered. However, what hadn't recovered was her reputation. She was already the local 'witchy woman,' and now her husband had died of poison. Her herbalism business dried up overnight. She changed her name, moved to Argleton, and made a new start for herself.

Sylvia explained to the police and to us that Ginny had discovered her true identity by accident while digging for more dirt on Dorothy Ingram. She'd been helping Harold Winstone with his hospital history project, which was how they met, and so she had access to all the old hospital records, including death certificates.

Sylvia also explained that Mrs. Winstone had purchased one of her walking sticks a couple of weeks ago as a gift to Harold for when he returned from a research trip to London. Analysis by Jo revealed the dried blood on the stick belonged to Harold. It was the murder weapon, which Brenda Winstone had also used to beat herself and then thrown in the bushes in the hope it would incriminate Dorothy Ingram when the police discovered it. Since they overlooked her carefully-planted evidence, she'd had to direct me toward it.

Jo said Mrs. Winstone would be unlikely to go to jail. Her lawyer would be arguing for insanity, and the jury would be sympathetic, given her age and state of mind.

As for Greta, she wouldn't get off so lightly. A search of her home revealed some containers and equipment with an arsenic residue. The chimneys in Helmut's forge were scraped clean, and the collected powder compared to the poison found in Mrs. Scarlett and the Terror of Argleton. They matched perfectly.

That was that. Another mystery solved, another couple of murderers brought to justice. All in a day's work at Nevermore Bookshop.

If only we were closer to solving the biggest mystery of all. The mystery I cared about most, because it involved three people I adored. Why did Nevermore Bookshop bring fictional characters to life? What did the time-traveling room upstairs have to do with it? And why did Mr. Simson instruct the guys to protect me, and from *what*?

I slipped into the shadows of the first floor, clicked on my newest purchase – a fuzzy Snoopy lamp with a glowing red nose – and returned to the stack of books I was shelving in the Aviation section. I nearly reached the end of my stack when a noise behind me made me look up.

At first, I couldn't see anything amiss. No one was up here snapping pictures of book covers to buy on their e-reader later, no kids climbed up the bookshelves, no cheeky shop cats darted between the stacks. "Hello? Is someone there?"

No one answered. I squinted into the room beyond. In the middle of the floor sat a small leatherbound book.

My skin prickled. The air in the room chilled, raising goosepimples along my arms.

Did one of the guys leave it here or something? I hadn't left that book there, and it was a weird place for it to have fallen – the shelves weren't close enough for it to have toppled into the center of the room. It sat at an exact right angle to the door, facing me so I couldn't help but notice it.

It looked… as if it had been placed there.

But by whom? And why?

"Hello?" I called again, crawling across the floor on my hands and knees to stare down at the book. The prickling along my spine increased as my fingers traced a stamped design in the leather. *The same design on the cover of that empty book in the occult room.* The spine had been hand-stitched, and the edges of the pages were rough and yellowed. This book was old. Antiquarian. Maybe valuable.

Maybe… maybe it was connected to Herman Strepel's old bindery—

"I'm off, dear!" Mum called up the stairs. "Thank you for arranging this today."

"It was all you, Mum. I'm all dusty so I won't come down. I'll see you tonight!" The shop bell rang, signaling her departure. My heart racing, I slid the book into my lap and flipped open the cover. The pages were hand-written – rows of Greek letters and bright illustrations of a mouse and a frog. In another image, an entire army of mice marched into battle armed with swords and shields.

I flipped to the back of the book. A gasp escaped my throat as I recognized the name and markings. I scrambled to my feet and rushed downstairs.

Downstairs at his desk, Heathcliff was barely visible behind a wall of animal language dictionaries. "I see my mother has recruited you into her pyramid scheme," I said.

"That woman is the real Terror of Argleton," he growled. "What's a pyramid scheme?"

"Never mind that now." I threw the book down on the desk. "I think the shop is trying to tell us something."

"How do you figure that?"

"First that mouse shows up and terrorizes the neighborhood, the upstairs room opens up, the mouse re-appears in our suspect's house, you reveal to me that Mr. Simson told you about me all along, and just now I found *this* lying in the middle of the floor upstairs."

"So some wanker left a book on the floor. They do that all the time."

"I don't think so. *Look* at it."

Heathcliff slid the book across the desk and flipped open the cover. "Yes. As I suspected. It's an old, smelly book."

I jabbed my finger at the pictures. "Look. Mice! And here…" I flipped to the back and showed him the bookbinder's markings. "Herman Strepel. Don't you see? It's a sign."

Morrie wandered in from the other room, his eyes lit up with curiosity. Quoth fluttered over from the armadillo and settled on the till. All four of us peered at the book as Heathcliff flipped through the pages. "A sign of what?" he snarled.

"How should I know? As well as a lack of Medieval Latin, fashion school also didn't prepare me for reading Ancient Greek or deciphering cursed bookshops."

Morrie whipped the book from Heathcliff's hands and held it up. "I've heard about this. This work is called the *Batrachomy-omachia,* supposedly written by Homer."

"Homer Simpson?" I grinned.

Heathcliff glowered at me. "I'm going to pretend you didn't just say that."

"Sorry, couldn't help it."

"Homer, of course, is regarded by scholars as one of the oldest and finest storytellers of all time." Morrie flipped to the back and studied the last page. "And the fact that this is a Strepel edition cannot be a coincidence."

"Croak," Quoth agreed.

"I thought Homer wrote those epic poems, the *Iliad* and the *Odyssey* – about Achilles and Paris and the Trojan war. I don't remember any mice or frogs."

"So you *did* take Classical Mythology at fashion school?" Morrie lifted a perfect eyebrow.

"No," I stuck my tongue out at him. "I saw the Brad Pitt movie. Ashley had a huge crush on Orlando Bloom."

Morrie sighed, as if there was just nothing he could do with me. "*Batrachomyomachia* means 'The Frog-Mouse war.' In this story, a mouse goes to the lake to have a drink, and he meets the Frog King, who invites him to his house on the other side of the pond for tea. The mouse hops on the Frog King's back and they start to swim across the river. Halfway across, the Frog King meets a fearsome water snake. Terrified, the Frog King dives to safety, forgetting all about the mouse on his back. The mouse drowns."

Heathcliff leaned back in his chair. "That's a terrible story."

"Agreed." I followed the illustrations over Morrie's shoulder. "Where's the farm-mouse who grows up to save the world, or the tavern-mouse with a heart of gold?"

"Croak!" Quoth interjected.

"It's not over yet." Morrie flips to the next page. "Another mouse witnesses the first mouse's death. He goes back and tells all his mouse friends what the Frog King did. They arm themselves and head to the water. The frogs mobilize. The gods watch all of this and have an argument about whether they should get involved, as gods are wont to do. They agree just to watch. The mice win the battle and they're slaughtering the frogs and doing their victory dance over the tiny frog corpses or whatever, when Zeus summons a force of crabs out of the water to attack the mice. The mice are afraid of the crabs and retreat, and the battle is over. A few frogs live to fight another day. The end."

"I retract my earlier statement," Heathcliff said, a glint in his eye. "Give that author a Pulitzer."

"Do you think Homer might be the next fictional character to come to the shop?" Morrie's eyes lit up in excitement.

I took the book from him and studied the carefully-drawn images of mice and frogs duking it out. "Unlikely. Homer was the author, not a character."

"Not necessarily. It depends on where you stand on the Homeric Question."

"What question is that?"

"Oh, gorgeous," Morrie sighed, flopping down into his favorite velvet chair. "Brad Pitt hasn't taught you a thing. The Homeric Question is one of the biggest debates in Classical scholarship. Did Homer really exist, or was he just another character in Greek mythology? Was he one person or many people? Was he a she? When did he or she pen the epic poems? Oh, this is too exciting. I'm going to make a list of questions for when he or she arrives."

"Don't get your expensive knickers in a twist. We've had plenty of fictional visitors, and a book has never randomly preceded their arrival before." Heathcliff lifted his head, and his black eyes fixed on mine. "It's not a new fictional character showing up. It's Mina."

"What about me?"

"This is all *your fault*. Ever since you answered my ad… in fact, ever since Mr. Simson told us to watch for you, things have been strange around here. Quoth can speak to you telepathically. The bedroom door flies open. Random books appear. Murder victims stack up."

"I've had nothing to do with the murders, and I'm not doing anything! There's something weird about the shop. Maybe there always has been. Now we know there's been a bookshop here for nearly a thousand years, and that the previous owner kept a room of occult books and seems to have some fortune-telling powers, I wonder if this site is like the bookstore version of an Indian Burial Ground. It's haunted by the spirits of books that have gone before."

"That's preposterous," Heathcliff scoffed.

"Do you have a better explanation?" Morrie asked him.

"Of course I don't." Heathcliff threw up his hands. "Between the two of us, we've read every bloody book in that blasted occult room. There's no explanation for what's happening, no reference in any text to fictional characters coming back from the dead. Everything about wormholes comes from naff science fiction. There's no reason for any of it."

"All the mathematical simulations I've run show that this shop and its properties are a theoretical impossibility," Morrie added. "If you have an idea for how we might be able to get some answers, we'd be intrigued to hear it."

"Actually, I do." I folded my arms and glared at each of them in turn. "I think all four of us should spend a night in the bedroom upstairs."

TO BE CONTINUED

It's murder and manners, petticoats and plots when Mina and her boys attend the annual Jane Austen Weekend. Grab book 3, *Pride and Premeditation.*

Can't get enough of Mina and her boys? Read a free alternative scene from Quoth's point-of-view along with other bonus scenes and extra stories when you sign up for the Steffanie Holmes newsletter.

FROM THE AUTHOR

Another book, another note from me. As if you're not sick of me by now!

In *Of Mice and Murder*, I introduce the Banned Book Club – a bunch of quirky ladies who spend their days enjoying literature that has been banned or censored at some point in history.

Every year, when Banned Book Week rolls around, I'm saddened by the amount of books still challenged or banned from our libraries. According to the American Library Association, more than 11,300 books have been challenged in that country alone since the 1980s!

The Diary of Anne Frank, banned for passages considered 'sexually offensive'. *The Bell Jar* by Sylvia Plath has been repeatedly banned because of its content dealing with mental illness and suicide. In a cruel twist of irony, Ray Bradbury's *Fahrenheit 451* – a book with a central theme of censorship and book burning – has been repeatedly challenged.

Of Mice and Men, by John Steinbeck – the book Mina reads and loves – is one of the most challenged books in history. It's usually banned because of "vulgar" language and "offensive" characterisations.

When you read between the lines, you see that these books upset people because they challenge beliefs and shine a light on aspects of society those at the top would like to ignore. They are powerful, and that power makes them dangerous.

As a writer, whenever I feel as though my words don't have meaning, or that what I do is pointless, I think back at all those books that have been banned because they challenged the status quo. Books that dared to show queer people enjoying their lives, books that shed light on poverty, books that questioned religious moral codes, books that used language to shock and enrage.

If I can bring a little of that fire and fury to my romance books about a cursed bookshop, then I've done my job.

It's important to continue to read challenged books, to talk about their themes, and to encourage our friends and families and children to look beyond the 'safe' words and embrace new ideas.

Read widely. Read books that will make you look good if you die in the middle of them, read wicked books with pages so hot they singe your fingers. Read books that open your heart and your mind, and especially books by *USA Today* bestselling author Steffanie Holmes, because I've heard they're quite good.

Xxx

Steffanie

PRIDE & PREMEDITATION

"*I* have my doubts about the sagacity of this plan," Morrie said as he hitched a pile of pillows under his arm.

"If your sagacity is so offended, you don't have to come with us," I reminded him, tying back my hair and smoothing down the front of my Snoopy pajamas. "You could go back downstairs and finish off that display I started for the Argleton Jane Austen Festival."

"Don't joke, gorgeous. This room has confounded me since I arrived in your world. I won't be tying ribbons around frivolous books while the rest of you discern its secrets." Morrie reached under my shirt and rolled my nipple between his fingers. "Besides which, the opportunity to spend the night with you should never be overlooked."

"Jane Austen isn't frivolous," I shot back, grabbing his wrist and twisting it, so his hand slid off my nipple and I could think straight again. "You shouldn't say things like that around Argleton right now. The whole village has gone Austen-mad."

It was true. Ten years ago, a famous local scholar by the name of Algernon Hathaway discovered a record of Jane Austen spending a Christmas at Baddesley Hall, the grandest of the grand stately homes overlooking Argleton, now owned by the Lachlans. Ever since the discovery of their famous temporary resident, the village has celebrated with an annual Regency Christmas festival that has grown ever more elaborate over the years. There were tea parties, dramatic readings, a costume promenade, and a Regency-style dance at the community hall, as well as a book drive where villagers donated reading materials to poor children.

This year, the Lachlans were even hosting the Jane Austen Experience – an academic conference and immersive event where guests paid hundreds of pounds to stay at Baddesley Hall for a weekend, dress up in silly costumes, attend fancy balls and tea parties, and go about proposing marriage to each other. This year, the famous scholar Professor Hathaway himself was the guest of honor.

Of course, Heathcliff wanted nothing to do with the Jane Austen Festival. He rebuffed all my clever ideas – hosting Professor Hathaway for a free public lecture in the World History room, putting together a Pride & Prejudice quiz night, dressing Quoth up in a tiny bird-sized bonnet (actually, Quoth was the one who vetoed that one). Heathcliff's blatant lack of mercantile interest was probably why he'd suggested the eve of the festival to make good on my idea to spend the night in the magical room and attempt to discern its secrets.

"I'll say what I please," Morrie winked at me as he affected a posh accent. His hand slid beneath my shirt again. "You haven't minded before."

No, I don't mind at all. Morrie's lips fluttered along the edge of my neck. His hand cupped my breast, the fingers pinching and teasing my nipple. *If this is any indication of what tonight might offer, the past better watch out—*

"Out of the way, lovebirds," Heathcliff bellowed from his

bedroom. A moment later, an enormous brown duvet sailed through his doorway and slammed into the wall above our heads. I tore myself from Morrie's embrace and leaped away as it slid to the floor to join the large pile of Heathcliff's stuff already piled against the door.

He's hoping we don't emerge again until next week.

"We'd better take this elsewhere, in case Sir Pricklyton starts throwing his whisky bottles." Morrie led me aside, his hand skimming the small of my back in a possessive way that made my heart flutter.

Morrie's lips had barely grazed mine when we were interrupted again. Quoth clattered down from his attic room with his gear. As usual, he wore the minimum amount of clothes – in this case, a pair of black boxers that left nothing to the imagination. I wet my bottom lip. How was I going to survive the night with all three of them without things devolving into a Bacchanalian orgy?

Why did the thought of a Bacchanalian orgy with the three of them make heat pool between my legs?

Remember why we're doing this. Don't get distracted by Quoth's beautiful eyes or Heathcliff's strong hands or Morrie's wandering tongue—

"This is all I need." Quoth handed me a bag of berries. I tucked it into my snack pack and emergency supplies.

"You sure we should bring along all this gear?" Morrie frowned at the tote bags I'd stuffed with dehydrated food, a camping stove, water bottles, emergency flares, and boxes of tampons. Heathcliff wasn't the only one in Girl Scout mode. "It's not very conspicuous, or very historical."

"There's no telling what we're going to encounter on the other side and how long it's going to take us to get the door open again into the present day. I want to be prepared for anything."

"Agreed." Heathcliff stumbled out of his room. Under one arm, he carried three bottles of whisky and a package of Wagon

Wheels. Under the other, a long, pointed sword with an elaborate hilt.

"What are you going to do with that thing?" Morrie frowned at the sword.

"Roast marshmallows," Heathcliff grunted. He shoved his bottles into my bag, tucked the sword into a scabbard on his belt, and pulled out his key. "Are we doing this or not?"

I nodded. We needed answers, and the only way to find them was to unravel the secrets of Nevermore Bookshop, starting with the room that traveled through time… or something.

Morrie smoothed down the collar of his Armani pajamas. "Which room do you think we'll see on the other side? I propose a wager – the loser has to clean the bathroom. I'm hoping for a Regency boudoir, complete with Edward VII's infamous Le Chabanais sex chair."

"I vote the empty attic," Heathcliff said.

"Of course you do."

"I want Herman Strepel's offices," I added. "But I'm not participating in this bet, because there is no way in Hades you're getting me to even step foot in that bathroom."

"I'm hoping for dinosaurs," Quoth added.

"You're *hoping* for dinosaurs? You're an idiot. Good thing Heathcliff has his sword." Morrie grabbed the key from Heathcliff and shoved it in the lock. I blanched at his insult, although Quoth didn't seem to care. The last couple of weeks, Morrie's comments to all of us – usually friendly teasing – had become more barbed. It was as if he wanted to keep reassuring all of us he didn't really care about us, that he thought himself superior in every way. It was starting to wear me down a little, especially when he did it to Quoth, who never snapped back and seemed to internalize every comment.

The door turned with an ominous click. Morrie stepped back and gestured to the door. "After you, gorgeous. This was your *clever* idea."

Yes, it was. And if it gets us closer to figuring out what's happening in this shop, you'll be thanking me.

I sucked in a breath and pushed the door open.

It's murder and manners, petticoats and plots when Mina and her boys attend the annual Jane Austen Weekend. Read book 3, *Pride and Premeditation.*

NEVERMORE BOOKSHOP 3

PRIDE AND PREMEDITATION

READ NOW

It is a truth universally acknowledged, that a single man in possession of a good fortune will be gruesomely murdered at the ball.

Mina's excited to attend the annual Argleton Jane Austen Experience at the stately Lachlan Manor. It's just what she needs after all the recent murders – a whole weekend of dancing with Morrie, attending poetry readings with Quoth, and helping Heathcliff field marriage proposals from adoring fans.

But murder and intrigue follow Mina everywhere. When an eminent Austen scholar is run through with his own sword, Mina and her boys must solve the mystery before the killer claims another victim.

The Nevermore Bookshop Mysteries are what you get when all your book boyfriends come to life. New from *USA Today* bestselling author Steffanie Holmes, this book bursts with petticoats and plots, steamy scenes and scandalous liaisons, manners and mystery, magical books and time-traveling rooms, and a healthy dose of Jane Austen humor. Read on only if you believe one hot book hero isn't enough!

READ NOW

WANT MORE REVERSE HAREM FROM STEFFANIE HOLMES

Dear Fae,

Don't even THINK about attacking my castle.

This science geek witch and her four magic-wielding men are about to get medieval on your ass.

I'm Maeve Crawford. For years I've had my future mathematically calculated down to the last detail; Leave my podunk Arizona town, graduate MIT, get into the space program, be the first woman on Mars, get a cat (not necessarily in this order).

Then fairies killed my parents and shot the whole plan to hell.

I've inherited a real, honest-to-goodness English castle – complete with turrets, ramparts, and four gorgeous male tenants, who I'm totally *not* in love with.

Not at all.

It would be crazy to fall for four guys at once, even though they're totally gorgeous and amazing and wonderful and kind.

But not as crazy as finding out I'm a witch. A week ago, I didn't even believe magic existed, and now I'm up to my ears in spells and prophetic dreams and messages from the dead.

When we're together – and I'm talking in the Biblical sense – the five of us wield a powerful magic that can banish the fae forever. They intend to stop us by killing us all.

I can't science my way out of this mess.

Forget NASA, it's going to take all my smarts just to survive Briarwood Castle.

The Castle of Earth and Embers is the first in a brand new steamy reverse harem romance by *USA Today* bestselling author, Steffanie Holmes. This full-length book glitters with love, heartache, hope, grief, dark magic, fairy trickery, steamy scenes, British slang, meat pies, second chances, and the healing powers of a good cup of tea. Read on only if you believe one just isn't enough.

Available from Amazon and in KU.

OTHER BOOKS BY STEFFANIE HOLMES

This list is in recommended reading order, although each couple's story can be enjoyed as a standalone.

Nevermore Bookshop Mysteries

A Dead and Stormy Night

Of Mice and Murder

Pride and Premeditation

Memoirs of a Garroter

Prose and Cons

A Novel Way to Die

How Heathcliff Stole Christmas

Kings of Miskatonic Prep

Shunned

Initiated

Possessed

Ignited

Broken Muses of Manderley Academy

Ghosted

Haunted

Briarwood Reverse Harem series

The Castle of Earth and Embers

The Castle of Fire and Fable

The Castle of Water and Woe

The Castle of Wind and Whispers

The Castle of Spirit and Sorrow

Crookshollow Gothic Romance series

Art of Cunning (Alex & Ryan)

Art of the Hunt (Alex & Ryan)

Art of Temptation (Alex & Ryan)

The Man in Black (Elinor & Eric)

Watcher (Belinda & Cole)

Reaper (Belinda & Cole)

Wolves of Crookshollow series

Digging the Wolf (Anna & Luke)

Writing the Wolf (Rosa & Caleb)

Inking the Wolf (Bianca & Robbie)

Wedding the Wolf (Willow & Irvine)

Want to be informed when the next Steffanie Holmes paranormal romance story goes live? Sign up for the newsletter at www.steffanieholmes.com/newsletter to get the scoop, and score a free collection of bonus scenes and stories to enjoy!

ABOUT THE AUTHOR

Steffanie Holmes is the author of steamy historical and paranormal romance. Her books feature clever, witty heroines, wild shifters, cunning witches and alpha males who *always* get what they want.

Before becoming a writer, Steffanie worked as an archaeologist and museum curator. She loves to explore historical settings and ancient conceptions of love and possession. From Dark Age Europe to crumbling gothic estates, Steffanie is fascinated with how love can blossom between the most unlikely characters. She also writes dark fantasy / science fiction under S. C. Green.

Steffanie lives in New Zealand with her husband and a horde of cantankerous cats.

STEFFANIE HOLMES VIP LIST

Can't get enough of Mina and her boys? Read a free alternative scene from Quoth's point-of-view along with other bonus scenes and extra stories when you sign up for the Steffanie Holmes newsletter.

Come hang with Steffanie
www.steffanieholmes.com
hello@steffanieholmes.com